A Very Novel Murder

ELLIE ALEXANDER

Paperback ISBN: 978-1-83700-309-9

Cover design: Dawn Adams
Cover images: Dawn Adams

Published by Storm Publishing.

For further information, visit:
www.stormpublishing.co

This book is dedicated to public libraries everywhere. If it weren't for my childhood library (shoutout to Fort Vancouver Regional Library), I never would have discovered Agatha Christie and gone on to write a series inspired by her stories. Libraries are the cornerstone of democracy, so please take this as your sign to visit your local branch and show your library some extra love.

CHAPTER 1

"Please tell me things aren't going to be this slow forever?" Fletcher flopped down onto the couch, stretching his lanky legs over one armrest and leaning back as if settling in for a therapy session. He scowled and ran his finger along his sharp jawline pensively. "Where are all the clients, Annie? Where?" There was a rare touch of anxiety in his tone.

I looked up from my screen and smiled confidently, excited to share my news. "Don't worry. They're coming." I closed my laptop and reached for my navy blue spiral-bound notebook with our logo embossed on the front. My best friend, Pri, had designed it. The whimsical logo, with a pair of crows and a magnifying glass, perfectly captured the vibe we wanted to create at the Novel Detectives agency. "These things take a while, but the tides are turning…"

It wasn't lip service—I truly believed it. In just a few weeks, word of our venture had already begun to spread. I surveyed our cozy and inviting space. Our new office could pass for a therapist's retreat—calm, comfortable, but with a hint of intrigue. Large arched windows offered a view of the English garden. Walnut bookshelves brimming with collections of mysteries, reference books, and maps of Redwood Grove lined the pale blue walls. Soft gold accent lamps provided a touch of extra warmth near the plush chairs and couch, where clients could make themselves comfortable with a cup of spiced chai. A fake crow perched on top of the bookcase, an homage to the two crows living on the grounds, aptly named Jekyll and Hyde, who watched over us like our own guardians.

When Fletcher Hughes, my friend and business partner, and I purchased the Secret Bookcase, the largest mystery-themed bookstore on the West Coast, we'd also taken the plunge into a new venture—the Novel Detectives. I'd studied criminology in college and had intended to pursue a career in the field. That dream was put on hold after my college best friend, Scarlet, was murdered right before graduation. I took a detour and ended up at the Secret Bookcase, where I'd spent the past decade connecting books and readers, running events and slowly gathering enough evidence to bring Scarlet's killer to justice. Now it was time for a new chapter.

I sighed contentedly at the thought.

Fletcher and I had transformed an old storage room on the second floor of the massive country estate into our private detective agency. Boxes of advanced reader copies, book merch, stickers, and overstock items found a new home in the basement. We'd given the space a deep cleaning, polishing the original hardwood floors and adding a touch of color with a large crimson rug and throw pillows. New artwork hung on the walls—a watercolor painting of 221B Baker Street, bookish prints, and an illustration of the Secret Bookcase, hand drawn by a local artist.

The space was warm and inviting, a place where our future clients could confide in us privately. There had been just one problem until now—clients. Or the lack thereof.

We officially opened the Novel Detectives three weeks ago, and until today, our client count had been at zero. I had been trying to assure Fletcher for days that these things take time. We were building a new business. Clients would find us, eventually. But this was Redwood Grove; after all, an off-the-beaten-path little village in Northern California wasn't exactly a hotspot for murder and mayhem. We just needed to be patient.

But my bit of good news would cheer him up. He'd been occupied setting up chairs in the Conservatory for an author, so I hadn't had a chance to share an update yet.

"What do you mean the tides are turning?" He perked up, shooting me a sideways glance like he wasn't sure whether I was messing with him or not.

I wasn't. I would never toy with his emotions like that, especially when it came to our burgeoning business venture.

I flipped through my notebook until I landed on the right page and held it for him to see, tapping the page while I shot him an eager grin. "You ready for this?" I paused dramatically and strummed my fingers on the desk. "I'm pleased to report that we have our first official client. The Novel Detectives are on the case."

"What?" Fletcher shot up like a rocket. His gaze darted around the office, like he expected I had stashed our client away behind one of the bookshelves or under my desk. "When? How? Where? Annie, spare no detail—tell me everything!"

"Are you just tossing out questions?" I teased with a chuckle, pushing my glasses back up my nose. I've worn glasses since the second grade. Classmates loathed the idea of wearing glasses, but I distinctly remember buzzing about choosing from the rainbow of frames at the doctor's office. My first pair were bright orange with blue polka dots. They were game changers not only because I could finally see my teacher and the whiteboard but because, even at an early age, I knew I was different—not in a bad way. More like in a bookish way, preferring to spend time traveling to far-flung locations and trekking on adventures in fictional worlds in the well-worn pages of my favorite paperbacks.

"Answering questions is the very essence of what we do here, yes?" He cracked his knuckles. "Out with it. My deductive senses are tingling with readiness. I can't believe it. A client. A real client!"

Fletcher's enthusiasm was contagious. I appreciated how invested he was in our shared success, but our first client wasn't exactly a stranger off the street. "Don't get too excited. It's someone we know," I cautioned.

Fletcher smoothed his houndstooth vest and crossed one leg over the other, doing his best to contain his enthusiasm. "So who is the mystery client? Or should I guess? Is this a test? Are the clues lying in plain sight? Time to break out my magnifying glass?" He gestured to the far wall where a prop magnifying glass hung at the ready. "Don't tempt me, Annie."

I grinned and shook my head. "Let's leave the wall art in peace for now." Fletcher was a true Sherlockian. His obsession with the fictional detective knew no bounds. He ran a local Sherlock fan club and had studied every piece of work produced by the late great Sir Arthur Conan Doyle. While I had practical training and my private investigator's license, Fletcher had a treasure trove of bookish knowledge and innate deductive skills honed from years of living inside the Sherlock canon. "There's no need to guess. I got a call about an hour ago from Caroline while you were setting up downstairs. She wants to stop by soon to discuss a potential case with us."

"Caroline Miles?" Fletcher's brows tugged into a frown. "What kind of a case would Caroline have for us?"

I shrugged and shut the notebook. "No idea. She didn't say more, other than requesting we don't mention anything about the meeting with Hal. I assured her we would keep everything in the strictest of confidence."

Fletcher's scowl widened. He pressed his fingers together and stared at me with concern. "You don't think it could have to do with Hal?"

"I don't know," I answered truthfully. That thought had crossed my mind during my brief conversation with Caroline, though I'd immediately told myself there was nothing to worry about. Hal Christie, the former owner of the Secret Bookcase and our dear friend and mentor, had been dating Caroline for well over a year. She owned Artifacts, a small boutique in the village square. Nothing about their relationship raised any red flags for me. If anything, Hal's attachment to Caroline had been part of his decision to sell the store to us and scale back. She and Hal were a good balance for one another. She'd brought Hal out of his shell a bit, or at least out of the store. They'd traveled recently, spending a week wine tasting in Napa, cruising through the Channel Islands, and snowshoeing in Lake Tahoe. Hal had taught her how to play chess and made her a home-cooked dinner a few times a week, where they'd enjoy a three-course feast and friendly chess match.

They gave the impression of being ridiculously happy and seemed to have found the right note of managing time together and time for themselves. Finding love later in life looked good on both of them, and like Fletcher, I hoped Caroline's call wasn't a sign that maybe their relationship wasn't all rainbows and unicorns. But I couldn't imagine a scenario where the two of them weren't blissfully content. No, there had to be another reason Caroline had reached out.

"She's coming soon?" Fletcher stood, glancing at the antique clock next to the bookcase. "Do we need to prepare?"

"You could boil the kettle for tea," I suggested, pointing to the electric kettle on the portable gold cart near the windows. We stocked it with an assortment of herbal teas and ceramic mugs with whimsical detective-themed images like fingerprints and crime scene tape. "I'll print our client agreement and rate card."

Fletcher turned on the kettle and stood gazing out the window. An unrelenting January fog had rolled in from the Pacific Ocean days ago, refusing to release its grip over Redwood Grove. The lush garden, with its topiaries, pathways, and native California flowers, was shrouded behind a gray haze.

I shivered, pulling my sweater tighter. "Maybe we should turn the heat up a notch, too? Is it chilly in here, or is it just me?"

"Annie, you're always cold." Fletcher rolled his eyes but moved to adjust the thermostat. "You wear gloves in the middle of summer. It could be eighty-five degrees outside, and you'd still have a blanket over your lap."

"True." I rubbed my fingers together for friction. "But that's because of my Raynaud's."

"Or because you're cold-blooded." Fletcher wiggled his eyebrows and turned up the dial on the old wall heating unit. "Nah, you know I'm kidding. No one has a bigger heart than you."

"Aww, you too." I grinned and pressed my hand to my heart.

I put together the paperwork and an intake file for Caroline, then heard a timid knock on the door. Fletcher swept over, swung the door open, checked the hallway, and quickly ushered Caroline in like she was some kind of a spy here to share covert documents. In fairness, Hal's private quarters were on the opposite side of the second floor, but Fletcher didn't need to overdo it.

"Annie, Fletcher, thank you so much for making time for me with such short notice," Caroline said with a smile that made her dimples crease. She was in her late sixties with thick white curls and an elegant, understated style. She wore a long chocolate tweed skirt, knee-high boots, and a thick cream cashmere sweater. Her doe-like eyes scanned the room. "Wow, I can't believe what you've done to this space. The last time I saw it, it was floor-to-ceiling boxes." She moved closer to the seating area. "I had no idea these windows were so stunning. You probably have a view of the entire village—well—that is if this fog would ever lift."

"The view is incredible," I replied, stretching to my tiptoes to peer outside. Being short had its disadvantages. As did the fog. There wasn't much to see behind the bank of thick, charcoal gray mist.

Fletcher jumped in, ever the gracious host. "Can I pour you a cup of peppermint or chamomile tea? We have biscuits, or I could run downstairs if you're in the mood for something more substantial. I'm happy to raid our author talk snacks."

"Oh, peppermint would be lovely. Don't go to any extra trouble." Caroline paused as if trying to decide if she should sit or stand.

"Please have a seat." I followed her, bringing my file folder and notebook and gesturing for her to pick a spot on the couch or the chairs.

She opted for the couch, resting her oversized brown leather purse by her feet. "You two have outdone yourselves. This is charming. Absolutely charming. I love the artwork. Is that cinnamon I'm smelling?" Her gaze drifted to a cinnamon-spice candle flickering on the coffee table. "I recognize that tin."

"I got it at your shop," I said with a smile, sitting beside her. The spicy and slightly sweet aroma filled the room as the wood-wick flame flickered and crackled like a real campfire.

Fletcher brought her a cup of steaming tea in a Novel Detectives mug. "Be careful. It's hot." He set it on a vintage Nancy Drew ceramic coaster next to her.

"I feel so special. I wasn't expecting the star treatment." Her soft lips, accentuated by a burnt orange lipstick, pressed into a thin smile. "Really, you didn't need to go to any extra trouble."

"It's part of our service." I spoke as if we had a line of clients out the door. We would soon enough, and in the meantime, Caroline was a perfect test subject, a chance for us to find our flow.

"Well, lucky me." She sighed and stole a glance toward the door. Her eyes hardened as she reached for her tea, making the fine lines around her eyes deepen. She studied the mug with newfound interest, as if she was buying time to figure out how to start. After a minute, she let out a slow sigh and looked at both of us. "I'm sure you both have plenty to do, so I'll get to the point. Let me start with an apology. I feel bad putting you in the middle of this, but as I mentioned on the phone, I'd prefer that we leave Hal out of this, at least for the time being. I think it's better this way, but I do understand if that's a conflict of interest. My feelings won't be hurt if you don't want to take the case."

Fletcher caught my eye. We shook our heads in unison. "Not at all," I answered for both of us. "Discretion is our priority."

"Good. Wonderful." Caroline let out her breath. "I just don't want to get his hopes up."

"Hopes up?" Fletcher asked.

"Yes, I suppose it would help if you have a clear picture of what I need. You're aware of his claim that he's Agatha Christie's long-lost grandson?" she asked, pausing to blow on the tea. Already knowing the answer, she continued without waiting for our response. "It's been a topic of discussion for us since we first met, and frankly, I find it incredibly endearing."

I agreed with her. Hal was convinced that his mother was the world's most popular mystery writer's love child. Agatha had gone missing for a stretch of time. To this day, the mystery of her disappearance has never been solved. She simply vanished from her home in Sunningdale, reappearing eleven days later at a hotel in Harrogate with no memory of what had occurred while she had gone missing. Theories abounded, from the disappearing act being a publicity stunt to her attempting to seek revenge on her husband for having an affair. Hal's theory was more—unique? Outlandish? He believed the world's most prolific and popular mystery writer—to this day—had intentionally retreated from the spotlight to give birth. According to his research, the timing lined up with his mother's adoption. He postulated that Ms. Christie had her own affair, which resulted in a pregnancy and the subsequent adoption of his mother. Unfortunately, he had no proof, and none of the Christie scholars even so much as hinted at the possibility she could have been pregnant.

That hadn't dissuaded Hal from his conviction.

"He's quite obsessed, and I believe as he's getting older, the need to understand his roots is growing even stronger,"

Caroline continued, taking a timid sip of the tea. "I've listened and been there as a support for him. I suggested he reach out to the adoption agency that arranged his mother's placement. He told me that he tried years ago, but so much time has passed, the agency has since disbanded, and his mother's records remain sealed."

I nodded. I'd heard as much from Hal over the years, and I could only imagine how challenging it must be for him not to know much, if anything, about his lineage and family tree.

"I wouldn't say this to him, but I never quite bought the theory." She bit her bottom lip. "I hate to admit it, but Agatha Christie?"

"It would be a game changer if it were true," Fletcher added with a shake of his head. "Can you imagine the press coverage? It would be breaking news everywhere. The story of the century, you might say."

"Exactly, which is one of the reasons I'd like to keep this private." She paused, set down the tea, bent over, and unzipped her purse. She gently removed something wrapped in an elegant, silky handkerchief. "I was trying to nudge him down a different path. I thought if I could help him find his mother's birth mother, maybe he could let the Agatha theory go, but then I found this." She carefully unwrapped the item, cradling it gently in her hands for us to see.

"Ooh." I let out a gasp. The overhead light danced on the shiny object, sending ribbons of blues, greens, and gold rays toward the ceiling.

"It's a brooch," Fletcher said, stating the obvious.

"An expensive brooch," I added, leaning closer to get a better look. I'd never seen anything like it. It wasn't just any brooch, but a brooch that looked like it belonged to royalty, with a stunning sapphire gemstone the size of my thumb surrounded by tiny multicolored stones and intricate metalwork patterns.

"It's gorgeous," I said, bending over the table to examine it. The dazzling brooch was truly a piece of art, but I was curious what it had to do with Hal or Agatha Christie.

Caroline handed it to me. "It's unlike anything I've seen. I found it in an old box of Hal's things while we were cleaning his closet to make space for some of my clothes. When I asked him about it, he said it belonged to his mother. That might not sound like much, but there's more."

I passed it to Fletcher, unsure where Caroline was going with her story, but I was already completely intrigued. She reached for her phone and scrolled through her photos. "A few days later, when I was looking into Hal's mother's adoption dates and when Agatha went missing, I found this." She positioned her screen so we could see the photo. "This was taken three days before Agatha disappeared. Look what she's wearing." She zoomed in on the picture, tapping the screen with a manicured nail.

I scooted even closer. In the photo, Agatha was seated at her desk, posing in front of her typewriter, wearing a brooch that looked remarkably like the one Fletcher was holding pinned to her chest.

"Now I'm not so sure. Could Hal be right? What are the odds that he has this very brooch in his possession? It's the same brooch, don't you think? Is he Agatha Christie's grandson?"

My breath caught in my chest. Could this be it? The smoking gun Hal had been waiting for his entire adult life?

"This is why I want to keep your investigation between us." Caroline's eyes darted to the door again like she was worried that Hal might burst in at any moment. "I don't want him to get his hopes up until we have more to go on. I want to hire you to prove once and for all whether Hal Christie is related to *the* most famous Christie of all time."

CHAPTER 2

"Will you take the case?" Caroline asked with wide, pleading eyes, looking from me to Fletcher hopefully.

"Yes, of course," I answered without thinking, my heart rate picking up speed. I wanted the case. I knew it would bring Hal immense peace if Fletcher and I could find definitive proof of his genealogy. Hal was like a grandfather to me. He had done so much for me over the years, from hiring me when I first arrived in Redwood Grove, heartbroken and lost from Scarlet's murder, to championing the Novel Detectives and providing Fletcher and me with his steadfast support in this next phase of the Secret Bookcase. If I could return the favor in any small way, it would feel like a huge gift.

And I wasn't immune to getting swept up in the mystery either. I'd read nearly every article and book published about the incident. The detective in me was ever curious about how Ms. Christie pulled off the stunt and why. "But I'm not sure we can make any promises. Agatha's disappearance has been part of cultural lore for decades. Dozens of experts have attempted to solve the mystery of her vanishing act and failed."

"Yeah," Fletcher agreed, studying the brooch with new interest. He held it to the light and twisted it from one side to the other. "It's right up there with finding Amelia Earhart."

Caroline nodded, her face shifting. "I understand, but my faith is in you. You're both highly qualified. I can't think of a duo better prepared for the job. The brooch is new evidence, or at least a trail to follow, don't you think?"

She was right. It wasn't much, but it was something.

Fletcher returned the piece as if he were handling explosives.

"No, no, you should keep it." She waved him off. "Please keep it. I trust you to keep it safe."

"What about Hal, won't he miss it?" I asked. Not much got past Hal. He was astute and quick-witted. A few years ago, we'd thrown him a surprise garden party for his birthday, and he sniffed out our plans before we hung the first streamer. He kindly played along, pretending to be shocked and delighted to discover his friends gathered on the Terrace with cake and champagne.

"I already thought about that, and I came up with a cover story, which I think you'll appreciate." She shot me a coy smile, pressing her hands together and softly clapping like she was applauding her craftiness. "I told him I wanted to get the brooch professionally cleaned and appraised for insurance purposes. He agreed without so much as batting an eye. I don't think he has the faintest idea what I'm up to, and I want to keep it that way."

"Well done." I was impressed with Caroline's stealthy tactics and relieved she wasn't hiring us for other purposes. She wanted to bring Hal some permanent closure about his family of origin. It was a romantic gesture and a case I was already personally invested in wanting to solve.

"Great. Excellent. What do we do next? Where do I sign?" She sounded relieved.

We reviewed the paperwork and agreed to give her an update as soon as we had more information to share. She thanked us profusely and snuck out to meet Hal for dinner. Once she was gone, Fletcher let his jaw hang open in shock. "Annie, what just happened? Am I actually holding Agatha Christie's brooch in my hands? It's a good thing we invested in a professional safe. How much do you think this is worth?"

"Antique jewelry is not my area of expertise, but I agree with Caroline; I think our first step is to have the brooch appraised.

Obviously, we won't mention anything about a potential tie to Agatha, but if that turns out to be true, whatever its value, we probably have to double it."

"Or triple it." He folded the handkerchief over the brooch and walked to the safe, disguised by a smaller bookcase, a nod to our bookstore roots. Every room in the bookstore was themed after the grand dame of mystery—the Sitting Room was a replica of the one in Miss Marple's house in St. Mary Mead; the Parlor was designed to resemble Hercule Poirot's Art Deco style; the Conservatory, an ornate ballroom where we hosted events and author signings; and the Dig Room based on her popular novel *Death on the Nile* was an adventurous spot for our youngest readers, with a sandbox and archeological dig supplies mixed in with picture books. By far, the most popular place in the store was the secret bookcase located amongst the many shelves in the Sitting Room. I always loved watching readers trying to sleuth out how to open the hidden door. When Fletcher and I renovated the storage room, it had been his idea to replicate the concept with a safe. We anticipated—and rightfully so—that some of our clients might share sensitive and valuable documents with us, and we needed a place to secure them. Hal's family heirloom was the first item, tucked safely away for the short term.

The faintest flutter of nerves washed over me. I hated the thought of keeping a secret from Hal, but I agreed with Caroline. It was better to do our due diligence first. Getting his hopes up only to shatter them would be so much worse.

Fletcher and I spent the remainder of the afternoon discussing our action plan before we headed downstairs for the author event in the Conservatory. We decided our best bet was to divide and conquer. He would tackle the brooch—getting a formal appraisal and seeing if he could trace the jewelry maker. I would look into the adoption agency and records. It felt good to have an official case and our first puzzle.

The next morning, I was sifting through dozens of articles and books on Agatha's disappearance when the phone rang.

"Hello, is this the Novel Detectives agency?" a shaky, aging voice asked with a hint of trepidation when I answered.

"Yes, this is Annie Murray, how can I help you?" I pushed aside the Agatha Christie case notes and reached for a pencil and a piece of paper.

"Oh, lovely, wonderful, dear. My name is June Munrow. I read about you in the newspaper. You closed that case—your friend Scarlet and her murder. Very impressive. And so much news coverage. I've seen the story everywhere."

"Yes, that's correct." I could feel heat creeping up my cheeks. The arrest of Scarlet's killer had been headline news for weeks. Publications as far away as the East Coast and Canada covered the story.

"I've clipped every article and story about your heroics," June continued. "You're a regular media darling, aren't you?"

I wasn't sure I would go that far. I had tried to keep my name out of the news. I didn't need accolades. I didn't want accolades. I had closure for Scarlet's family and myself, the only thing I'd been desperately seeking, but it was inevitable that the press had jumped on the story given the high-profile nature of the arrest and subsequent trial.

"You've gained quite the following. Consider me a fan." June cleared her throat. "I have a matter that I believe you can assist me with. Would it be possible to arrange a meeting? It would be better to speak about this in person."

"Sure, would you like to come to our office? Fletcher Hughes, my partner, and I have flexible hours. We're located at the Secret Bookcase. Are you familiar with the store?"

"Yes, I know, dear. I've done my homework, but I wonder if meeting at my cottage wouldn't be too much trouble? I don't get around much these days. I have so many newspapers and clippings to show you that will likely be of assistance to your investigation, and it would be a burden to gather them together to bring to you."

"Okay." I wasn't about to turn down a client. "Where are you located?"

June gave me an address on the opposite side of Redwood Grove. "This matter is extremely urgent. Can you come today?"

"Today?" I glanced at the clock, hesitating briefly. There were still a few hours until closing, but no evening events were scheduled for the night. We could probably make it work. "I can check with my partner. Maybe we can drop by later this afternoon?"

"Yes. Fine. I'll be here. See you then." She hung up quickly.

I was taken aback by her abruptness but called Fletcher upstairs. Not surprisingly, he was more than enthusiastic about the prospect of a new client. "Even if I had plans, Annie, I'd cancel them." He fired up his computer and got straight to work researching June Munrow to see if there was anything we could learn about her.

The fog had shifted to a full-blown rainstorm, so we opted to drive to June's place to avoid trekking through the soggy pathways of Oceanside Park. As fate would have it, I'd driven to the bookstore because I'd stopped on my way in to pick up shipping supplies. I rarely needed a car since everything in the village was within walking distance of the Secret Bookcase, but today it came in handy for carting book boxes and now for paying a visit to a potential client.

"June Munrow, age seventy-six," Fletcher reported as fat raindrops splattered on the windshield and I hurried to unlock the car. He jumped into the passenger seat, buckled his seat belt tight, and rattled off a list of facts about Ms. Munrow. "Retired nurse. Never married. No children. Her name appeared in several searches regarding her neighbor who died under mysterious circumstances about three weeks ago."

We'd gone over the details in our office, but Fletcher was ever thorough and liked to be overprepared. That was fine by me. I navigated through the village square as he recounted the little we'd garnered about June Munrow in the short amount of time we'd had to prepare.

Downtown Redwood Grove looked charming as always, even in the drizzle, with its quaint shops and restaurants, even under the blanket of fog and drippy January skies. An eclectic mix of architectural styles gave our town its unique character with Spanish-style buildings with terra-cotta-tiled roofs, mid-century modern designs, and old-world English estates all mixed together. The square was lined with trees—minty eucalyptus, leafy palms, and ancient redwoods. Banners announcing the upcoming festivals hung from lampposts, and planters overflowed with winter succulents—blue agave, Red Velvet echeveria, and dazzling bunches of plum sedum.

"Do you think June wants to hire us to investigate her neighbor's case?" Fletcher asked as we passed Oceanside Park. The spacious grounds looked almost mystical, with heavy clouds clinging to the redwood trees. Rain began pouring down in sheets, washing everything in a glossy silver. While the Pacific Ocean was technically about thirty miles to the west, we benefited from the sea breezes that wafted over the village, leaving a hint of salty brine in the air and providing natural cooling year-round. "June's name came up in some of the articles about it. It has to be that, don't you think?"

"I think we'll know in a few short minutes." I tapped the clock on the dashboard and turned onto a small lane leading to June's neighborhood. It was a newer development, built about ten years ago when Redwood Grove had experienced a brief boom when a major winery opened a production facility nearby. Most of the area surrounding the town consisted of organic farmland—family-owned vineyards and orchards. The neighborhood itself was quintessentially Californian with a coastal cottage vibe with neat gardens, brick and stone pathways, and gated arches dripping with greenery and wisteria.

June's house was at the end of a dead-end street where every cottage was a mirror image of the other. The only point of differentiation was that each was painted in colors reflecting the natural California landscape—seafoam green, buttery yellow, and sky blue.

"There it is." Fletcher pointed to a sage green two-story cottage with a shingled roof and paved brick pathway. The exterior of the house was neat and tidy, with a fake turf lawn and planter boxes hanging from the windows. A welcome mat and vintage mailbox greeted us at the door.

My eyes wandered to a large bay window where a sturdy figure stood staring back at me. I jumped, startling as my foot slipped on the wet steps. I caught myself on the railing.

"What?" Fletcher asked, following my gaze.

"Nothing. I'm guessing that's June." I moved on to the door, stepping slowly as I tried to shake off my unease.

Before we could even knock, the door swung open. "You must be Annie and Fletcher. You're right on time. Come in." June waited for us with a stack of faded newspapers tucked under one frail arm. She was short and stocky with thinning white hair piled in a bun. She could have passed for Miss Marple with her sensible shoes, tweed skirt, and cardigan. "I've been expecting you. Follow me to the living room." She shuffled inside, using the wainscotting to steady herself.

Two well-worn couches with hand-knit, multicolored afghans draped over the back were arranged in front of a gas fireplace, blazing with heat. The arched window offered her a view of the entire street and the neighboring cottages. I caught a whiff of buttery bread and brewing tea.

"Can I get you anything? Coffee, tea, water?" June asked. "I've baked a loaf of my famous sourdough this morning if you're hungry."

"No, I'm fine," I politely declined, looking at Fletcher. I had a feeling he wanted to skip any pleasantries and find out why June was interested in hiring us.

"Thank you, but no." He shook his head as well, patting the folder under his arm like he was ready to get to work.

"Okay, then do sit." June eased herself onto a creaky rocking chair next to the fireplace. She made room on a rusted TV tray cluttered with prescription pill bottles and used teacups. I surmised that she must be on a variety of medications because there were at least half a dozen clear orange pill bottles with white caps resting on the TV stand. I wondered about her physical health. Perhaps that's why she had insisted we come to her. She didn't appear to be in poor health. Maybe a touch frail.

She carefully inched into the chair and rested the newspapers on her lap. More newspaper and magazine clippings, notebooks, and photos were piled on the coffee and side tables in what I could only describe as organized chaos. There seemed to be a method to her madness with the dozens of stacked bundles arranged in semi-neat piles. "Thank you very much for coming. As you can see, I've amassed quite a lot of material regarding the case I'd like to hire you to investigate."

That was an understatement. From the looks of it, June had been at work on her own research for quite a while. I counted at least four legal yellow notepads with shaky, cursive handwriting and stacks and stacks of photos. To my surprise, I spotted several old articles about Scarlet's case sitting face up on top of stacks of dozens of others. The pages were flagged with sticky notes, and some of the text was highlighted in bright neon.

Fletcher opened his Novel Detectives notebook and clicked his ballpoint pen, shifting into professional mode. "How can we be of service?"

"You cut right to the chase, don't you, young man?" June studied him briefly before giving him a curt nod. "I like that.

There's much to do and no time to waste. With every passing day, the case grows colder, and I fear that public interest has faded even in these short weeks, since it's no longer in the headlines. You two are my last hope, as the police seem to have little motivation to close the case." She reached for one of the pill bottles, struggling to open the childproof cap. I was about to offer her assistance, but she set it back with the others like she'd changed her mind. What medication was she taking? Something for her heart? I hoped our questions and doing a deep dive into her neighbor's death wasn't going to exacerbate any medical conditions.

"It might help if you start at the beginning," I nudged, motioning to the articles in her lap. "We had a feeling this might be regarding your neighbor's death?"

"Yes, that's correct." June's eyes brightened. "My instincts were right to call you." She tapped the papers. "My neighbor Kelly Taylor slipped and fell in her bathtub three weeks ago. It was such a tragedy. She was so young and bright with her whole life in front of her." June paused and closed her eyes briefly. "But the police have been absolutely incompetent. Her case remains open because they can't seem to determine whether it was an accident or suicide."

I flinched internally but forced my face to remain neutral. Dr. Caldwell, Redwood Grove's lead detective, was one of the most competent and brilliant people I knew. She had been my criminology professor in college and had closed countless investigations in record time. Last year, she offered me a position on her team. It was a huge honor, but ultimately, I decided I wanted to carve out my own path—blending the two things I loved most: running a bookstore and investigating cases. Dr. Caldwell was exceptionally gracious when I turned her down, offering to hire us as consultants whenever she needed an extra or fresh set of eyes on a case or assist us with materials and support (within the bounds of the law, of course).

Fletcher paused from taking notes. "And you'd like us to determine the cause of her death?"

June's lips pressed together in a fine line as she slowly shook her head. "No, I want you to help me prove she was murdered."

CHAPTER 3

"You think Kelly was murdered?" I repeated, watching as June rifled through the newspapers on her lap. The case had made headlines, and I'd followed it loosely. In the limited research we'd done prior to meeting June, there had been nothing in the media reports about foul play. Hints about suicide, yes. But murder? No.

"I don't think she was killed. I *know* she was killed." June handed me the bundle of newspaper clippings, her hands trembling slightly. "Have a look. I've highlighted sections you should read."

I took the papers from her. The living room was unbearably warm and stuffy, even for me. It was probably due to the fact that June had the fireplace turned to its highest setting. I tugged off my raincoat and unbuttoned my sweater. "What makes you suspect she was killed?"

"Did you know she was a world-class surfer?" June's eyes seemed to almost bore into me as she watched me leaf through the articles. "She had signed a deal with a major sponsor shortly before she died. You cannot convince me she drowned in her *bathtub*." She made a ticking sound and moved her finger back and forth. "Kelly loved the water. She spent every waking minute in the ocean. There is not even the wildest chance she drowned. The police think I'm a batty old lady, but I won't let this go."

"But according to the reports, she slipped and hit her head. She was probably unconscious, hence the drowning," Fletcher said, setting his notebook to the side and reaching for one of the articles on the coffee table. He fanned his face subtly and dabbed his forehead with the back of his wrist.

"That's a load of rubbish." June waved him off with the toss of her hand, knocking over one of the bottles of prescription medication on the TV tray. "She was killed. I'm sure of it, but now that a few weeks have passed, no one cares any longer. I've taken everything I've gathered to the police, who dismissed me like a neighborhood gossip." She shook her head in disgust. "That's why I want to hire you. You need to get to work on Kelly's case immediately. There isn't a single second to spare."

"What was your relationship with Kelly?" I asked, thumbing through the articles as a tiny bead of sweat dripped down my neck. June had highlighted sections where a neighbor who asked to remain anonymous was quoted as saying she spotted a man sneaking into Kelly's house the night she died as well as her surfing coach loitering around the neighborhood. I didn't have to stretch my imagination far to determine who the "anonymous" neighbor was. Several articles cited reports of a neighbor seeing someone inside Kelly's house and overhearing heated arguments between Kelly and her ex-boyfriend.

"She was a dear." June's eyes turned glassy as they drifted to the window. "She made a point of looking after me, checking in. She knew I lived alone and treated me like her grandmother." She paused, growing emotional. She reached for a tissue on the TV stand and wadded it up to dab her eyes.

I gave her a moment to collect herself before continuing. We needed as much information as she could recall if we took the case. "What makes you suspect it was murder?"

"Where to start?" She tossed the tissue on the TV tray. "Kelly was a sweet young woman but had terrible taste in men and, frankly, friends."

Fletcher resumed his notetaking. His cheeks were bright red from the heat. "Can you give us some specifics?"

"Thank you. It's about time someone took me seriously." June pointed to the table again. "Yes, I have pages and pages and photos. You can look through any of this. You can even take it. I would like it back eventually, but anything I can do to assist you and ensure that Kelly isn't forgotten. The police refuse to listen to me. As I said, they dismiss me as a lonely, elderly woman, but I've seen things… I know things…" She trailed off.

I felt a swell of empathy and understood June's need to keep Kelly's case in the forefront. When I had been trying to solve Scarlet's murder, I felt almost a kinship to her, like she was right there with me again, cheering me on. It was also impossible to explain to even the people dearest to me what it was like to carry that grief—to be responsible for keeping Scarlet's memory alive. But I was also curious about Dr. Caldwell's perspective. I couldn't imagine her simply dismissing June either.

June spread photos printed on eight-and-a-half-by-eleven sheets of paper out in front of us. Each photo had names, dates, and personal details. "You should start by looking into her ex-boyfriend, Jake Harken. He's a surfer. That's how they met, but Kelly quickly exceeded his abilities. She was a breakout star, and he didn't like sharing the spotlight with her. They got into some nasty fights right out there for everyone in the neighborhood to see."

"Which house was hers?" I craned my neck to see around a blooming peace plant, stretching toward the window light, its leaves drinking in the sun. The telescope aimed at the neighborhood did give me pause. How much time did June spend in front of the window spying on her neighbors?

"That one." She pointed with a wobbly finger to a house three doors down. "The one painted like an apricot."

Fletcher made another note. "You witnessed the argument?" I asked.

"Not argument, *arguments*," June corrected. "They fought all the time. He was bullish. A beast. I don't understand what she saw in him. Maybe it was the muscles or that he considered himself a god among their surfer friends. I encouraged her to break it off with him. She deserved so much better."

"You think the man you saw that night could have been him?" I made mental notes as Fletcher scribbled frantically to keep up with June. We had agreed it would be best if one of us were the designated notetaker while the other led the questions.

"Yes. He was snooping around her place earlier that day. She had finally followed through on my advice and broken up with him. He wasn't happy about that."

"Did they fight again?" Fletcher looked up from his notes.

"Oh, they did, and it was awful. Other neighbors, her room-mate, and her surfing coach had to hold him back. I warned her to get a restraining order against Jake immediately, but by the next morning, she was gone." June sighed, letting her eyes drift from the window back to her suspect pile. "He wasn't the only one, though. Her entire circle of friends was up to no good. I don't know why a nice young girl like her made such bad choices. I don't trust Brogan Blears, her former coach. He was harsh with her, too, making her take unnecessary risks and pushing her too hard. She told me she was considering quitting, but she was scared he would kill her. Those were her exact words." June tapped Brogan's photo. "I don't like her roommate, Allison Irons, either. They were not a good match. Allison is rude, possessive, and snippy. She didn't like Kelly stopping by to drop in on me. Why? I'll never understand." She swept a shaky hand around the stifling living room. The space was void of anything personal—no family photos or trinkets, just stacks of newspapers, magazines, and grainy pictures June had shot from her front windows of the neighborhood and anyone passing by. "Why would she care that her roommate liked to drop by and have a cup of tea with me?"

June's suspect list was rapidly expanding. She had done half her legwork for us. I was about to say as much when she snatched the last photo, holding it with her crooked fingers for us. "The

other person you should interrogate is Harvey Wade, her landlord.
I don't trust him as far as I could throw him, which I suppose
isn't that far." She laughed at the thought. Harvey was a burly
guy in his mid-sixties who looked like he could snap June like
a twig. "I have photo evidence of him entering Kelly's house at
unauthorized times when she wasn't home."

"You've done a lot of research." I flipped through her notes on
each of the suspects. She'd listed dates and times on each page,
reporting summaries of what she'd witnessed and overheard. It
was extensive, to say the very least. I couldn't shake the feeling
that this could be a case of a nosy neighbor. June lived alone. She
had a bird's-eye view of everyone's cottages. The telescope and her
personal surveillance photo collection were red flags. Just how
much time did she spend in front of the window?

June's suspect list was almost too convenient—too perfect.
Everyone she mentioned sounded equally credible and worth
investigating. Could they all possibly be as suspicious as June
made each of them sound? Doubtful. Was it all just a story she'd
concocted to keep her mind active?

I also wondered about June's perspective on the police and
how they'd handled the case. Dr. Caldwell was one of the best
detectives in California. I couldn't imagine she would overlook
even the tiniest detail that might have hinted at Kelly's death
being a murder.

It sounded like Kelly had befriended June. And it also sounded
like June may have inserted herself into Kelly's personal life.
Whether Kelly wanted that remained to be seen.

As if reading my mind, Fletcher asked, "What makes you
believe Kelly's death was a homicide?"

"Don't take that tone with me, young man." She wagged a
bony finger at him.

Fletcher looked at me with concern, like he'd said something
wrong. I gave him a quick shake of the head to let him know

he was fine. He cleared his throat and sat up straighter. "Sorry, I didn't mean to take a tone. We need to ask questions and paint a complete picture before proceeding. I haven't read the police report yet, but what's been publicly reported in the news makes it sound like there weren't any obvious signs of a struggle."

A brief flash of irritation crossed June's face. She inhaled deeply through her narrow, pointy nose to regain her composure. Her cheeks pinched in as she rounded her lips and exhaled slowly. "That's what the police want us to think, which is why I want to hire you. Kelly was murdered, mark my words. And as a certain brilliant mind once suggested, the so-called impossible should be mastered and made to obey."

"Let me guess," I said, turning to Fletcher. "Sherlock Holmes?"

"Hmm, that's in the style of Sir Arthur Conan Doyle, a brilliant mind, indeed," Fletcher said with an imaginary tip of his cap. "But I don't believe that's an exact quote."

"June, if you start referencing anything involving Sherlock, you'll have Fletcher eating out of the palm of your hand." I gathered her documents into a neat stack. "I'm intrigued by the case, and I think we're both eager to take a deeper dive, but I do have to warn you that if the police haven't been able to determine an official cause of death, that could mean there's simply not enough evidence. We will explore every angle, but there's a chance you won't like the outcome. It's important to take a beat and consider whether you want to move forward. How will you feel if we find proof that Kelly did kill herself? Something like that could come out in our inquiries."

"It won't. I don't need to take a beat. I need urgency." June snapped her fingers together and motioned to Fletcher's paperwork. "I'm ready to sign a contract and prepared to pay you handsomely." June cleared her throat and pushed herself to stand, putting an immediate end to that line of thought.

Fletcher and I followed suit.

Take this." She flicked her hand over the coffee table. "Your new purpose is to conquer the impossible in this case. Prove that Kelly didn't drown—prove she was murdered, and then figure out who did it."

CHAPTER 4

"Well, what do you think?" I asked Fletcher once we were out of earshot. I tugged my raincoat over my head as we walked toward the car. The rain was splattering on June's brick walkway and forming puddles in the turf. The cottages lining the cul-de-sac looked sweet and welcoming, but I couldn't help but wonder what secrets might be lurking behind their cozy exteriors. A prickly feeling ran down my spine as I felt June's eyes boring into my backside.

He ran his finger along his angular chin, a pensive gesture I'd learned was his tell. "Something's bugging me, but I can't put my finger on it."

"Literally." I mimicked the gesture, with a grin, yanking my attention away from our new client and trying to shake off the feeling of being watched.

He yanked his finger away from his face and stuffed it in his pocket. "I guess I need to work on my poker face, huh?"

"No, you're fine. Tell me more about your impression of June. I have a feeling we might be thinking the same thing." We got to the car. As I unlocked it, I caught June staring at us from the front porch and briefly raised my hand to wave bye.

"Like she's lonely and has nothing better to do with her time than stare out the window and take photos of her neighbors?" Fletcher scowled as he set the box of materials June had sent with us on the backseat. "I mean, Annie, some of this is over-the-top. She's been full-on spying on her neighbors."

"Yeah, exactly." I caught another glimpse of June watching us in the rearview mirror as I started the engine and pulled away from the curb. A cold shudder ran up my neck. I wasn't sure if it was my body's reaction to the cool air after being inside or from June's ever-watchful eyes. "Even right now, but don't turn around."

Fletcher ducked to check out the view from the passenger's side mirror. "I rest my case."

"Do you think we should have turned her down?" Now I was second-guessing myself. I wanted to investigate Kelly's death, but not at Fletcher's expense. We probably needed to work out a secret code for future clients—a way to tell each other yes or no without being obvious.

"Not at all. She's a legit client. A paying client, no less. In a week, we suddenly have two clients, and I'm never going to turn business down, but I guess I'm concerned she could be leading us on a wild goose chase. It reminds me of *Rear Window*. Has she spent too much time watching the neighborhood, and now she's created a story that Kelly's death was a murder because she misses the only friend she had?"

"That thought crossed my mind, too." I turned off June's lane, setting the wipers on high as the rain battered down and the wind sent palm fronds scattering over the road. "But if we're using *Rear Window* as an example, no one believed Jimmy Stewart's character, and he turned out to be right."

"Exactly, maybe June is right. I'm not ruling it out. It sounds like she had some contentious relationships, and there's plenty of documentation for us to go on. Do you think Dr. Caldwell will let us access the police records of the crime scene and autopsy report?"

"I'll call her as soon as we're back at the store." I was very eager to get Dr. Caldwell's take on the case and confident she would be more than willing to loop me and Fletcher in on everything she knew about Kelly Taylor's death. "Did you notice all those prescriptions? I hope she's in okay health. I almost wonder if we need to create a medical waiver for our clients. I would hate for our investigation to cause her undue stress."

"Yeah, she practically has her own pharmacy. Although maybe that comes with being a retired nurse. She seemed cognitively sharp. Perhaps a tiny bit unsteady on her feet, but otherwise fine." Fletcher made a face, pausing as he thought it through. "You don't really think we need her to sign a waiver."

"No, no." I shook my head.

"Okay, where should we start?" he asked, peering behind him toward the box cautiously like the documents might jump out and bite him. "I'm halfway terrified of June's notes. How much gossip will we need to wade through to get to the good stuff? Or is there any good stuff?"

"I think we should start with her suspects—the ex-boyfriend, surfing coach, roommate, and landlord. If we question each of them, we should quickly develop a sense of Kelly's state of mind and get a read on whether any of them seem cagey or like they're hiding something, but I'm with you on June's box of fun." I steered into the village square, feeling an immediate sense of calm wash over me as the red roofs and redwoods filled my line of sight.

"Should we call it the box of fun?" Fletcher interjected. "I could make a sign."

"Do it." I laughed as the village came into view, and the scent of the wood-fired grill at State of Mind Public House made my stomach rumble. Thankfully, I wouldn't have to wait terribly long to satisfy my sudden craving for one of their signature flatbread pizzas. I was meeting Liam and Pri and her girlfriend, Penny, later for a double date. Liam Donovan and I had been dating for a while now and growing closer by the minute. He owned the Stag Head pub and was classically handsome with chiseled features and a wry sense of humor. The more time we spent together, the harder I was falling for him. "No, but seriously, I vote we divide and conquer. We can each tackle a stack and then regroup and formulate a plan."

"That works for me." He closed the box again and gave it a pat. "The game is most definitely afoot."

I smiled at the Sherlock reference. Fletcher was such a dear, tender heart, but he couldn't help himself when it came to his obsession with anything involving his fictional hero. It was like the very essence of Conan Doyle's words flowed through him, slipping effortlessly from his lips as if it were second nature. His vast Sherlockian knowledge knew no bounds. He ran a local Sherlockian society and would talk endlessly to any interested customers at the Secret Bookcase about Sir Arthur's history in medicine and how it influenced his work, or the revival of serial fiction.

We strategized for the remainder of the short drive. When the Secret Bookcase came into view, my heart did a familiar little flop of happiness. The English estate, with its long pea gravel drive with teal-and-navy blue bunting stretching from the eves to the garden, was nothing short of magical. Ancient ivy snaked up the side of the creamy stucco as rain dripped from the eaves. A sandwich board propped outside near the front door welcomed readers inside for an afternoon of respite. Pretty chalk snowflakes and raindrops decorated the board, along with a quote handpicked by Fletcher from one of his favorite online ode-to-Sherlock sites: IT'S A CURIOUS THING, WATSON, HOW A SMALL MATTER MAY SOMETIMES HOLD THE KEY TO THE MOST VITAL ISSUE.

I hoped that sentiment would ring true for our investigation into Kelly Taylor's tragic death. The bell above the door tingled melodically as Fletcher opened it and gave me a half bow. "Beauty before brains."

I punched him in the arm and rolled my eyes. "You wish."

"If it isn't my two favorite people," Hal said, waving us inside with two fingers from behind the cash register. "You better get in here quickly, it's dumping out there." Hal was seventy. His enviable full head of thick white hair and neatly trimmed beard made him look like he belonged in one of the oil paintings lining the hallways. There was a natural kindness in his eyes and a spark of mischief, like he was always plotting his next move. Hal was an expert chess player, so it wouldn't surprise me if he were.

"How's the afternoon been?" I asked, shrugging off my wet coat and hanging it on the rack by the curved bay windows. Paper snowflakes hung from the ceiling at various lengths, dangling in front of the windows as if they were actually falling. We'd decked out our front-of-store displays with the coziest of winter reads and collections of candles scented in warm tones like cardamom, orange, balsam, and cedar. Stacks of new paperback and hardcover releases were arranged amongst stickers, bookmarks, journals, and fancy writing accoutrements—pens, colored pencils, and wax seals. Reading accessories for the season, like scarves, plush blankets, hot cocoa packets, and ceramic mugs with images of skulls and bloody knives, finished off our mystery-themed reading winter wonderland.

I went straight for a cup of coffee, pouring our rich house blend into a ceramic Secret Bookcase mug and topping it off with a splash of hazelnut cream. The Foyer's tea and coffee cart was more robust than the small set-up Fletcher and I had upstairs. We offered readers a selection of herbal teas, coffee, and treats like spiced sugar cookies to enjoy while they browsed or curled up in one of the bookshop's cozy nooks and crannies with a new read.

"Fairly slow, to tell you the truth, but you know me, I don't mind a lazy afternoon with a classic." Hal's eyes crinkled as he sheepishly held up a well-loved copy of *Murder on the Orient Express* like he had been caught sneaking in a read instead of doing homework. "We sold out of the new thriller you ordered, Fletcher, and we've had quite a few book club members drop in to pick up this month's novel, but otherwise, it's been a slow but steady stream of book lovers and me and good old Poirot." He ran his finger over the faded cover gently.

While Hal had officially retired as the sole owner of the store, he enjoyed working a few shifts each week and consulting with us, which was a win-win for everyone. We'd recently hired three part-time staff: Ash, a local high school student and cross-country runner who was tall and lanky with limbs and baggy clothes he had yet to grow into. Ash was a huge graphic novel and manga fan, which was great for helping us build out that section of the store and bring in more teen readers. Hardy, a college student studying creative writing, had a particular interest in historical mysteries and crime novels that tended to sway a bit more literary. He was named after the Hardy Boys, but he made it abundantly clear he much preferred it if we didn't mention that fact broadly. I thought it was sweet, but I could also understand how it might get old, especially working at a mystery bookshop. And Mary Jane, a midlife mom who was ready to restart her career as she prepared for an empty nest, had jumped at the chance to take the lead on our children's programming, although her reading taste leaned much darker.

Having well-rounded new staff with unique reading interests was a huge win for the store. It allowed each of us to claim a niche among subgenres to recommend a wide array of titles and introduce readers to new authors.

So far, things had been running smoothly. The extra help freed Fletcher and me to spend more time with clients like June while still allowing us ample opportunities to work in the store and grow our events and author signings.

"I can do a walk-through before closing," I said, cradling my coffee cup and taking a long sip. "Have you made the announcement yet?"

Hal rounded his lips into a guilty circle and wiggled his eyebrows. "It may have slipped my mind while I was riding the rails with Hercule, but Hardy is cleaning up the Dig Room from the preschool birthday party as we speak, and Mary Jane left shortly before you returned. She finished inventory and restocked the Sitting Room with a new shipment of cozies that came in."

"No worries. I'm on it." I laughed and rested my coffee on the long countertop, reaching for the intercom system. "Guys, gals, and nonbinary pals, this is your friendly book slinger, notifying you that the Secret Bookcase will be closing in—" I paused to check the vintage typewriter clock hanging behind Hal. "Ten minutes. Please bring your purchases to the Foyer so we can package a lovely stack of sinister reads for the weekend."

"Sinister reads, you're speaking my language, Annie." Fletcher stepped behind the counter and turned on the computer. "I knew that thriller would be a hit. I should have reserved a copy of *Blood on the Page* for myself. I figured we would sell them quickly, but not this fast. I'm ordering double. This is thriller season, after all, and it's as thick as pea soup out there." He motioned to the dewy window. The basalt clouds were so thick they nearly stretched all the way down to the ground.

"Just the cover alone haunts me." I pointed to the now-empty display with a shudder. The only thing remaining was the poster of the cover art the author's publicity team had sent. The dark and moody image of a blood-stained book in deep reds, blacks, and muted grays evoked a sense of urgency, but the kicker was the title. The font was runny and jagged, with the killer's fingerprints smeared in more red ink.

Our traditional mysteries were more my speed. I preferred my murder on the light side. Yet another reason Fletcher and I were a good team. He enjoyed spine-tingling reads that left him up at night. Not a day went by when I didn't find him chatting up customers about our noir and true crime titles or offer a dissertation about Sir Arthur Conan Doyle's medical expertise and how his years practicing medicine had led him to create characters like the brilliant Dr. Watson and ever-evil villainous James Moriarty.

I'd had enough murder in my real life. I was perfectly content to let my reading reflect that. Although I couldn't ignore the tiny niggling in the back of my mind that taking on Kelly Taylor's case might put us in danger again. If June was right about her accident being murder, inserting ourselves into the investigation could put us at risk.

CHAPTER 5

"The Dig Room is functional again," Hardy said, joining us in the Foyer as Hal shuffled upstairs.

Hardy was in his early twenties with a bushy, strawberry blond mustache that made him look like he was auditioning for the role of a 1970s detective show. "There was sand everywhere. I swear the kids must have had a sand-throwing contest. I found granules on the bookshelves—in between the pages of Nate the Great and Cam Jansen. How?"

"That's the fun of catering to our young readers," I said with a grin. Hardy had been working for us for a little over a month, and I couldn't believe how well he fit in. His mom was an English lit professor at Redwood College and had encouraged him to apply for the job, knowing that she had raised him on mysteries and that spending time in the bookstore would lend itself well to his goal of becoming a published author after graduation.

"I thought my college roommates were messy. The preschoolers? Next level." He brushed off his hoodie. "That place was a full disaster zone, but it's all good now."

"Thanks for your help," Fletcher said, offering him a hand wipe. "I hope we didn't keep you too late. Don't you have class this evening?"

Hardy ran the wipe over his hands and checked the typewriter clock. "I'm good. It's a guest lecture tonight on the golden age of mysteries. One of my mom's colleagues, who's starting a summer intensive on mystery and suspense in literature, is speaking in hopes of signing up more students. I would skip it, but I can't. My mom is introducing him. I love the program, but sometimes it sucks to go to the same college where your mom is department chair." He made a face and grabbed his backpack from behind the counter.

"What's the summer intensive?" Fletcher asked, sounding casual, but I noticed his shoulders stiffen a bit as he waited for Hardy to answer.

"It's pretty sick, actually." Hardy flung his backpack over one arm. "My mom's friend is a professor at UCLA. He's working on a graduate track for an MFA with a focus on the mystery genre. It sounds like it's the first of its kind anywhere in the country. It could be worth checking out. I'll hear more tonight and fill you in tomorrow." Hardy shot us both a wave and took off for campus.

"An MFA in mystery?" Fletcher repeated with a touch of awe, watching Hardy cut through the gravel path toward the gardens. "You know that was my goal before I dropped out of school."

Fletcher had mentioned that he'd taken classes at Redwood College before his funds ran out. Like me, he'd found his place at the bookstore many years ago. Hal offered him a job and took him under his wing.

But Fletcher had never mentioned that he regretted not finishing his degree. Come to think of it, he rarely said much about his short stint in college.

"You should sign up," I said, shooting him an encouraging smile. If he wanted to complete his degree, there was no time like the present.

"Annie, I'm going to be thirty-six this year. Can you imagine me mixing in with a bunch of kids Hardy's age?" He brushed his hand toward his button-up shirt and vest as if his attire were proof he was too old. "I don't think I would fit in."

"Fletcher Hughes! Don't even go there," I scolded. "It doesn't matter if you're thirty-six or eighty-six. It's never too late to pursue your passion."

He smiled, but only to appease me. "Yeah, I know, but that ship sailed a while ago. I wish I could have found a way to make it work at the time, but with housing costs and tuition, I couldn't swing it. I guess I've always regretted not having a degree. It's probably why I'm so annoying about my Sherlockian lore sometimes."

"You're not annoying," I interjected.

"I am." He nodded like we both knew it was true. "It's my own issue. I feel like I need to prove myself since I don't have a diploma, so sometimes I lean too hard into my scholarly knowledge about the one niche subject I feel like I am a bit of an expert on."

My heart broke for him. I never realized Fletcher cared so much about finishing school. I felt terrible that there was even the tiniest piece of him who thought he needed to prove his value or worth. "Nothing could be further from the truth," I said, placing both hands on my chest. "You are absolutely brilliant, and you don't need a piece of paper to prove anything." He started to interrupt, but I cut him off. "No, seriously, hear me out on this. I met students in college who were completely phoning it in. Sure, they might have a framed diploma on the wall, but that doesn't make them smarter than you. Your worth isn't based on a degree. You have nothing to prove, *nothing*. Understood?"

He stared at the floor but nodded again.

"I think you should sign up for the intensive this summer, though. It's perfect timing, and I promise you're not too old."

"I don't know." He hesitated, shifting his weight from one foot to the other. "Summer is busy here, and we're gaining steam with clients like June and Caroline."

"You can do both," I insisted. I wasn't letting him off easy. If this was important to Fletcher, it was important to me, too. "We have help—Hardy, Ash, Mary Jane, Hal. And Redwood College is in our backyard. You can't pass up this chance. Promise me, you'll at least consider it, like really consider it."

"Okay. Fine." He held his hands up in surrender. "You sound like Victoria."

"Good, I'm going to call her so we can team up on you," I threatened with a playful smile. Fletcher's girlfriend, Victoria, owned a bookmobile that traveled to underserved communities throughout the region, bringing stories and special literary events to readers who might not otherwise have access to a local bookshop or library. They had been dating long-distance for a while and seemed to be making it work. I was glad, although not the least bit surprised, that Victoria was encouraging him, too.

"I'm in trouble now," Fletcher said, throwing his hand to his forehead dramatically before he started running end-of-day sales numbers.

I dropped the subject for the short term and finished a walk-through of the store, but I was going to follow up with him soon and keep pestering him to sign up for the summer course.

After we finished closing the store, Fletcher headed home, and I went upstairs to call Dr. Caldwell and check in about the case.

"Annie, to what do I owe the pleasure?" she asked.

I filled her in on our meeting with June, including my concerns about the elderly woman's spying tendencies. "Would it be possible to review the case files, and do you think there's any merit to June's theory?"

Dr. Caldwell was quiet for a moment while she considered my questions. "I will gladly send over the case files and welcome your input. I was at a conference at the time of Kelly's death, so one of my colleagues has been the lead on her case. Let me see what I can do. There might be a way to bring you in officially, and I'll take a look at my colleague's notes before I send everything your way so I'm in the loop, too."

When we hung up, my body buzzed with excitement—this was exactly the kind of collaboration I had hoped for with the Novel Detectives, and I was glad Dr. Caldwell was willing to entrust me with the case files.

Since I was meeting my friends for dinner shortly, I didn't have much time, but I wanted to at least take a quick look at Kelly's files and get a baseline to build from. I made myself comfy on the couch in our office, tucking a throw blanket over my legs as I scanned the documents from Dr. Caldwell.

According to the police reports, Kelly was found unresponsive by her roommate, Allison.

Allison worked the night shift at the hospital and discovered Kelly the following morning upon her return home, making an exact time of death harder to pinpoint, especially since the body had gone cold in the bathwater. The police took statements and interviewed each of the suspects June had mentioned in depth but had yet to make an arrest or seriously consider foul play.

As I read on, I was struck by Kelly's many surfing accolades. She had moved to California from Michigan after two years of college. Her family was still in the Midwest, but she, like many young water lovers, had ventured to the West Coast in search of big waves and a laidback lifestyle.

Not only was she a rising star in the sport, but she volunteered her time to mentor young surfers and appeared to be a fierce advocate for preservation. I skimmed dozens of articles about her advocacy for ocean conservation. She was an active and vocal member of the Save the Waves Coalition and had testified at the state senate on the importance of saving the coastal ecosystems for future generations, as well as speaking at local schools on stewardship and raising awareness of the growing threats to the surf breaks, seagrass beds, and coastal forests.

A photo of Kelly surrounded by tiny surfers in brightly colored rash guards and swim trunks at a beach cleanup made me feel teary. She was obviously a crusader for good and a staunch ally of the wild spaces along the California coastline.

As I learned more about Kelly Taylor, I felt the sadness at her life being cut short so brutally rising in me—it gave me even more resolve to solve the case for her sake. This was exactly why I'd wanted to become a detective. Kelly had her whole life and endless dreams waiting for her. Someone had shattered her future. She deserved justice, and I was determined to see this through; whether an accident, suicide, or murder—Fletcher and I would figure it out.

CHAPTER 6

I carried thoughts of Kelly with me as I left my car at the bookstore and made the short, soggy walk to the village square to meet up with everyone for dinner. The familiar energy of being on a case—a case I felt personally invested in—hummed through me. Excitement wasn't quite the right word. More like a combination of nerves mixed with a strong resolve to find answers for June, for Kelly's friends and family, and for myself.

I wasn't usually prone to paranoia, but twice on the quarter-mile walk to the restaurant, I thought I saw a flash of movement in my peripheral vision. Both times, I froze, checking over my shoulder, only to be greeted by nothing more than the slight breeze rattling the leaves in the trees.

Jumpy much, Annie?

What was wrong with me?

I shook it off, chalking it up to frayed nerves, and quickened my pace.

The electric buzzy feeling only strengthened when I spotted Liam, Pri, and Penny gathered at a corner table of the busy restaurant, but fortunately, seeing my friends shifted the energy into something a bit more palatable.

"Annie, tell us everything." Pri, or Priya Kapoor, my best friend, deepest confidant, and favorite barista, patted the seat next to her when I arrived at the public house. She grinned at me with her dark, bright eyes, glittering with a touch of golden eye shadow. She practically glowed under the soft lighting. Her dark curls fell in loose waves at her shoulders, and her butterscotch turtleneck and matching blanket shawl brought out the warm notes in her skin. "We've been dying for you to get here. What took so long?"

I caught Liam's eye, feeling an inescapable pull to want to be wrapped up in his arms. He held my gaze briefly, sharing a reciprocal look of longing before he stood and scooted his chair forward to make room for me. "You look nice," he said, pushing a strand of hair from his face and looking at me so tenderly that my heart wanted to melt in a gushy puddle right there in the middle of the crowded restaurant.

Liam Donovan and I had been dating exclusively for many months, and he still made my stomach flutter, and my breath catch in my chest. He was tall and lanky with unruly wavy hair, a chiseled jawline, tattoos, and a crooked smile. We were the ultimate odd couple. I was short and petite with reddish hair, a smattering of freckles that no amount of makeup could conceal—not that I ever attempted to conceal them—and hazel eyes flecked with brown, gold, or green, depending on the light.

Penny, Pri's girlfriend, nodded in agreement. "You always look like you stepped out of the pages of a novel and in case you're wondering, I mean that as a compliment."

"I'll take it from you," I said, squeezing past Liam and resting my hand briefly on his shoulder. Penny was sophisticated and polished but approachable and easygoing. She was the perfect calm and centered counter to Pri's bold and wild energy. Her long hair fell loose on her shoulders, and her pale purple sweater made her eyes look almost amber under this light.

They'd already ordered appetizers. The table was filled with an array of mouth-watering small plates—bacon-wrapped puffed pastry twists, crisp baby potatoes smashed with olive oil and rosemary, and creamy lemon artichoke dip with crusty bread. I scooped a piece of bread into the dip as Liam handed me a cocktail in a short and squatty glass with a lemon slice and cherry.

"I took the liberty to order you a drink—a snowball. It's their winter special with brandy, simple syrup, and ginger ale." Liam draped his arm around the back of my chair and nodded to the pretty cocktail waiting for me.

"You're a dream. I could kiss you." I blew him a kiss, slightly tempted to reach over and plant my lips on his scruffy cheeks.

"Your text mentioned a case. Give us the goods," Pri said, crunching a puffed pastry twist.

"Let the poor woman breathe." Penny shook her head in mock disgust at Pri's pushiness. "She hasn't even had a chance to take her coat off yet."

"I know, so needy, right?" I shot Penny a wink and rested my coat on the back of my chair, settling in to tell them about my meeting with June Munrow and her theory that Kelly Taylor didn't drown in her bathtub.

"Do you want to order first?" Liam asked, studying me as if trying to assess whether I had skipped lunch. He had a habit of looking after me—checking to make sure I'd eaten, dropping by with homemade blueberry bran muffins, and practically demanding I stop by the Stag Head after work for soup and a pint. It was his love language, and I wasn't sad about it. After so many years of holing into myself and obsessing over Scarlet's murder, Liam, Pri, and Penny were all part of my cracking-open process. I was grateful for our connection. I never took their support and encouragement for granted; I knew how fleeting time could be and how your life could turn upside down in an instant.

"I'm happy to stuff my face with apps for the moment," I said, intentionally scooping more dip onto the bread and licking my lips.

Pri scowled at me over her pomegranate martini, tapping her wrist like she didn't have all night. "Stuff your face, and then out with it, okay? Prying minds want to know what's up."

"Okay, okay, I'll put you out of your misery. The rumors are true. I am happy to announce Fletcher and I signed our first client at the Novel Detectives this afternoon." I raised my glass in a toast as everyone applauded. I left out the part about Caroline hiring us. That was a secret for just Fletcher and me. "No, seriously, thanks to all of you. I wouldn't have taken this step if it wasn't for you." I felt my eyes start to well and a lump beginning to swell in my throat. I gulped a small sip of the drink. The brandy warmed my throat as I blinked away a tear. "I'm sorry to get emotional, but you know what a long road this has been, and I guess I just need to say aloud how lucky I am to have you."

"Damn, Annie," Pri said, brushing a tear from her face. "I wasn't prepared to cry tonight."

"It's happy tears. The thing is, I've been telling Fletcher not to worry—the clients would eventually come, but having our first client makes it real, you know?" I dabbed my eyes with my napkin. "Sorry. I won't gush anymore, but just know I love you."

"The feeling is entirely mutual." Liam's eyebrows lifted toward his forehead as he gave me a smoldering look that made me nearly spill my drink. "Now, out with it. Who is this mysterious client?"

"It's surprisingly a legit case," I said, brushing away one last tear. "Fletcher and I assumed we'd have to cut our teeth on missing cats and cheating spouses, but this is a murder. I'm sure you've all followed the story about Kelly Taylor. She's the young surfer who drowned in her bathtub a few weeks ago. It's so sad and even sadder once I've started to get a handle on her personal life—she was a huge advocate for conservation and was leading the charge as an agent of change to ensure that future generations have places left to surf."

"Oh, my God, yes. I totally remember reading about her efforts to save the coastline and her bizarre death." Pri stirred her drink with a swizzle stick. "It's the ultimate irony—a surfer drowning in a foot of water. She was really good, too, right? Wasn't she competing nationally?"

I nodded. "Yeah, and it sounds like she had signed endorsement deals shortly before her death."

"Can you give me the highlights?" Penny asked in an apologetic tone. "I'm the newbie here."

"Of course." I took a second to swallow the savory dip. "Kelly Taylor was a twenty-four-year-old surfer. She trained here but surfed all over the globe. And like Pri mentioned, she was destined for great things until she slipped in her bathtub one night, hit her head, and drowned. The police haven't been able to determine whether her death was an accident or if she could have killed herself. They found traces of a sedative in her system. Dr. Caldwell sent me the autopsy report and case files right before I came here tonight. I only had a chance to skim them. One thing stood out—there was no water on the floor or anywhere in the bathroom, no trail of blood, so the police aren't focused on the case being a homicide. They have a few theories. The first being that Kelly was dazed from the sedative and bumped her head, slipping under the water and never recovering. Another theory is that the hit knocked her unconscious, and then the last thread they're pursuing is that it was suicide. The problem is that the amount of sedatives in her system wasn't enough to kill her, and the coroner doesn't believe the head injury was fatal either. Drowning is the official cause of death."

"Is that where you and Fletcher come in?" Liam asked, giving me his full attention. It was one of the things I loved most about him—I never had to question whether he was really listening. He leaned in, letting his eyes linger as he waited for my response.

"Yes and no. June Munrow, is—was—Kelly's neighbor. She and Kelly were close, at least according to June." I wavered, still unsure how I felt about my client and her relationship with her neighbor. "And June is convinced that Kelly was murdered. She wants us to prove it and find the killer."

"Holy crap, Annie." Pri's mouth fell open. "You're not kidding. So much for missing cats and philanderers. Your first case is a murder investigation."

"An unsolved death," I corrected. "Neither Fletcher nor I are convinced. June is your classic neighborhood gossip. You should have seen her house. It was like a Sherlock murder board on steroids."

"Fletcher must have loved that," Liam said with a half grin.

"I think that's why he wanted to take the case. He saw a kindred spirit in June." I laughed and reached for one of the twisty bacon and puff pastry sticks. "No, June was even too much for him. She has a stakeout setup in front of her main window—multiple cameras, zoom lens, a telescope, the works. She can see the entire neighborhood, and it seems like she spends most of her time spying on the poor, unsuspecting people on her street. She basically gave us dossiers on everyone she considers to be a suspect. She believes Kelly was killed and has a lengthy list of theories as to why."

"Like what?" Liam flagged the server over to take our order. We paused the conversation long enough to order dinner. I could already almost taste the caramelized onion and turkey meatball flatbread and winter salad the kitchen would soon be preparing for me.

"June didn't like Kelly's boyfriend." I sipped my drink. "He's also a surfer. Jake Harken."

"Oh, I know Jake Harken," Pri said, twisting her lips into a grimace. "He comes into the coffee shop almost daily. I can tell you his order by heart—a triple-shot mocha with dark chocolate. He's super annoying, too. Instead of a mocha, he always says 'give me a choccy coffee' in a bad Australian accent. It was funny—once." She rolled her eyes and stabbed her salad with her fork.

"Any other insights?" I perked up, wanting to reach into my book bag and grab my journal to take notes but not wanting to turn our double date into a work session either.

"Uh, he has an inflated ego. It's odd that they were a couple because he doesn't strike me as the caring-about-the-ocean-or-anyone-except-for-himself type. He likes to make it known he's a surfer, not that you could miss it. Who else in Redwood Grove wears flip-flops and rash guards in the dead of winter?" Pri made a face. "Like, what's the deal? Did you come straight from the beach? It's a good thirty- or forty-minute drive. You didn't bother to take off your rash guard, my guy? Please."

I laughed. "Have you noticed any signs of a temper along with the ego? June mentioned the two of them fighting. She basically made it sound like he was borderline abusive."

Pri sighed, taking a minute to consider my question before continuing. "I've never seen him freak out over a coffee order or anything like that, but I will say he gives off stalkerish vibes."

Stalkerish sent warning bells sounding through my head. "How?"

Liam nodded in agreement. "Yeah, I'm curious what stalkerish vibes look like."

"Why, are you worried you're stalker adjacent or something?" She nudged him in the ribs.

"What? No." Liam recoiled at the mere thought.

"Relax, I'm teasing." Pri stuck out her tongue and tilted her head to one side, clearly enjoying his reaction. "He flirts with everyone, including me, even though I've made it perfectly clear I'm not interested, let alone I don't go for dudes. He wouldn't leave one of my younger baristas alone, so I had to warn him that if he kept harassing her, he was not welcome back—ever. I made it abundantly clear that we don't tolerate that behavior at Cryptic."

My skin tightened. I found myself curling my toes and pinching my lips together as I pictured Jake interacting inappropriately with Pri and her staff, feeling a natural protective instinct for my friend. Not that she needed my intervention. Pri could most certainly handle herself. "Did he stop?" This could be a critical piece of information. I'd have to fill Fletcher in tomorrow.

"I guess. Come to think of it, I haven't seen him since our little chat. Probably a couple of days or so."

Penny wrapped her arm around Pri. "Well done. You scared him off."

"Maybe." She pressed her lips together, thinking about it. "I'm fine with that. Cryptic is *not* a safe space for anyone attempting to harass my team—spread the word."

Our food arrived. I made space for my flatbread and a mental note to share Pri's insights about Jake Harken with Fletcher tomorrow. Perhaps June was onto something. Could the surfer have killed his ex-girlfriend in retaliation for breaking it off with him?

CHAPTER 7

The flatbread was even better than I remembered. I devoured two slices, not caring that it was scalding the roof of my mouth and tongue.

"It's too bad you don't like it," Liam noted with a grin.

"I hate it." I kept my tone and face as deadpan as possible. "Where is our server? I'm sending it back." I couldn't maintain the act for long. "Fine, I love it. I could marry it right now."

"You wouldn't dare." Pri swiped my hand away from my plate. "At least let your vampire slink off into the night before you propose to a pizza."

She had deemed Liam my vampire ever since he dressed up as Dracula for Halloween, at my encouragement, I might add—something he'd never let me live down after the nickname stuck, much to his chagrin and not for his lack of trying.

"What's your gut feeling about the case?" Liam asked, ignoring Pri's attempt to goad him into a friendly battle.

"It's too early to say. We have quite a few people to speak with. I need to get a sense of Kelly's mental health at the time of her death. Maybe the stress and pressure of surfing put her over the edge, or maybe she took something to relax, got in the tub, and bumped her head—it could have been the trifecta of fatal errors."

"Or she could have been killed," Pri added, stabbing a roasted red pepper with her fork. "Who are the other suspects?"

"Her roommate, Allison, who June claims was very possessive; her surfing coach, who was seen in the neighborhood the day she died; and her landlord, who apparently has a history of entering her property when she wasn't home."

"Sounds like you have your work cut out for you," Liam said, swirling his drink pensively.

"True, and is it bad that I'm excited to tackle this case and see if Fletcher and I can find a new angle or lead?" I gave everyone a sheepish shrug. "Dr. Caldwell said she's happy to have our assistance, and she said her colleague who's the lead on the case seems to be of the mindset that Kelly's death was nothing more than a tragic accident, but both Fletcher and I had this gut instinct that something doesn't feel right."

"Not at all." Penny replied first. "It shows that you are on your path of purpose—this is what you're meant to do."

"Thanks." I smiled, feeling warm from the cocktail, yummy food, and hanging with the people I loved most in this world. "Enough about me. I want to hear news about you. What's new at the farm?" I turned my attention to Penny.

Penny had purchased the old Wentworth family farmhouse and vineyard and had been painstakingly restoring the property to its original glory brick by brick and acre by acre.

"Things are continuing to progress—finally," Penny said, sounding upbeat as a soft smile spread across her naturally serene face. Penny didn't rattle easily, which was good because the process of renovating the aging estate had been much more costly and time-consuming than she had originally estimated. "You'll have to come to see the barn. You won't recognize it. The tasting room is taking shape. Now I have to hire a winemaker, which is making it start to feel real."

The next phase of her renovations included opening a tasting room and bottling her own wine with estate-grown grapes.

"Did you ever get in touch with my industry contact?" Liam asked. Running the Stag Head for years made him well-connected with regional vintners and brewers.

Penny's face lit up as she smiled and nodded. "I did. As a matter of fact, we're meeting next week. I'll keep you posted.

It's been surprisingly hard to find someone qualified. Part of the issue is that housing is hard to come by in Redwood Grove. I spoke with my contractor about the possibility of adding a small house. Free rent might be a good incentive. I don't want to hire just any winemaker. I want to find the best vintner—someone who knows the craft and can be a true partner as I grow the business."

"You will," Pri said encouragingly, patting her knee. "And if you don't, I'll take up winemaking. It can't be too far off from coffee. Beans, grapes—what's the difference, really? It's all small things that we smash into deliciousness."

We all laughed. The conversation shifted to Pri's latest ventures at Cryptic—cupping classes—and Liam's winter game nights at the pub. We lingered over decadent chocolate bread puddings smothered with vanilla bean ice cream and decaf coffee until I started to blink to keep my eyes open.

"Hey, that's our cue, Annie." Liam paid the bill and grabbed his coat, reaching for my hand and pulling me to my feet.

I didn't resist. The day had been long, and I wanted to be fresh to tackle Kelly's case first thing in the morning. We said our goodbyes and promised to meet up again soon.

On the short walk, Liam wrapped a sturdy arm around me and guided us past the enormous puddles and muddy sections of the paths that cut through Oceanside Park. The feeling that someone was watching me returned again.

A branch snapped in the distance. My senses spiked on high alert as an emptiness spread across the pit of my stomach. I froze and swiveled my head in that direction, my mind running through every worst-case scenario.

Was someone following us?

Why was I suddenly plagued by irrational fear?

"What is it?" Liam stopped and stared into the darkness, squinting hard.

I second-guessed myself, rubbing my hand over the back of my neck and taking a quick breath. "Nothing. I'm just tired and chilly."

"Let's get you home and warmed up." He wrapped his arm tighter around my waist as we continued. I felt grateful to have him nearby; I just wished I could figure out why I was so on edge.

At home, Liam tucked me in under layers of luxuriously soft bedding. For January, I had swapped my regular sheets with cozy flannel sheets designed with a dainty pink-and-pale-green winterberry pattern. I had added extra throw pillows and a thick down comforter that Professor Plum, my tabby cat, had immediately nabbed as his new favorite napping spot. The coziness extended to my bookshelves, which were packed with well-worn paperbacks and signed copies from authors who had visited the Secret Bookcase, along with framed photos, vases with dried flowers, and winter candles in scents of forest pine and cardamom and orange spice.

"Tea?" Liam asked, kicking off his shoes and making a nest in the middle of the bed for Professor Plum, who was more human than feline. He'd been Scarlet's cat, but I adopted him when she died, and he'd been faithfully by my side ever since.

"No, thanks. I have a feeling the minute my head hits the pillow, I'm going to be out." I stretched as Professor Plum kneaded my chest and the blankets, attempting to carve the perfect cozy spot and claim his territory before Liam got into bed.

As predicted, I was fast asleep in minutes, dreaming about swells on the sea and bubbling bathtubs that transformed into caskets. Despite the unsettling dreams, my sleep was strangely restful and rejuvenating. I was no dream expert, but I had a fairly good sense my subconscious was already furiously trying to piece together what had happened to the young surfer.

Liam was snoozing peacefully with Professor Plum nestled up under his arm when I woke the next morning with Kelly Taylor still on my mind. I left them both sleeping, tugged on a pair of leggings and an oversized knee-length sweater, and tiptoed to the kitchen. The fog and drizzle had finally loosened their grip. Golden sunlight flooded in through the window above my farmhouse sink, embracing my pots of basil, cilantro, and rosemary in a warm hug. Finally, a reprieve from the oppressive fog—maybe it was a sign that Kelly's case was going to be smooth sailing and Fletcher and I would have an answer for June quickly.

I made a pot of coffee—Cryptic's house blend—and toasted slices of sourdough.

My kitchen was comfy with a breakfast nook with a small table, window bench, bright throw pillows, and a view of my cul-de-sac. A vase of yellow snapdragons and white daisies sat in the center of the table. Pictures of me, Liam, and our circle of friends hiking in the redwoods, posing on the pier on a sunny summer afternoon, and dressed up in elaborate Halloween costumes were stuck to the fridge with a variety of bookstore magnets—a reminder of how much my world had expanded since moving to Redwood Grove.

I slathered butter and local wildflower honey on my toast and curled up with a mug of coffee, watching the sunrise over Oceanside Park in the distance. My neighborhood, like June's, was a collection of two-story houses with covered front porches and small, fenced yards. I was one of the younger residents in the community, which meant that my retired neighbors tended to dote on me—leaving plates of hot-from-the-oven chocolate chip cookies and baskets of apples and peaches from the farmer's market on my porch. I appreciated that they looked after me, and as far as I knew, no one had telescopic lenses pointed at my house.

I peered out onto the cul-de-sac. At least, I didn't think any of my neighbors did.

Liam shuffled downstairs as I was putting my dishes away. "You weren't kidding. You're up and at 'em early." He ran his fingers through his hair and scrunched his eyes, trying to adjust to the light. "Annie Murray is back on a case, and there's no stopping her now, huh?"

"Something like that?" I hid a grin. He knew me too well. I poured him a cup of coffee and shook Professor Plum's bag of kibble. An instant later, the cat joined us, making a beeline for his food dish. "There's a palpable energy that comes with being on a case. It's like my body is saying, 'Come on, get to work already.'"

"Don't let us stop you." Liam moved out of the way, lifting his coffee cup to his lips and tapping his phone. "Professor Plum and I will hang out for a while and enjoy a leisurely morning with my word games and your coffee." Since Liam worked later shifts at the pub, he tended to sleep in and get a slow start to the day with his crossword puzzles and word games.

"Sounds good." I stood on my tiptoes to kiss him and grabbed leftovers from the fridge for lunch later. "I'll see you at Stag Head when I'm done."

"Good luck, and don't do anything dangerous," he called after me.

"Me? Never." I scurried outside before he could say more, loving the fact that he had nailed my emotional state. When I was on a case, it was all-consuming. It was like I *had* to find the answers, even if it meant putting myself in harm's way. I didn't think there was too much danger involved in digging into Kelly's death, but then again, if June was correct about someone else having a hand in her drowning, I needed to remain vigilant and proceed with caution.

I couldn't shake feeling bothered by the circumstances surrounding her death. What had really happened to the young surfer? Even if she'd taken something to help her sleep, wouldn't she have jolted awake the minute her head slipped under the water?

Unless whatever she'd taken had knocked her out—intentionally.

We could be dealing with a clever killer.

But what could have put her in harm's way? A jealous boyfriend, possessive roommate, abrasive coach, or creepy landlord? Any death was unsettling, but Kelly's felt eerily similar to Scarlet's—a life cut way too short, with no chance for her to reach her full potential or continue to be a force of good in the world.

This is on you, Annie.

You can solve this.

I quickened my pace, energized by the thought, as I took the path through Oceanside Park. The spacious jewel of Redwood Grove was empty at this hour. My boots sunk into the pressed-bark walkways that cut through clusters of eucalyptus trees, which gave the park its refreshing herbal aroma. There were benches and picnic tables tucked under towering redwoods, open grassy spaces for outdoor yoga and Tai Chi, a pavilion and amphitheater, a children's play area with swings, and a splash fountain that was highly coveted in the summer.

Yesterday's rain left everything smelling renewed. Sunlight danced off the soggy, dewy grass, making everything look like it had been dusted with glitter. I breathed deeply as I turned onto the trail that led to the Secret Bookcase. Hal had insisted the grounds surrounding the estate remain open to the public when he purchased the property.

Jekyll and Hyde swooped overhead, cawing and stretching their velvety feathers as they glided over the gardens in a gracious morning welcome. Their obsidian shadows danced on the ground as they sailed effortlessly overhead.

"Good morning," I called to our resident birds, reaching into my book tote for a handful of peanuts. Fletcher and I kept stockpiles of peanuts everywhere—book bags, at the sales counter, and stashed in a locked outdoor container on the Terrace. In exchange for feeding them, they left us shiny trinkets, pebbles, and sometimes even cash. They'd gotten bolder and braver as time wore on and they realized we weren't a threat. Not a day went by that they didn't sail overhead, riding imaginary waves in the sky and chattering happily as I tossed them peanuts on my way into the store.

I paused long enough to scatter peanuts on the ground and watched them dive-bomb the grass, snatching up the unshelled nuts with their sharp beaks and then doing a flyover as if saying *thank you*.

Fletcher and I had a shared goal to get them eating out of the palms of our hands by the end of the year. It wasn't out of the realm of possibility. Whenever I took a lunch break on the Terrace, they would bounce along the retaining wall with their dinosaur-like feet, watching my every move and inching ever so slightly closer.

Last week, Fletcher was able to get Hyde to stay perched on the iron front railing while he put the sandwich board sign out.

"Who's ready for breakfast?" I called to my guardians, continuing through the lush English garden.

There was never a dull season at the Secret Bookcase or in the gardens. I loved watching new flowers and sprouts push up through the ground in the springtime, blooming in tidy rows of jewel-toned tulips and daffodils. Summer brought a bounty of roses, the intoxicating scent of jasmine and wisteria, and a symphony of birds and pollinators. Autumn ushered in a kaleidoscope of colors—burnt orange, taupe, and flaxen yellow leaves creating a carpet beneath my feet. And then winter, ah, winter. There was nothing like it. Bountiful citrus trees, heavy with clementines and Meyer lemons, a touch of frost on the topiaries and fountains, and snowdrops in bloom made me acutely aware that winter in Northern California was distinctively different than other regions.

"Don't eat those all at once," I cautioned the crows and headed down the gravel drive to the front of the store. As expected, I was the first to arrive. I went through the opening procedures, turning on the gas fireplaces in the Sitting Room and Library, propping pillows, turning featured titles face-out, starting water for tea, and making sure everything was ready once we turned the sign on the door to OPEN.

I used the opportunity and quiet to begin my initial case notes. The sooner we dove into interviewing the suspects, the better, especially since Kelly's case had already been stagnant for the last few weeks. Technically, Kelly's case wasn't considered cold yet. Police departments had various criteria they used regarding the length of time before a case was classified as cold, depending on the size of the department and the nature of the crime. Typically, if a case sat unsolved for more than three months, it had gone cold. We were still within the critical window, but we needed to move quickly and press everyone associated with Kelly's death now while details were still relatively fresh.

The first person I wanted to speak with was Jake Harken, Kelly's ex-boyfriend. According to the police report, the detective assigned to the case noted his short temper and that Jake and Kelly had a volatile history, but there was no direct evidence linking him to her death. Jake admitted he visited Kelly the day she died and that they fought, but that wasn't a crime.

Pri's insight about Jake from dinner last night was added to my spreadsheet, along with his current address. While I researched the surfer, scouring his social media pages and public records, I found an interesting link. Brogan Blears was now coaching Jake. The two were roommates, and he had been instrumental in launching Jake's career and signing lucrative sponsorships with major brand partners. One was the very same partner Kelly had signed with shortly before her death—TideBreak Apparel. The trendy brand offered stylish, durable surf apparel that was equally functional, fashionable, and sustainable. They were one of the top sponsors of the WSL, the World Surf League, and a huge donor to causes that protected the environment. The partnership between the brand and Kelly seemed synonymous, but given what Pri told me about Jake, I had some questions.

I paused to consider the implications of Jake landing the same sponsorship. Could there be a financial angle? I made a note to reach out to the company to see how many brand deals they offered each year and what they might be able to tell us about Kelly.

Brogan Blears had been a World Surf League coach and board member for ten years, helping countless surfers break out into major stars not just in the more niche world of surfing but in the broader sports marketplace, making surfing mainstream and bringing in a swell of sponsor money.

The good news was I should be able to speak with both of them at the same time since they were roommates.

Next, I moved on to Allison Irons, Kelly's former roommate. Allison worked as an ER nurse at the hospital. If there was any truth to Kelly's death being a homicide, Allison was likely going to be ruled out quickly because the police report documented she worked a night shift the evening of Kelly's accident. Her alibi appeared to be airtight. The hospital administrator shared Allison's rotation—she'd assisted in three surgeries and attended to countless patients that night. Still, I intended to speak with Allison as soon as possible. She had lived with Kelly and could likely provide us with the best insight into her former roommate's mood and well-being leading up to her death.

Last was Harvey Wade. My screen lit up like a Christmas tree when I searched his name. Dozens of complaints and online reviews painted a clear picture of the landlord. He seemed to take very little care of the properties he owned and managed. Tenants complained about rat infestations, broken water pipes, and entering their premises without permission.

What a gem.

Ugh.

I wasn't looking forward to having a chat with Harvey. I could tell from Kelly's files that the detective and team had similar feelings about Mr. Wade. They investigated his activities, pursuing the angle that he had violated tenant rights, and handed his case over to the local housing authority. That case had to be handled separately. I knew as much from my studies and private detective exams. If a police officer or detective uncovered other criminal activity during an investigation, they typically referred it to another department because they had to prioritize the primary case, unless they happened to have the resources or legal justification to pursue multiple cases at once.

The cheerful jingle of the doorbell made me look up to see Fletcher waving for a hand. A tower of tippy boxes was precariously perched on his arms, waiting to topple over at any minute.

"What's all this?" I asked, propping the door open.

He kept his grip tight, heading straight for the counter and resting the stack with a huge sigh of relief like he'd just accomplished a monumental feat. "Whew, I thought I was about to lose these halfway up the drive." He shook his arms, letting them flail to his sides like soggy, wet noodles.

"What's in the boxes?" I repeated.

"As my dear Sherlock would say, 'Data, data, data! I can't make bricks without clay.'"

"Fletcher." I scowled, giving him my best "get on with it" look.

"Fine. Call it research." He tapped the side of a box. "I was up most of the night giving my printer a run for its money. Once I got started, I couldn't stop."

"You printed all of this last night?" I said, not able to mask the awe in my tone, counting three corrugated file storage boxes. Each was lidded and marked with the words: KELLY TAYLOR CASE FILES.

"Not all of it. I went to the library first and reviewed every article published in local, regional, and even national newspapers.

The staff was gracious enough to let me make copies there, too. Did you know that Kelly's death made headlines in surfing publications around the world? I didn't realize she was quite the rising star. June mentioned that, and as you know, the local news had plenty of coverage immediately after her death, but surfing isn't exactly my sport. Her death sent ripples through the surfing community."

"I've garnered the same thing from what I've been reading this morning. I didn't realize the kind of money attached to surfing sponsorships either." I filled him in on what I'd discovered about Jake and Brogan, as well as my conversation with Dr. Caldwell.

"Follow the money." Fletcher shot his finger to the cash register.

"My thoughts exactly." I was glad we were in agreement. "I want to pay a visit to the surfing bros today. Maybe during my lunch break."

"Excellent. I have much to wade through, as you can see." He ran his hand over the boxes.

With that, we were off and running. The investigation into Kelly Taylor's mysterious drowning had begun.

CHAPTER 8

Mary Jane arrived shortly after Fletcher. She was tall with long brown hair that curled softly on the ends, glasses, and the kind of energy that exuded a natural calm that was in complete opposition to her bookish addiction to dark psychological thrillers. When she'd interviewed for the position, Fletcher and I were in immediate agreement that her easygoing style would be an excellent match for the store and to guide more programs for our youngest readers—story time, crafts, mini cooking-from-the-book classes. She'd thrown us for a loop when he asked where her reading tendencies swayed. I had assumed she'd reply with something along the lines of golden age mysteries or culinary cozies, but instead, she'd given him a wicked, impish smile. "Dark. The darker, the better. Horror, true crime, psychological thrillers—they're all my speed."

It just went to show you couldn't judge a book by its cover, or a reader by the book.

Her teenagers were in high school, and she'd put her career on hold to be home with them. She was looking for a job that would allow her the flexibility to attend soccer games and help with homework but also fill her with a sense of purpose. It was a match made in bookish heaven and a win for all of us.

"How is everyone?" she asked, sweeping inside with a plate of homemade cinnamon and currant scones. "I'm on math-club snack duty today, so I made an extra batch for the store. Please, help yourselves."

"Math was never my subject, but I won't turn down a *scone*." Fletcher used one of the more proper British pronunciations, which sounded more like "gone," as he grabbed one from the plate.

"Hey, speaking of school, did you look into the summer course?" I was eager to loop Mary Jane into my master plan to convince him to sign up for the mystery intensive. I knew she would back me up.

"What course?" she asked, making room for the scones near the tea cart.

"Annie's trying to force me to attend a summer program at Redwood College as a first step toward going back to finish my MFA." Fletcher ripped a piece of the scone and popped it in his mouth.

"Oh, do it! Yes, great idea." Mary Jane smiled brightly.

"I don't know, I think I'm too old," Fletcher said, sounding like he was already trying to talk himself out of it.

"Too old?" Mary Jane scoffed and caught my eye before shaking her head at Fletcher. "I'm forty-five. Do you have any idea how nervous I was about applying for this job? I figured you would laugh at my application. I've been out of the game for so long, and I was even more nervous on my first day, but I love every minute of being at the store. I'm so energized. Being around books and bookish people is the best, and I get to talk to customers about what they're reading and help them discover new reads. I've been hand-selling *Blood on the Page* like you wouldn't believe. Telling readers how it kept me up all night, turning the pages and checking under my bed."

Fletcher chuckled as he broke off another piece of the scone. "So you're the reason we can't keep it in stock."

"That's right. Consider me a book pusher." Mary Jane gave him a proud nod. "I hope you'll consider taking the course. I tell my kids that investing in yourself is always worth it. Use me as an example. I'm starting a brand-new career in my mid-forties, and it's making me feel like I'm twenty again."

"Okay, okay. I'll think about it," he said, stuffing the rest of the scone in his mouth so he didn't have to say more.

I hoped he was serious and not just trying to get us off his back, but I let the conversation shift to the daily schedule and upcoming events.

The morning breezed by. I chatted with regulars, helped customers find titles, made book recommendations—my absolute favorite part of the job—and wrapped new reads in craft paper, finishing packages with our signature Secret Bookcase stickers. By the time the lunch hour arrived, I scarfed down my leftovers and checked in with Fletcher and Mary Jane before grabbing my notebook and venturing off to see if I could get Jake and Brogan to speak with me about Kelly's death.

Their house wasn't far from the library. I was surprised they'd opted to live in Redwood Grove rather than closer to the beach, but I found their place easily. I didn't have to stretch my sleuthing skills to figure out which one was their house. A stack of surfboards was propped on a custom-built rack in front of the garage. Two SUVs were parked in the driveway, each plastered with surfing bumper stickers with sayings like HANG LOOSE, JUST SURF, SURFER DUDES, and NO KOOKS. The yard was littered with more surfing gear—wet suits and damp towels soaking up muddy water on the patchy grass.

I had no idea what "No kooks" meant or what color either of the vehicles was underneath the bumper sticker graffiti. Rash guards and wet suits hung near the surfboards, drying in the afternoon sun. The house was in decent shape. There were no obvious signs of neglect, but it gave off frat-party vibes. I could almost smell the stale beer and weed.

I knocked on the door, pounding to be heard over the music blaring inside. The porch was dusted with sand. Another surfboard was propped against the side. Tubes of sunscreen and wax were piled on a plastic table. Swim trunks and board shorts hung along the railing that enclosed the porch, transforming it into a permanent drying rack.

It took a couple of minutes before anyone realized or heard my knocking. I was about to give up when the music finally shut off, and a guy slowly shuffled toward the door, peering out the keyhole first to make sure I wasn't a serial killer. Or maybe the cops?

He was shorter than I had imagined but rock-solid—all muscle—with sandy-brown, chin-length hair, naturally bleached from the sun and salt water. I deduced this must be the infamous Jake Harken from his coral rash guard and flip-flops.

"Hey, what's up?" His glassy eyes struggled to focus as he studied me, trying to decide if I was about to sell him something or here to proselytize.

"I'm Annie Murray from Novel Detectives. I was hoping I might be able to speak with you about Kelly Taylor for a minute." I offered him a business card. "Are you Jake?"

"Yeah, that's me." He stared at the card like it was written in hieroglyphics, flipping it over to check the back as if that might give him a clue. "Huh?"

"I'm doing some research into Kelly's death, and I heard you knew her."

"Kelly?"

How high is he?

Should I change my approach?

"Kelly was a cool girl." He handed me my card and leaned against the doorframe, letting it support his body weight. "What do you need to know?"

"Some new information has come to light in the investigation into her death—"

"Drowning. She drowned." He cut me off and grabbed a tube of expensive sunscreen. He twisted off the cap and squeezed some of the thick moisturizer into his hand, rubbing it into his skin like he was trying to soothe away the memory.

"Right." Had I hit a nerve? His body tensed slightly. "I've been hired to help with the case, and it sounds like you knew her well; I'd love to get a picture of who she was and her state of mind."

"Nah, I don't have time." He started to shut the door. "I already told the cops everything I remember about that night."

I stuck my foot in the frame.

Jake Harken was my top suspect. There was no way I was leaving without getting more information from him.

CHAPTER 9

"Hey, what are you doing?" Jake loosened his grip on the door. "I said I don't have time to talk. What's the deal anyway? Like I said, she drowned. End of story."

"We're not so sure about that." I yanked my foot free and held my ground.

"Huh?" He squinted, scrunching his face tight. "You don't think she drowned?"

This wasn't exactly how I had intended for our conversation to go, but I needed to draw him out. He wasn't going to talk without some pressure, and the only way to do that was to make him sweat a little. To make him think he was a suspect, which he was, at least in my book.

"I'm a private detective, working with the local police to re-examine the case. There's been new information that's come to light that has us considering new possibilities. You don't have to speak with me, but it would be better if you did. Otherwise, the police can bring you down to the station." That wasn't entirely true. Although now that Dr. Caldwell was involved in the investigation, I didn't doubt that she would call Jake in for further questioning at my directive.

"No, no. I don't want to get the cops involved again. What do you want to know?"

Jackpot!

I have him right where I want him.

"Anything you can tell me about Kelly, especially in the days leading up to her death."

"Yeah, I mean, she was always chill. Super chill. But then she changed—like that." He snapped his fingers together but missed. He tried again, forcing the motion like he couldn't figure out why it wasn't working.

"When did she change?" I pressed.

He shrugged, fiddling with the sunscreen cap like it was a Mensa puzzle. It took every ounce of control not to grab it from him and twist it back on the tube. "Uh, I don't know. Maybe a few weeks before her accident. She broke it off with me. We'd been hanging for a year, and then she went silent. She ghosted me. Wouldn't talk. Wouldn't even look at me when we were surfing."

"That must have been hard for you." I softened my tone, hoping I could connect with him. If I wanted him to open up, I needed to build rapport.

"Yeah, it sucked." He kicked a rock off the porch with his flip-flop.

I wanted to ask if we could go inside and sit down, but I didn't want to push my luck. I had a feeling that if I broke out my notebook, he would clam up.

"A neighbor mentioned you were there the day she died."

"Oh, God, not that old lady." He scraped his hands through his hair and squinted again. "She was always watching us. Staring out the window. Like, do you have nothing better to do? She didn't like me. I'm sure she's part of the reason Kelly broke it off."

This was a new tidbit. How much influence had June had over Kelly? If Kelly had confided in June and reached out to her for advice, that potentially made June's concerns and perspective on Kelly's death more valid in my book. There was a difference between a nosy neighbor, stirring up gossip and excitement, and someone who Kelly may have turned to for help.

"She tried to tell the cops I had something to do with Kelly's accident."

"Why would she do that?" I played dumb. I'd already read all of this in the police report, but I wanted to hear Jake's perspective.

"Because we got in a fight. I hate that she died that day. Things got kind of heated." He kicked the ground twice and looked off in the distance. Then he tightened the cap on the sunscreen and tossed it in the pile.

I waited.

I'd learned it was often best to remain silent and let a witness or suspect feel the weight and uncomfortableness of the silence. Most often, they would rush to fill the empty space, hopefully sharing more than they intended.

Jake did that now. "She got in her head. Had a bad crash. It happens. It's part of the sport. You pick yourself up and get back on the board. But she couldn't take it. The pressure got to her. She was quitting—giving it all up."

I nodded, not wanting to interrupt his thoughts. Giving it all up certainly sounded like Kelly might have been in emotional distress at the time of her death.

"We did fight that day." He ran his tongue along the inside of his cheek as he shook his head. "It wasn't because I was trying to get back together with her. That's what the old creepy neighbor lady told the police. They came down hard on me. Yeah, sure, I was still into her, but that wasn't why I was there. Brogan asked me to talk her off the ledge."

Again, his choice of words made me wonder if this case was a tragedy. Whether intended or not, Kelly might have succumbed to drowning due to her mental health. It wasn't uncommon in highly competitive sports. Recently, several high-profile Olympic athletes had used their platforms to speak out about the role mental health plays in their lives and the importance of therapy to balance the demands of the pressure to perform.

"Was Brogan concerned about her?" I asked.

"He didn't want her to quit, if that's what you mean." His nose turned up into a half snarl as he scrunched his face and shook his head. "She signed with TideBreak Apparel. She was about to go nuclear. He thought maybe I could convince her to stay."

"That's what you fought about the day she died?" I tried to glance inside. I could hear the low murmur from the TV and smell something burning. Was Brogan here? Was he listening to our conversation?

"Yep. I begged her not to quit. I told her she was ruining her life by opting out, but she wouldn't listen. She'd already made up her mind. Nothing I could say was going to change that, and I only made it worse. She got pissed. Told me she was done with me and surfing and that if I ever came by again, she would go to the police. Then she was dead. It wasn't supposed to be like that. Kelly was chill. She was cool. I still can't understand why she flipped out."

"Do you believe she killed herself?" I asked gently. I knew it was a touchy and potentially triggering question.

"No. No way. No chance. Never. She wouldn't." He balled his hand into a fist and punched the doorframe twice. "I should have been there. I could have saved her."

"What do you think happened that night?" I believed that he didn't think she killed herself, but that still didn't mean it was true.

"The same as always. She took an edible to relax and slipped in the bath. She had terrible insomnia. She barely ever slept more than a few hours every night without her cocktail of supplements, which she would use to knock herself out. She had a strict routine—light dinner with lots of protein, take an edible, and get in the bath to relax. Sometimes, it helped her sleep. Sometimes, it didn't." He shifted his body weight, walked to the railing, and yanked off a pair of floral board shorts with much more force than was necessary like he was taking out his aggression on the shorts. "Isn't that what the cops think happened?

I don't get it. I already told them all of this. They won't let it go. Let her RIP, you know?"

I noticed the deep veins in his neck throb as he wadded the still-damp shorts, wringing them out like a dish towel. "The police report is inconclusive," I replied, carefully examining his body language. His knuckles had gone as white as the snowdrops pushing up through the ground, and his left eye started to twitch. He was nervous. Was it because I was asking questions about Kelly's death, or was it a natural reaction—his body's response to raw grief? Kelly had only died a few weeks ago.

"What does that mean?" He sounded put out that I'd even brought up the topic. "She's dead. It was an accident. Why does it matter now?"

"That's what I'm here to find." I needed to remain calm and collected without giving away any specifics. I wanted him to know we were helping with the case but not *why* we were helping with the case. I couldn't risk scaring him. That was a guaranteed way to shut him up.

"I don't get it." He discarded the board shorts, flinging them to the ground. "Why? Why won't they just let her rest in peace?"

"As I mentioned, some new details have come to light. It's standard protocol for cases like this. They don't want Kelly's case to go cold."

"Cold cases." He recoiled away from me. "Isn't that for murders and stuff?"

"Not necessarily." I tried to sound noncommittal. "The police haven't been able to determine whether Kelly's death was an accident or suicide, so that's where I come in."

He massaged the top of his thighs with his thumbs. "Seems weird to drag it up again. We just had the funeral."

"I understand. I've lost someone I cared for deeply, too."

"Yeah." He stared at his feet and went silent.

I took that as my cue that he was done with the conversation. "Well, I appreciate your time. Is Brogan here by chance?" I peered around him. The entryway mirrored the porch. It was cluttered with surfing gear and two more boards. How many surfboards did these guys need? "I'd love to chat with him for a minute, too."

"Uh, yeah, I'll get him." Jake moved slowly, stepping deliberately and keeping one eye on me as he backed away.

While I waited for Brogan, I made a few quick notes. There was nothing in the police report about Kelly quitting the sport. Had they failed to ask those questions? Doubtful. It was more likely that Jake and Brogan had intentionally left out that critical piece of information. But why?

CHAPTER 10

Brogan Blears was a carbon copy of Jake, only about ten years older and significantly taller. Otherwise, he sported the same surfer wavy hair and lackadaisical movements. He was a mix of lean muscle mass and thick, red hair, with glassy, bloodshot eyes. He'd either had a stint of sleepless nights or maybe he'd been crying recently?

"Hey, I wondered where Jake had disappeared. What's up?" He flashed me a toothy grin that was too practiced, too bright, like he was putting on a show. His tanned cheeks only enhanced his brilliant white smile. Given the smattering of freckles and red spots on his cheeks, I guessed he'd had plenty of sun damage.

"I'm Annie Murray," I said, reaching to shake his hand. "I was asking Jake a few questions about Kelly Taylor and was hoping I might get some insight from you, too. You were her coach, correct?"

He clasped my hand tighter and let out what almost sounded like a whimper. "Ah, Kelly Taylor. She was one of a kind. The real deal. Killer talent. Natural instincts. Fearless." He released his grasp, seeming to realize he'd been holding on to me too long. "Sorry. Yeah, what do you want to know about Kelly?"

I gave him my rehearsed story about being hired to look into Kelly's death, new information about the circumstances surrounding her drowning, and working in conjunction with the police to close her case. "I heard you were her coach, and she was considering quitting. Is that true?"

His demeanor changed radically. He shook his head and backed away, glancing behind him and then back at me. Gone was the polished, dazzling smile.

What had I said that triggered such a strong reaction? Kelly quitting? Something else?

"Uh, hey, yeah, I can't talk…" He struggled, trying to find the right words, keeping his head swiveled toward the doorway. "Not here. Not now." He lowered his voice, refusing to tear his eyes away from the door. "You know that coffee shop downtown, the one with the cool roll-up garage doors?"

"Cryptic?" I offered. "My friend is the head barista there."

"Yeah. That. You want to grab a coffee there? Maybe tomorrow? Same time?" He glanced behind him, not bothering to conceal that he didn't want Jake to hear us.

"Sure." A zillion questions bombarded my brain, but I wasn't about to turn down a chance to have some of them answered. "Tomorrow afternoon. I'll meet you there, thanks." I gave him a business card. "Here's my contact info in case anything changes."

"Catch you later." Brogan raised his left hand in a wave, flashing the hang loose sign.

I turned to make my exit but stopped in mid-stride. "Before I go, I need to know, what does 'No kooks' mean?" I pointed to the Jeep.

He tossed his head back and laughed. "Surfer lingo—no newbies."

"That's rough for anyone starting the sport, yeah?"

"Nah, it's not like that. Anyone is welcome, but kooks is more about disrespectful, inexperienced surfers. You know the type; they pretend to know everything, but they don't. Total lack of awareness about the waves and the surfers around them. They get themselves and all of us in dangerous positions. It's mainly a joke, but after years of coaching, I can spot a kook right away from their brand-new big-box gear."

"So Kelly wasn't a kook," I said, hoping to glean a bit more from him while he was more relaxed.

"Nah, Kelly could never be a kook. She was a goddess from day one," he said with a touch of longing in his voice. "God, she was gorgeous when she surfed, like totally one with the water. A queen."

His choice of words wasn't lost on me—*goddess, queen, gorgeous.* Could that explain why he wanted to meet at Cryptic? I created a new potential narrative in my head on the drive home. What if Brogan and Kelly were having an affair? That would explain why he didn't want to talk about her with Jake nearby which could have led to even more stress. Keeping a secret like that might have added to her mental health and sleep challenges.

It was too soon to jump to conclusions, though. We were in the early phases of an investigation, which meant any and every possibility was on the table until we could prove or disprove a theory.

Fletcher was packing a stack of books for a customer when I returned to the Secret Bookcase. I waited for him to finish before launching into what I'd learned.

"This is good, Annie." He gestured to the stack of files near the cash register. "I've been weeding through everything I can between customers. Do you know how much some of these surfers make?"

"I'm guessing it's a decent amount?" I paused to rearrange the candle display, filling in gaps where customers had taken French vanilla and lavender tins from the tiered stack.

"The top-ranked pros earn millions with their sponsorship deals," Fletcher said. "From what I've garnered, it sounds like Kelly was on that trajectory. She earned nearly a half million her last year, and she was in a position to make an even larger cut of the sponsorship money headed her way. She donated a substantial amount to various conservation charities and still had plenty left in the bank."

"But who would kill her for the money? I checked the case report earlier. Her parents were listed as the beneficiaries in her will. None of our suspects would have received anything from her death, and there's the issue that her sponsorship required her to actually surf. That money would have gone away upon her death."

"Agreed." Fletcher scowled and tapped the side of his chin with a bony finger. "Unless someone else seized the opportunity to sign with the same ad sponsor—killed her to get her out of the way and then slip in and sign the deal that was meant for her."

"Someone like Jake Harken, perhaps?" I returned a lid to one of the candles. It was a common occurrence in the bookshop. Customers would test candles and forget to put the lids back on. The bane of my existence as an indie bookstore owner was constantly having to reshelve misplaced books and merchandise. But I could deal with our daily reshelving in exchange for the plethora of amazing things that owning a store offered. "I'll be eager to hear what Brogan can add when I meet with him tomorrow. Jake didn't try to lie about snagging the TideBreak sponsorship, but I don't trust that I got the full story either."

"Who's next on your list?"

I went behind the counter and tucked my bag in one of the cubbies underneath the cash register. "I'd like to speak with Allison Irons."

"Yes, yes." Fletcher held up a finger to stop me and leafed through his notes. "I happened to see her schedule in this stack of documents. According to her interview with the police, she's worked the same shift for five years. She's working tonight, so you can probably catch her on her break."

"Perfect. That's great timing. I'm hoping to track down Harvey Wade this week, too."

"I'll come along with you on that one. I can't go to the hospital because it's my Sherlockian society meeting tonight, and I'm hosting it." He tilted his head back and craned his neck toward the ceiling, tapping his shoulders. "But I don't think you should meet with Harvey alone."

"No, let's definitely do that one together. Trust me, I'm dreading that interview the most. The online reviews are atrocious. I don't know how he's still in business. I'm surprised the housing authority hasn't shut him down already. He has two pending civil cases in small claims court from tenants claiming he failed to return their security deposits."

A customer looking for a recommendation for a birthday gift interrupted us. I showed her to the Mary Westmacott Nook where we housed our selections of romance novels. The room was a nod to the pen name Agatha Christie used when writing love stories. It was on the smaller side, with tall walnut bookcases, illustrations of Mr. Darcy and Elizabeth Bennet, dried pastel flowers in bookish vases, and heart string lights. I suggested a few titles for the customer and sent her on her way with a sweet stack of reads for her friend's birthday. Connecting books and readers always felt like magic. There was something innately special about being a tiny part of a reader discovering a new book that would hopefully transport them to a far-off corner of the world or help them uncover an untouched part of themselves in the pages.

I'd always believed that books have the power to create points of understanding in ways that nothing else could. Opening pages yellowed from the years and venturing into an author's head was the only time we ever had an opportunity to see things from someone else's viewpoint. If that wasn't magic, I didn't know what was.

Liam liked to tease me that I was a book romantic, and he was right. I wouldn't put up a fight when it came to my bookish obsessions or the belief that my job was to change lives one book at a time.

I spent the remainder of the afternoon mapping out our event schedule for February and March. In addition to our weekly story time for our youngest readers and book clubs, we were planning to host another Valentine's matchmaking weekend at the store. Several bestselling mystery authors were lined up for a Dark and Stormy event, and we were launching our first Flash Fiction contest. The idea had been suggested by an author who was generous enough to send us some prompts to get started. Customers would use the prompts, including a motive, setting, and murder weapon. Then they'd have one hour to write a one-hundred-word story on note cards that we would provide.

At the end of the event, we would post the note cards throughout the store and let customers vote on their favorites. The winning story would receive a Secret Bookcase tote brimming with literary goodies. I penciled out everything on the calendar, double-checked my dates, and posted each event on our social media pages.

Then I drafted a newsletter featuring the upcoming events, new releases we were excited about, and our customer reviews. Customer reviews were a recent addition to our newsletter. We asked some of our regulars and book club members to share short reviews about books they loved. It was an instant hit. Their recommended titles had been flying off the shelves. We learned we needed to double our order before we sent out a newsletter, which, as a small, independent bookstore, was a great problem to have.

Once I finished the event schedule, it was nearly time to close. I took a leisurely walk through the store, returning misplaced books to their spots and rearranging furniture. I never cared if a reader moved one of the chairs closer to the fireplace or window to curl up for an afternoon of getting lost in the pages. That was the gift of a shop like the Secret Bookcase. We encouraged readers to stay and linger.

Darkness settled in over the grounds and gardens, casting a midnight blush on the bookstore. Usually, I enjoyed the routine of going room by room and tucking the shop in for a good night's sleep. I never felt unsafe at the Secret Bookcase, but tonight, I had to admit my anxiety was slightly spiked. I was probably running on high due to Kelly's case, but every creak of the floorboard or flicker of my shadow sent my heartbeat thudding against my chest.

You're overreacting, Annie.

I shook it off, squaring my shoulders and ignoring the damp, cold chill spreading down my arms. The long corridor stretched ahead, lined with portraits whose painted eyes seemed to be watching my every move.

What's wrong with you, Annie?

In the Sitting Room, I returned a stack of books to their spot on the shelves and checked the secret bookcase to make sure we didn't have any stowaways attempting to hide out in the store overnight. Thankfully, the coast was clear.

As I turned off the antique Tiffany lamp near the bay windows, I caught a flash of movement outside and jerked backward, throwing a protective arm over my chest.

What is that?

I crouched down and squinted, only to catch my own reflection staring back at me through the glass.

Geez, Annie.

Get it together.

I stood up and wiped my sweaty palms on my leggings just as something hit the window with an echoing thud, sending my heartbeat skyrocketing and me to the floor.

CHAPTER 11

I screamed and threw my hands over my mouth.

The tapping on the glass grew louder, sharper, and more insistent.

Who was it?

I slowly lifted my head, just enough to see above the windowsill, and came face-to-face, or face-to-beak, with Jekyll and Hyde rapping their talons on the glass.

"Oh, my God, you two scared me to death." I pushed to my feet with a shaky exhale.

The crows.

It's the crows.

Thank goodness.

But also, maybe it was time for Fletcher and me to rethink our training protocols. Were we giving them too many peanuts? Were they *too* comfortable around us? Too tame?

"That's it for tonight. Sweet dreams. I'll see you in the morning," I called to them as I switched off the lights and headed for the front.

Fletcher was moving the sandwich board sign inside and turning off the accent lights when I made it to the Foyer. "Where did the day go?" He tapped his watch but then stopped when he caught my eye and looked at me with concern. "Are you okay? You look like you've seen a ghost."

"Do crows count?" I shuddered, rubbing my shoulders and wrapping myself in a tight hug. "Jekyll and Hyde just scared the living daylights out of me," I said, pointing down the hallway. "They were at the window begging for treats. I thought someone was trying to break in. Nope, just our winged warriors begging for evening snacks."

"They're coming to the window now. Interesting." Fletcher considered this for a minute, his eyes drifting to the ceiling and then outside again like his mind was making rapid connections. "Maybe we need to invite them inside? Build them a crow's nest in the Parlor?"

"No chance." I laughed, breaking the tension. It was silly of me to get spooked by our crow friends, but we were in the middle of an investigation into a suspicious death. Having my senses on high alert would serve me well when it came to interviewing suspects. "I'm glad to hear you feel the same about the day. I can't believe it's this late. I thought maybe it was because I left for an extended lunch. It wasn't even particularly busy."

"I suppose that's January for you." He pointed to the ebony sky. "It feels like midnight out there, but it's just a little after five."

"Have fun with your Sherlockians. Is there a theme for your festivities?"

"Is there a theme? Please. Annie, have you met me?" He tipped his head to the side and frowned. "Of course there is a theme."

I chuckled. "Care to share?"

He propped the sign next to the coffee and tea cart and whipped out his phone. "This is my menu—Baker's Street Bruschetta, Dr. Watson's Chicken and Veg Pasty, and Irene Adler's Grapefruit Meringue Tart."

"You're making all of that? Tonight? You better hustle, my friend." I shoved him toward the door.

"I will be on my way, but not to worry. I spent the weekend prepping. Everything is ready to go—a bit of assembly, warming, and a quick outfit change."

"You're breaking out the deerstalker and your plastic pipe, aren't you?" I wrinkled my brow and scowled. Fletcher would use any opportunity he could get to dress up like his favorite fictional character.

"Elementary, dear Watson." He gave me an exaggerated wink, using his fingers to serve as a pipe. "Good luck with Allison. I'll be eager to hear what illumination she may be able to shed on the case."

"Give the Sherlockians my best. I'll finish closing." I waved with two fingers. "And don't forget to sign up for summer school!"

"Until tomorrow." He scurried down the hallway toward the back entrance, ignoring my comment.

I felt good about my progress with our store events and was ready to return my full attention to the case.

> Making a quick pit stop at the hospital before dinner

Three dots appeared right away.

> Hospital?!?

I realized I should have clarified the reason for my stop.

> Checking in with a suspect, btw. I'm fine.

The dots stopped and then reappeared.

> Don't do that to me, Murray. The hospital nearly sent me into a panic.

> Sorry.

I included a sorry and a kissing emoji.

> Should be there in 30.

And you call yourself a word lover.

He added a winking emoji.

See you when you get here. Good luck.

He had a fair point. I finished closing the bookstore and cut through the garden. There was no sign of Jekyll and Hyde. They must have flown off in search of greener pastures, or the hope that someone may have dropped part of a bagel or a leftover snack in the park.

Even though I knew it had been them tapping at the window, the jittery feeling stuck with me on my walk. I kept checking over my shoulder at the sound of a twig snapping in the distance or the breeze rattling through the trees.

Solar lanterns dangled from the trees and lined the pathways, lighting my way. The hospital, like everything else in Redwood Grove, was located not far off the village square. One of the many perks of living in a walkable community was rarely needing to drive to work, for shopping, or a dinner out. Even hiking trails were accessible from town. Liam and I had developed a routine of getting out early on Sunday mornings, starting at Oceanside Park, and trekking deep into the coastal forests for miles on the network trails that led to sweeping views of the sea.

My thoughts turned to the Pacific Ocean as I picked up my pace, wanting to get to the hospital before complete darkness enveloped the village. The far side of the square wasn't as well-lit, aside from vintage streetlights. How many surfers lived in Redwood Grove? Had Jake and Brogan followed Kelly here? I added it to my list of questions for my coffee date tomorrow.

If Brogan and Kelly were having an affair, Allison might have known about it. June mentioned Allison was protective; could that be because she was in the loop on Kelly's love life and was helping to keep their tryst quiet?

I didn't have more time to ponder the many questions vying for space in my head because the hospital came into view. It was a long two-story building with a round, glass atrium. A tranquility garden with benches and a water feature made the entrance look more like a spa than a hospital.

I found the main desk and asked if Allison Irons might have a few minutes to speak with me. The volunteer checked and told me I could find her in the cafeteria. I followed the smell of grilling burgers down a sterile corridor with fluorescent-lit hallways. The hum of bustling activity and beeping machines surrounded me. Stepping into the busy dining area, I could see a sea of people, most of them in scrubs, moving between tables and filling trays at hot food stations. I scanned the busy dining area. I'd seen Allison's picture online and in the articles June had shared about Kelly's death.

I weaved through the long tables, finally spotting Allison. She was seated alone with her head buried in a novel. That was a good sign. She was a reader. I had an instant "in."

"Sorry to bother you," I said, leaning to the side to catch her eye behind her book. "Are you Allison Irons?" She was tall and slender, with long dark hair pulled into a high ponytail. Her maroon scrubs, lanyard, and tennis shoes made me confident I'd found the right person.

Interrupting reading time was the worst. I wasn't surprised to see a frown tug at her lips and her eyes narrow as she reluctantly dragged her eyes away from the pages. Her tone had a touch of accusation like she was already on the defensive. "Yeah, what do you need?"

"Seriously, I'm so sorry for barging in on your reading time. I own the Secret Bookcase, so trust me, I'm uber-protective of my reading time, too."

"You own the Secret Bookcase?" She lifted a familiar bookmark from the back of the book and flipped over the cover to show me. It was none other than the thriller *Blood on the Page*. "I bought this from you. Your staff has the best recommendations."

"I'm so glad to hear that, and you're lucky. That title has been so popular—we can't keep it in stock." I motioned to the empty chair. "Do you mind if I sit for a minute?"

"Go ahead." She tucked the bookmark to hold her place and closed the book.

"I'm Annie Murray." I slid one of our business cards across the table. "I was hoping to speak with you about Kelly Taylor."

She sucked in a gasp of breath. "Kelly? What? Why?"

"My partner and I have been hired to help with her case."

Was it just my imagination, or did she look like she'd just seen a ghost? Her face lost all its color. Her eyes grew wide as she leaned away from me and shook her head.

"Kelly, you want to know more about Kelly?" Her voice cracked and broke. "I don't know if I can handle talking about it again…"

CHAPTER 12

"I don't mean to poke at wounds," I said softly to Allison. "I doubt it's much consolation, but I went through a very similar loss. My best friend and college roommate was murdered shortly before graduation, so I do have some sense of how difficult it is to move on and how the grief lingers. In fact, one of the reasons I was drawn to Kelly's case is because it reminds me of my friend. She died too soon, too young. I'm really sorry for your loss."

"Thanks, yeah. It's been rough." She leaned her elbows on the table and rubbed her forehead with her fingers. "It's such weird timing. I mean, I think about her all the time. She's always on my mind, but I just got a call from her ex-boyfriend. I haven't heard from him since she died."

"You received a call from Jake?" I would say that the timing was more than weird. I spoke with Jake a few short hours ago. He must have called Allison right after I left.

Had I spooked him?

"Yeah, you know him?" She sat up and studied the card. Upon closer inspection, she was a bit older than she looked from the articles in the newspaper. I'd put her in her mid-thirties, probably ten years older than Kelly. "Wait, you're the detective? He told me the police were asking a bunch of questions again."

"Private investigator," I corrected her. "The police are still trying to determine the cause of death, so we're reviewing the files, speaking with witnesses, people like you—friends, family, neighbors, to see if there could be something that's been missed. It's common in cases like this to get fresh eyes, so to speak." I wanted to put her at ease, especially if Jake had already reached out to her. Why would he have contacted Allison? It didn't make sense.

"Why?" Allison inserted the business card into her book. "She drowned." She touched the lanyard clipped to her chest. "I'm a nurse. I found her in the tub."

Again, I was struck by how everyone I spoke with insisted Kelly's death was a drowning. It was almost like they were all reading from the same script.

"This tends to happen with accidents. The police have limited resources, so often private investigators will be called in when they can't officially rule out whether it was an accident or suicide." I didn't go into any specifics about June hiring us. "Can I ask, what did Jake say?"

"He was pissed. That's typical—nothing new for him. He wanted to know why I had hired you. I told him I had no idea what he was talking about. Now it makes sense. I figured he was high or on one of his rants." She adjusted her ponytail.

"Did he rant often?" I reached for my notebook. "Do you mind if I take a few notes?"

"No, go for it." She shrugged like she was still trying to connect the dots between her call with Jake and me sitting next to her. "And as to your question about Jake, the answer is yes. He's a hothead. He always has been. I warned Kelly about him, but she wouldn't listen. I don't know what she saw in him. She was focused on making surfing and the world better for everyone else. He's focused on himself. It took me years to convince her to dump him. She could have done so much better, but she dragged him around like dead weight."

There was something about her dismissive tone that made me wonder if she was holding back. "I want to ask you more about their relationship, but before we get into that, can you tell me exactly when Jake called you and what he said?"

"Sure." She picked up her soda and swirled the ice in her glass with a straw. "It was around two thirty. I can check the specific time on my phone, but I know it was about then because I had just finished my yoga class. I saw his name flash on the screen, and I couldn't believe it was him. The last time we spoke was at her funeral. He didn't seem very broken up about her death. He was surfing the next day." She sighed slowly, her shoulders sagging at the memory. "That was already bad enough, but then when I heard he signed her brand deal—well, I couldn't stomach that. She had big plans for how she was going to use that money to help preserve the beach. He's going to blow through it on expensive surfing gear and who knows what else? I've gone out of my way to avoid bumping into him. It's fairly easy. We don't hang out in the same places, and as far as I know, he's still surfing, so I would guess he's usually out at the coast."

I took notes. Jake called her at two thirty, literally minutes after I left. Why?

"He didn't even give me a chance to speak. He just launched into how dare I get the police involved. He accused me of sending them—well, you—to his place. He said something about letting Kelly rest in peace and not dragging her name back into the media—that she didn't deserve this, and then he hung up. I didn't even get a word in. It was bizarre, but I guess now it makes more sense."

"Got it. Thanks. This is helpful." I paused as a team of Allison's co-workers decked out in colorful scrubs passed our table with friendly waves.

Allison sipped her soda, pressing her lips around the straw and sucking slowly like she was processing everything. "I never liked the guy. He was such an ass to Kelly. I think he hated that she was a better surfer than him. He couldn't handle her being the media darling. She had so many superfans. The press loved her. Sponsors loved her. Other surfers loved her. The charities and nonprofits she supported loved her. Everyone loved her." Her voice caught as she shook her head and looked past me.

I could hear the emotion in her voice. It made my throat swell thinking of Scarlet. Why was it that the brightest lights were taken from us when serial killers roamed free? It served as a reminder of why I was drawn to this work. If I could provide closure for the people who loved Kelly, it wouldn't bring her back, but even if it made a sliver of a difference, I would feel like I was doing something worthy.

"Can you tell me about your friendship? How did the two of you meet?"

She dipped a fry in ketchup and gathered her thoughts. "I answered an ad for a roommate. Kelly had just moved to town. She couldn't afford the cost of renting a place on the beach—you know how outlandish leases are for waterfront property. She'd been living in a house with a bunch of other surfers, but they raised her rent, and she decided it was worth the thirty-minute drive to live here in Redwood Grove and commute to the beach. She left super early, before sunrise. It wasn't like there was ever traffic, and it was an easy drive. Anyway, she found the house, but it was too big for her, and she wanted someone to split the rent. It was great for me—a short walk to the hospital, and I liked Kelly instantly. She was easygoing and friendly."

"So the two of you didn't know each other prior to you moving in?" I wondered if there was any significance to the fact that Kelly had leased their cottage. June had mentioned their landlord as a potential suspect.

"Nope." Allison munched on the fry and shook her head, her ponytail swinging from side to side. "But we ended up becoming great friends—best friends. It's kind of a risk moving in with a stranger, but I had a good feeling about her. We weren't the same age, but we were close enough, and we both enjoyed the outdoors and cheesy romantic comedies. I'm not much of a partier. I don't have time since I work the night shift. I like to read, and our hours complemented each other. She was up and gone in the morning, so I had the place to myself most of the day, and I worked nights so she had space for herself in the evenings. When our schedules lined up, we'd do movie marathons in our PJs and eat cookie dough straight out of the package. It was the perfect setup. We both liked the company of having a roommate and also alone time."

"That does sound ideal." I paused as the intercom paged a doctor. "Please tell me if you need to go. I don't want to keep you from your work."

Allison checked her watch. "I've got another fifteen minutes or so."

"What about Jake? Did he hang around the house a lot?"

She rolled her eyes, shaking her head and rubbing her temples again. "Yes, unfortunately. It wasn't bad when they first started dating because he wasn't living here, but then he found a house in Redwood Grove, and suddenly he was like a leech, sucking every ounce of Kelly's lifeblood. I couldn't get rid of him."

"Did that become a point of contention between you and Kelly?" I asked pointedly since her reaction didn't leave much room for interpretation.

"Not really. As I mentioned, our schedules were opposite, so fortunately, I didn't see much of him, but the house reeked of pot and was littered with his crap anytime he stayed over. Kelly would apologize and clean up after him. I don't know what she saw in the guy. She was so confident and strong about surfing, but she let Jake walk all over her. She was ten times the surfer he was, but he would berate her, critique her every move, and tell her she was never going to break into the top twenty. It was hard to watch."

That lined up with what June had told us.

I felt for her. It had to be challenging to see a friend—or anyone you loved—make themselves smaller in a relationship. It also made me appreciate what I had with Liam. He was my steadfast supporter and champion. I couldn't imagine him not wanting me to succeed or vice versa.

"I encouraged her to break it off with him," she continued, reaching for another fry. "But she would come up with excuse after excuse, trying to normalize his behavior. He was the ultimate gaslighter, making her believe *she* was the problem, not the other way around." Allison bit into the fry and took a minute to consider her words. "He's the kind of guy who doesn't have any real talent or self-worth, so he goes around trying to knock other people down. It was gross. Terrible to watch, but Kelly finally came to her senses and kicked him to the curb a few weeks before she died."

"How did he take it?" I already had a good idea of what she was going to say, but I wanted to hear it from her.

"Not well. He turned stalker on her—threatening to ruin her career if she didn't take him back."

"How would he do that?"

"No idea." She shrugged. "That gives you a sense of his ego. He thinks he's some kind of surfing god, but no one else agrees."

"Did things ever get physical?" I made a few more notes.

"Not that I ever saw, but he was emotionally abusive for sure. He would wait outside our house for her to get home and they'd get into one-sided screaming matches. I told her to go to the police. She didn't want to. She thought he would calm down with a little time, but then…" She trailed off.

"Then she died?" I offered. "Do you think there's a possibility Jake could have been involved?"

"In her accident?" Allison scrunched her face in confusion. "How?"

I decided I might as well be direct with her. "What if it wasn't an accident?"

"Wait, what? What are you saying?" She put her hands up as if motioning me not to say more.

"Nothing yet. We're in the early stages of speaking with people who knew her."

"But she slipped in the tub." Allison pushed her plate away and stared at me, her face turning ashen. "I was there. I found her."

"I know. It must have been terribly difficult," I said, feeling a swell of emotion stirring as I thought about Scarlet. "I'm sure you heard that they found trace amounts of a sedative in her system."

"No, no, no, not a sedative." Allison shook her head as if begging me not to make her recount finding her friend's body. "It was one of her gummies. She took them to sleep."

Why was she suddenly defensive again? I didn't correct her. Jake had mentioned the gummies as well, but the toxicology report was clear—there wasn't pot in Kelly's system. It made me think about Allison's position at the hospital. She likely had access to prescription sedatives, like the one in the coroner's report.

"You weren't there that night," I continued, wanting to keep her talking. I didn't have much time before her break was over, and I wanted her to confirm her alibi. "You were working here, correct?"

She placed her napkin over the rest of her uneaten dinner. "Yes. I was here at the hospital. All night. I never left."

That was an odd response.

"Would you typically leave during a shift?" I asked casually, doodling on my notepad.

"Huh?" She pulled away, narrowing her eyes like she'd heard me wrong.

"You said you were here the entire night," I prompted.

She nodded rapidly like she was trying to convince herself. "Yes, I was here. That's in the police report, I'm sure. They spoke with the administrator and scheduler, which I don't understand, but what I meant was that if only I had forgotten something at home, I might have found her before it was too late." She stood, gathering her things. "Look, I need to get back to work. I'm sorry, it's hard to talk about, especially here."

"I understand. I appreciate your candor." It was true, although I had yet to decide whether Allison's reaction was due to her lingering grief or guilt. "Can I ask you one more thing on the way out? Do you think there's a chance Kelly killed herself? I've heard she was stressed about surfing—considering quitting even—and then with the breakup, were you worried about her mental health?"

"Not for a minute. Never. Kelly had big plans for her future, and she wasn't quitting—she was signing with a new coach. She was ready to break out and make the world-tour team."

CHAPTER 13

Was Kelly signing with a new coach? My mind went immediately to my odd interaction with Brogan. The more time I spent chatting with the people who had known the rising surfing star the best, the more I was inclined to believe that June might be onto something about Kelly's death not being an accident.

Allison walked with me to the lobby, decisively putting an end to our conversation. "My break is over. You know the way out, right?"

"Yes. Thanks again for your time. If you can think of anything else, it doesn't matter how big or small, please reach out to me."

"Yeah, okay."

"Would it be possible to look at your bathroom at some point?" I wasn't sure if I was pressing my luck. I still had more questions for her. I wanted to ask about Harvey, their landlord, and hear more about Kelly's future plans, but Allison had patients to tend to, and I was due to meet Liam for dinner.

"You want to look at my *bathroom*?" She scoffed and curled her lip in disbelief.

"Sometimes it's helpful to see the scene in person," I said. "I understand if it doesn't work."

"No, I guess it's fine. I don't know what you'll see. It's not like I preserved the space after the police finished their investigation."

"That's fine. I'll email you to find a convenient time." My words tumbled out in a rush, not wanting to give her a window for an out.

"Okay." She hesitated as if she wanted to say more but then turned and walked down the sterile corridor. "Yeah, fine."

My first impression of Allison was that of a grieving friend, but I couldn't rule out the possibility that she had the means and opportunity to kill her roommate—they lived together, and she had access to prescription drugs. She could have easily drugged Kelly. She likely knew about drug interactions and could have given Kelly something extra to help with the stress, knowing it would be a fatal dose or enough to render her roommate unconscious. The question was timing. Could she have slipped away from the hospital briefly, sight unseen? Or could she have helped Kelly into the tub before she left for her shift? There was a two-hour time-of-death window, but my coursework had taught us that there are many variables when it comes to calculating a specific time of death in cases like this—things like core body temperature, which the water would impact, as would the fact that Kelly wasn't found until the next morning.

The only problem was a motive. Why would Allison want Kelly dead? What did she stand to gain from her roommate's death?

That question niggled at my brain as I walked to the Stag Head.

My mind was deep in the case as I cut through the park. But when a text dinged as I passed the children's play area, it drew me back into the present moment.

The text was from a colleague I'd reached out to about Hal's case. We'd attended the criminology program together under Dr. Caldwell, and my former classmate, like me, ended up taking a meandering path that ultimately led him to work for an art recovery firm. He was well-versed in art-related crimes—theft and forgery—having done hours and hours of additional forensic art training for the role.

I'd sent him pictures of the brooch along with some background information about Hal's theory. If anyone could pinpoint the validity of the brooch's origins, it was him.

Quick update. Still reviewing documents and historical photos. All signs point to it being legit but need firm evidence. More to report soon. Didn't want you to think I forgot about you.

Thanks so much! No rush.

I was glad to hear Hal's case was progressing. Hopefully, we'd have more confirmation from the appraisal when that came back, too.

I picked up my pace and hurried on toward the welcoming glow of the village square.

The pub was located in a rustic, converted house on the corner of the square. Music spilled out the steamy front windows, along with the intoxicating aroma of roasted chicken and veggies. I was suddenly famished and couldn't wait to fill Liam in on my progress.

Inside, the space was crowded but homey and relaxed. Paper stag heads cut out of heavy cardboard hung from the walls. Some were colorful, painted with intricate designs and patterns, while others were simple, showcasing the artist's craftwork. A rustic wooden bar ran the length of the front, with counter seating and shiny rotating tap handles. Black-and-white photos of Redwood Grove and the surrounding area adorned the seating area with booths and more tables. A small stage took up the back, where tonight's band performed—a three-piece jazz trio. Liam hosted weekly trivia, lectures, and game nights. He kept a selection of board and card games on hand for customers to use while lingering over a pint or enjoying his rotating menu of pub fare.

I spotted him behind the bar. Our eyes locked, and a familiar heat crept up the nape of my neck as he shot me a seductive smile. I tried to ignore the burning sensation in my cheeks as I joined the line queuing for drinks. A specials board highlighted a roasted chicken platter served with root vegetables, smashed rosemary and garlic potatoes, and blackberry pie for dessert. The recommended beer pairing was winter pale ale, described as having a spicy finish and bright citrus notes.

Sold.

I didn't bother to consider any of the other choices. That sounded like perfection.

"Hey, you're right on time." Liam tossed a dish towel over his shoulder and leaned across the bar to greet me with a soft kiss on my cheek. "I've been watching the clock."

"I couldn't resist the siren's song of your roasted chicken any longer. My nose led me here."

He typed my order into his point-of-sale system. "You want the beer that comes with it or something else?"

"Definitely the beer. Spicy citrus? I'm intrigued."

"It's good." He gestured to a two-person table near the back. "I reserved that for us. Go grab a seat, and I'll bring you your beer." He dropped his voice into a whisper. "Don't look yet, but you're not going to believe who's here. He's in the second booth."

I waited for a minute, pretending to scan the dining room for a seat. My eyes briefly landed on the booth. Sure enough, Harvey Wade, Kelly's seedy landlord, was making quick work of a mound of nachos. Cheesy sauce dribbled down his chin. He wiped it away with his sleeve and gobbled another bite. He was seated alone—just him, the nachos, and three empty pint glasses. "Harvey's here? That's a stroke of good luck. He's next on my suspect list," I said under my breath to Liam. "When did he come in?"

"Maybe thirty minutes or so. I would have texted, but I knew you were interviewing the nurse."

"Is he a regular?"

Liam held a pint glass toward the Edison-style lighting above the bar, checking for any spots or residue. "Not a regular, but he comes in now and then."

"What serendipitous timing," I said with a sly grin, already developing a plan for getting him to speak with me in my head.

"Are you going to seize the opportunity?" Liam sounded unsure whether that was a wise idea. "Tread cautiously. He's rough around the edges—like sandpaper rough."

"I already gathered that from my preliminary research. Fletcher and I intended to arrange a meeting with him later this week, but this feels like divine intervention." I stole another glance in Harvey's direction. I couldn't pass up the chance to speak with him and I already had a fairly solid list of questions in mind.

"Don't get defensive, Murray, but I'm keeping my eye on you. If he tries anything, I'm kicking him out of the bar and banning him permanently."

"Is he that bad?" My jaw tightened. I wasn't worried about talking to Harvey in the middle of the crowded pub. There were dozens of people around, and I knew Liam wouldn't hesitate to rush to my defense if necessary. I prided myself on my independence and ability to fend for myself, but secretly, I thought his chivalry was romantic. Liam's perspective on Harvey made my spine tingle and my skin start to buzz. If he was concerned about my well-being, simply talking to the guy, what could that mean for Kelly's investigation?

"He's already knocked back three pints since he showed up." Liam raised one brow and turned to pour a pint. "Holler if you need a friendly bartender, okay?"

"Will do." I smoothed my sweater, twisted my hair into a ponytail, and filled a glass with cucumber water. Liam offered flavored waters in glass pitchers at the bar. Tonight's rotation included cucumber and mint, lemon and orange, and strawberry. From what I'd read about Harvey, I decided my best bet was a less direct route than I'd taken with Allison. I scurried toward his table, and once I was within a few feet of the booth, I purposely spilled half the water down the front of my sweater.

"Oh, dear. I'm such a klutz. Hey, could I grab a few napkins from you?" I pointed to the napkin container, tugging my sweater away from my body.

"Yeah, go ahead," Harvey grunted.

I set the water on the edge of the table and scooted into the booth, grabbing a stack of napkins and dabbing my sweater. "I can't believe I did that. Sorry to barge in on your dinner."

"It's fine." He looked up from the nachos he was systematically destroying with beady, dark eyes. He ran them over me, lingering on my chest area too long. I kept my face passive but shuddered internally.

Gross.

No wonder Liam wanted to keep an eye on him.

"Wait, you look familiar," I said, continuing to pat my dress. Thankfully, I'd managed not to fully douse myself. "Do I know you?"

"You could know me. We could get out of here and go somewhere more quiet if you want?" He licked salsa from his lips in what I could only interpret as a seductive gesture. The effect was anything but.

"No, I know you." I ignored his attempt at a pickup line and bad grammar. "I was just on your website. A friend suggested I check out your rental properties."

"You looking for a rental?" He smeared his greasy fingers on a napkin, slurring his words slightly.

"Yes, my lease is coming up for renewal, and I'm hoping to get a bigger place. My friend Allison Irons recommended you."

At the mention of Allison's name, he scowled and shook his head, jutting his chin forward like he'd heard me wrong. "Allison sent you my info?"

"She did." I stuck to my story. "She said she's been in her house for a few years and hasn't had any issues, well—except for the terrible accident with her former roommate, Kelly. That was tragic." I pressed my soggy napkins to my heart and closed my eyes. "That must have been awful for you as a landlord—to have a tenant die in your property…" I trailed off, hoping he would take the bait.

"Not my problem." He huffed, his Adam's apple bulging as he swallowed. "The bathtub didn't kill her. She killed herself. I read the news."

"Did she kill herself?" I pretended to be shocked by this. Acting had never been my strong suit, but in this line of work, I had to play many roles and perfect my responses depending on the situation. "Oh, God, that's terrible. I didn't realize that. I heard it was an accident. But killing herself, that's even sadder."

"Whatever. It doesn't matter. I had nothing to do with it."

His insistence that he wasn't involved was interesting, to say the least. I wasn't sure how I would respond if Kelly had been my tenant, but I knew I would show at least a glimmer of empathy. The other thing that immediately made me curious was that Harvey was the first suspect to mention Kelly killing herself. Everyone else had immediately said her drowning was an accident.

Harvey squirmed, loosening the top button of his pants and letting his belly hang out as he scooped another nacho off the platter.

I tried another tactic. "Did you know her well?"

"Who?" Harvey snarled. Drool spread down the side of his lip and dripped along his jaw. He slopped it up with the back of his hand.

"Kelly, the woman who died." I felt Liam's eyes on me across the room. I shot a quick glance toward the bar to let him know I was good.

"What's this got to do with me?" Harvey didn't bother to close his mouth while he chewed. "Why are you asking me this?"

"Oh, no reason. It just came up when Allison and I were talking about rentals and your property management company."

"She's stirring that up again?" Harvey flicked a piece of olive off his tooth. "She better knock that off. I already warned her I'd slap a slander suit on her if she does that again."

"Sorry, I'm lost. What do you mean?"

"I mean, she had better shut her mouth about things that are done and in the past." He tossed his napkin on his plate and pushed himself up, sucking in his gut to get out of the booth. "You can check the website for leases." He stormed away.

I caught Liam's eye again. He watched Harvey leave and then motioned to the table he'd reserved for us, holding a pint glass in one hand and a plate of salad in the other. I dropped the soggy napkins in a recycling bin and went to join him.

"I see you made quick work of him." Liam set the beer and salad on the table and scooted out a chair. "He got the full Murray treatment."

"What exactly is the full Murray treatment?" I scrunched my brow as I sat down.

"All I know is that you don't want to be on the receiving end of one of your soul-piercing gazes."

"Like this?" I squinted, narrowing my eyes as I formed my lips into a tight, determined circle.

"Yep, that's it." Liam nodded rapidly, pulling away from me like he was worried I might bite.

"Good, I hope I scared him. I see why his reputation precedes him." I filled Liam in on our brief yet revealing conversation. Knowing I rattled Harvey felt good and meant that Fletcher and I were on the right track. I had a new round of questions for Allison. In our short discussion, Harvey's name hadn't come up, but when I spoke with her next, he was going to be top of my list.

CHAPTER 14

June was waiting for me the next morning at the Secret Bookcase. She was dressed like a character from a BBC mystery with her long gray duster, sensible shoes, and knit wool cap. A well-worn satchel rested at her feet. Liam's teasing about my piercing gaze was nothing compared with the steely look June gave me as I approached the front door, where she was perched against the iron railing wearing a disapproving frown. He obviously hadn't met June Munrow.

An immediate rush of panic swirled in my stomach. Had I forgotten a meeting? What was she doing at the bookstore this early?

"There you are. I've been waiting for nearly a half hour." She bent over slowly to pick up the satchel and pointed to the door. "Are you going to stand there or invite me in?"

"Yes, of course, come in." I fumbled through my book tote to find my keys and unlocked the door. "We were supposed to be meeting this morning?" I hated feeling flustered, but a meeting with our primary client wouldn't have slipped my mind. There had to be another reason for June's impromptu visit.

June hurried inside in front of me, shuffling forward and pausing to signal me to hurry up. "I was under the impression that you and Fletcher encouraged input during your investigation."

"Absolutely." I flipped on the lights and considered my options. I needed to prep the store for opening, but clearly, June wanted to speak with me. "Sorry, it's chilly in here. Hal likes to tease that the estate has old bones. We can go upstairs to my office, or I can light the fireplace in the Sitting Room."

"The Sitting Room is fine." June looped her satchel over her arm and waited for me to put my things behind the counter. "I know the way."

What was her hurry?

"What updates do you have?" she asked as we walked through the dark hallway. I turned on the lights as we went, our footsteps echoing along the empty corridor. We passed framed portraits of some of the mystery greats—Agatha Christie, Dorothy L. Sayers, and Dashiell Hammett—along with collections of old photographs of the estate in its early days. Buttery-yellow sconces lighted our way.

"Have a seat," I said, opening the Sitting Room curtains and turning on the tea kettle. Sunlight poured into the cozy space, giving the room an instant boost. I lit the gas fireplace and pulled a chair beside her while the water warmed. "We've made nice progress thus far. We've already had initial conversations with each of the witnesses from the police files." I felt pretty pleased with what we'd been able to accomplish in such a short amount of time.

"Witnesses?" June snapped, her tone turning sharp. "Don't you mean suspects?"

"Potentially, yes." I nodded, staring at the floral wallpaper Hal had custom-designed to match Miss Marple's house in the classic BBC production starring Joan Hickson (his favorite of all the Marples). "But as Fletcher and I mentioned, it's too soon to jump to any conclusions. We're in the preliminary stages of the investigation."

June tossed her hand toward the fireplace like she was tossing away my thoughts. "You must have an idea by now. Kelly was murdered, wasn't she? I think you need to get the press involved. Get the story back in the papers. We need to scare the killer. If they realize that Kelly's murder is at the forefront of the public's mind again, they may slip up."

"True." I considered my words. Fortunately, the screeching of the tea kettle bought me a few extra minutes to think about how best to proceed with June. "Let me pour us some tea. Any preferences?"

"Whatever you have is fine." Her tone was crisp and nasally, growing in irritation.

Part of me understood her sense of urgency. There had been many times over the years when new information about Scarlet's death would surface and drag me right back into the frenetic feeling of needing answers immediately. But going to the press wasn't a wise idea. We wanted the suspects, as June suggested, to feel comfortable with us—to open up. Our method was already working: case in point, Jake calling Allison right after our chat and Harvey's reaction last night. We needed more time.

I poured boiling water into two deep red mugs with skull and crossbones designs and gathered an assortment of tea packets. "Take your pick." I placed the mug and tea dish next to June.

"I would think you would come up with something much cleverer. Pick your poison, perhaps." She drew in her cheeks in an odd attempt at a smile.

Was she trying to be funny? If so, it wasn't exactly hitting. The smile that spread across June's plump cheeks was wicked and without humor. Her face froze, suspended in the sinister grin, until she broke form with a slight nod of her head, unwrapped a tea packet, and plunged it into the scalding water. "You are in agreement about the press, then? Kelly's death should be front-page news."

"Actually, I'm not sure that's a good idea." I was about to say more, but June wagged a finger at me.

"Stop there. I would think you would be thrilled to have your detective agency front and center. It's basically free advertising for you. I don't see a line of clients at your door, do I?" She twisted her head toward the window.

I wouldn't argue with a client, but I wanted to remind her that the bookstore didn't even open for another forty-five minutes, and technically, our Novel Detectives office was upstairs.

She unbuckled her satchel and forced a sheet of paper at me. "I've taken the liberty to prepare a press release. I can certainly send it to the paper as a concerned local citizen, but I believe it would be better coming from the Novel Detectives."

I scanned the press release. It contained bulleted points about Kelly's death, highlighting the Novel Detectives as being on the brink of "cracking the case." From our research, I'd learned June had been a nurse in her working years, but the press release was so professional that it made me wonder if she'd also moonlighted in PR.

I rested the paper on my lap. "June, I appreciate your enthusiasm and understand how invested you are in solving the mystery surrounding Kelly's death. I assure you, Fletcher and I share your passion and urgency, and I want you to know we've already made good progress." While we sipped our tea, I told her about my conversations, next steps, and Fletcher's research. "If you can give us another few days to follow these threads, I think we'll have a much better sense of where things are at, and then at that point, we can consider other strategies, like press outreach."

She stood and wandered toward the nearest row of book-shelves.

Was she angry? About to drop us?

I couldn't get a read on her.

Her finger glided along the spines, as fluid and precise as a pianist's touch on the keys. She landed on a wildly popular series by a Swedish author, removing the first book and leafing through it like she was considering whether to buy it. Then she turned to me, clutching the book to her chest and rocking slightly from side to side. "I hear what you're saying, and I'm willing to give you more time. I apologize for being so pushy, but Kelly's death has gone unsolved for far too many days. I suppose hiring you has brought the terrible tragedy to the surface again, and I want you to find her killer and make them pay."

I nodded, breathing slowly and intentionally, choosing my words carefully. "I get it, I really do, and I promise Fletcher and I are as invested as you in discovering the truth."

She regained control of her emotions, pulling the book away from her chest and studying it with newfound interest. "What a title—*An Elderly Lady Is Up to No Good*."

I nodded to the miniature hardbound novel with its sweet crochet pattern. "Our cozy book club read that over the holidays and loved it. The main sleuth is, um, well, let's just say an anti-hero who takes justice into her own hands."

"It's good to see old ladies like me represented in fiction. Everyone forgets about us. That's why the police won't believe me." She sighed, tucking the book back in its spot. "Not Kelly. She was a good neighbor. A friend."

"She's lucky to have a friend like you to keep her memory alive."

"Yes, I suppose." June cleared her throat and picked up her satchel, abruptly ending our conversation. "I'd like an update by the end of the week."

"Absolutely." I handed her the press release.

"No, you keep that. You might need it." She didn't wait for a response before she began walking toward the exit. Her speech was clipped and short. "I'll see myself out. Thank you for your time."

After she was gone, I let out a long breath and pressed my hand against my stomach, feeling a jumble of thoughts that I couldn't quite put into words yet. That conversation hadn't gone as I expected. June was clearly intent on pushing the case forward no matter the cost. At least I'd bought us a little more time.

I picked up our teacups and put the room back in order. Once Fletcher arrived, I needed to fill him in on June's urgency. It wasn't as if we had wasted any time diving into the case, but I didn't want June to go to the press or to lose her as a client. Suddenly, it was like we had a ticking time bomb waiting to detonate, and if we couldn't come up with answers about Kelly's death, it was about to explode in our faces.

CHAPTER 15

"Why would she want to go to the press?" Fletcher sounded incredulous when I told him about June dropping by the bookshop later in our shared office. "That would be the worst possible thing we could do. There's a reason it's called a private detective agency—emphasis on *private*."

"I know, believe me, I know. I think I talked her out of it. I hope I did." I showed him the release June had written.

Fletcher scanned it quickly and shoved it into the desk drawer. Our workspaces could not be more different. Fletcher's desk was a cluttered mess of case notes, collectibles, water bottles, and used coffee cups. His Sherlock murder board loomed over him on the adjacent wall. He'd updated it with photos of Kelly and the pictures June shared with us. "It doesn't make sense. Why hire us just to blast it all over the news a day later?"

"She's upset, maybe?" I shrugged, organizing my case notes by color-coding the file folders. My desk had neat organizers for my Sharpies, paper clips, rubber bands, and lip gloss. "Perhaps hiring us to look into Kelly's murder—if it is murder—has her anxious. I think she believes she's helping us, but I tried to make it clear this would do the opposite."

"Seriously." Fletcher shook his head as he repositioned a LEGO model of Tower Bridge on the bookshelves. "I intend to spend the next few hours researching every financial breadcrumb. We're covered at the store until the late afternoon shift."

"I'm meeting Brogan at Cryptic soon." I glanced at the antique replica of Big Ben that Fletcher had found on an obscure online shopping site. "Hopefully, he'll be able to shed some light on their relationship."

"You're thinking they had an affair, right?" Fletcher returned to his desk and pushed around the clutter to make space for his laptop.

"It could be. I don't know for sure. That was literally the first thing that crossed my mind. His reaction was strange. He shut me down immediately and was super jumpy, like he was worried Jake would hear him." I paused and pointed to my files. "I've found quite a few photos of them at surfing events and press conferences where they look like a lot more than coach and surfer. They've got their arms draped all over each other. Big hookup vibes. It seems logical and would explain why he didn't want to talk around Jake, but as with everything, I'm remaining open and neutral until I speak with him directly."

Fletcher opened his laptop, which was graffitied with stickers. "Oh, hey, the report from the appraiser came in."

"Ooh, what does it say?" I leaned over my desk, trying to get a peek at his screen. "My friend who works for the art recovery firm texted last night to say he thinks the brooch could legitimately have belonged to Agatha, but he doesn't have solid proof yet."

"It's an Art Deco brooch in platinum and twenty-four karat gold. The period is between 1920 and 1924. A center round-cut sapphire in seven karats set with diamonds, rubies, and emeralds. Designed by Cartier." He gasped, covering his hand with his mouth as he read the next line in the report. "Get this, Annie. The estimated value is fifty-eight thousand dollars."

"What?" My mouth dropped open. I had a sense that the antique piece of jewelry was valuable, but not that valuable. "Are you sure?"

"That's what the appraisal says." He turned his screen for me to see. "Do you think Hal has any idea how valuable this is?"

"No clue." Hal was discreet about his finances. For a while, I'd wondered if he was in over his head at the Secret Bookcase. Sales had slumped before we got serious about expanding events and finding new ways to bring customers into the store. But when we negotiated the sale of the bookstore, I discovered he owned the estate and surrounding acreage outright. He'd had no qualms about Fletcher and me buying him out in installments, nor had he required a large down payment in the purchase process. He wanted us to take over the store and have his legacy continue.

But it was a conundrum. There had been rumors circulating Redwood Grove for years that Liam, among other business owners in the village, was interested in buying the property and transforming it into everything from a modern B&B to a luxury hotel and restaurant. I'd asked Liam about it, and he'd informed me that there was a brief period when Hal had entertained the possibility of selling but quickly and quietly changed his mind.

Was there a reason for that? Could he have come into money?

It wasn't the sort of conversation you had with your boss. It's not like over coffee in the morning, one of us would casually ask, "So, Hal, are you rich?"

"Fifty-eight thousand dollars for one tiny piece of jewelry," Fletcher said, tapping the screen. "And Hal had it stuffed in a box in his closet. I bet he doesn't know. Maybe he thinks it's a costume piece."

"Yeah, maybe." I dragged my teeth over my lip.

"What? What are you thinking? You're doing that thing." Fletcher waved his finger at me.

"What thing?"

"That thing where you gnaw on your bottom lip." Fletcher copied me.

"Guilty." I ran my finger over my lip and reached for a tube of lip gloss. "I'm not sure. There's something there, but I can't quite put my finger on it." I applied a thin layer of gloss. "Does it say anything about a connection to Christie?"

"No. They're checking with some colleagues and auction houses and will get back to us on that. I'm also sending it to a few more appraisers, just in case this valuation is an outlier." He shut the laptop. "The timing lines up. If the brooch was crafted in the 1920s, Agatha would have been in her thirties then. She went missing in 1926. Do you think we should tell Caroline about this?"

"Yeah, I'd love to hear more about how she found it and if there are other items like this or from the same time period. I'm also curious if she has any idea how valuable the brooch is."

"I'll get in touch and arrange another meeting, but I'll wait until then to tell her about the appraisal."

"Good plan." I checked the time—I was due at Cryptic. "All right, I'm off to have a one-on-one with Brogan. Want me to bring you back anything?"

"If he's the killer or involved in Kelly's death, a signed and sealed confession on a platter would be nice, preferably with a blood-red wax skull."

"Okay." I chuckled. "I'll see what I can do."

"I have the utmost faith in you and your methods, Annie." He gave me a two-finger salute.

I left him with a wave. The short walk to Cryptic was the refresher I needed. The coffee shop was in a converted garage with large roll-up doors connecting the outdoor patio and modern interior. Its soft and warm earth tones blended beautifully with the native California landscape. You'd never know it had poured relentlessly for days. The garage doors were open, allowing sunlight to flood into the artistic, industrial space.

The rich aroma of toasted almonds and richly brewed coffee hit me when I stepped inside. I scanned the seating options, plush armchairs, wooden benches, and industrial-style stools to see if Brogan was already there. He wasn't.

"Annie, hey, girl, hey!" Pri waved from behind the sleek marble coffee bar dotted with touches of tangerine and teal blue. There was an expensive commercial espresso machine, a glass pastry case filled with an assortment of drool-worthy delights, and stickers and temporary tattoos for sale. Pri was a talented artist, and after months of not-so-gentle encouragement by all of us, she'd finally started selling her designs at the coffee shop. "What brings you into my humble coffee house?" Pri asked, wiping her hands on her denim apron.

I surveyed the perimeter with one hand shielding my forehead, intentionally playing up the spy angle. "Secret detective work."

Pri rubbed her hands together with excitement. "Say more."

I lowered my voice and studied the menu. I don't know why I bothered; Pri always created special drinks for me. She liked to call me her crash test coffee dummy, and I was more than happy to fill that role. Her ability to layer complex flavors and bring out the subtle nuances in Cryptic's signature roasts was a work of art. I especially appreciated that her drinks were never cloyingly sweet or topped with copious amounts of whipping cream.

"I'm meeting with Brogan to discuss Kelly's death." I didn't go into detail.

"Secret detective work calls for something strong and moody. Hmm. Give me a minute." She picked up a glass bottle of house-made simple syrup. "French roast, this simple syrup, bitters, and a generous splash of oat milk. It should give you a bold, bittersweet flavor."

"Sounds great." Two of the couches opened up. "I'm going to snag a seat. Be right back."

"Don't worry. We're in a lull. The next rush will be when the high school gets out in an hour. Make yourself comfortable. I'll bring it to you."

"Thanks, you're a gem." I blew her a kiss and scooted over to grab a couch.

Eighties music played overhead. I settled into the couch, checking out the new artwork on display. Cryptic rotated art each month, featuring a variety of local artists. This month's gallery included watercolor paintings of the redwoods, coast, and mountains. One of the many things that made our location enviable was you could drive an hour or two in any direction and end up backpacking through a mossy, old-world forest, hiking along the stunning rugged coastline, or skiing on snow-kissed mountain peaks. The paintings captured California's ever-changing climate with a touch of whimsy. I was tempted to check the price tag to see if I could afford them.

Pri delivered my drink and a glazed ginger orange cookie. "No sign of the surf bro, yet?" She mimicked Jake and Brogan's lackadaisical speech style and gave me a hang loose sign.

"Nope." I chuckled, checking the entrance and my watch. Brogan was late. "I hope he didn't agree to meet me just to get me out of his hair yesterday."

"He's probably doing his hair. I swear those guys spend more money on hair products than the entire makeup department at the community theater. Do you know how much gel and product it takes to get those surfer curls?" She ran her hands through her natural waves, pretending to fluff them, and then tossed her hair over her shoulder like a model, posing with her chin up for effect.

"I guess I never considered it," I said with a laugh. "I'm surprised you have."

"Annie, these are the pressing things keeping me up at night. How does a guy like Brogan make his loose waves appear effortless and natural, as if he just stepped out of the ocean? Those highlights probably set him back a pretty penny, too."

"Why are we talking about surfer hair?" I scrunched my face into a puzzled grin and snuck a taste of the coffee.

"Wait, wait, this topic will have to be tabled because I see your surfer hair right now." She wiggled her brows toward the front door, backed away, and hurried to the espresso bar.

Brogan caught my eye and gave me a nod to let me know he was putting in an order. Good. He'd shown. That was a first step. I reviewed my list of questions while I waited for him to get a drink.

"What's up?" He plopped onto the couch, kicking one leg over the other. He wore long shorts, Uggs, and a ratty, faded hoodie. The look was intentional—as if he wanted everyone to be actually aware that he was relaxed and couldn't care less.

"Thanks for making time to speak with me. I'd love to hear more about your relationship with Kelly and anything you can tell me about her behavior and mood leading up to her death." I reached for my notebook. "Do you mind if I take a few notes while we talk?"

"Go ahead." He fiddled with the rope bracelet on his wrist.

"Anything and everything you can tell me about her will be great, but for starters, I got the impression you didn't want to say much in front of Jake. Is that because you and Kelly had a special relationship?"

"Special?" His leathery cheeks tightened into a scowl.

"Were you more than her coach?" I was confident I already knew the answer—between his reaction to not wanting to talk with Jake in earshot and the photos I'd found of him and Kelly, the evidence pointed to an affair. My strategy with him was to come right out with it and see if he would take the bait.

"No. God, no. No. No way. Not at all." He tossed his hands in the air in surrender. "Don't say that. No, I don't know where you heard that. I wasn't into Kelly, and that would be a violation of our work agreement. I don't cross boundaries like that. I mean, do women hit on me? Yeah. But you know, I'm a good guy. I don't do that. Not with my clients. No. No." He used the back of his hand to dab his brow.

My internal radar dinged. He crossed and uncrossed his legs like he couldn't get comfortable. I'd hit a nerve for sure. He was protesting too much. Way too much.

"Okay." I shifted direction for a minute. Once he calmed down, I would show him the pictures and try again. "Can I ask why you were so worried about talking about Kelly in front of Jake?"

He flicked the stringy bracelet, repeatedly flipping it against his wrist like a rubber band. "Yeah, that's why I came. I wanted to talk to you in private because if Jake hears what I'm going to tell you, he'll go freaking ballistic again."

CHAPTER 16

"What do you mean by ballistic?" I rested my pencil on the notebook, intrigued by Brogan's word choice.

"It's a long story."

"I've got time." I leaned back against the couch like I was ready to get comfortable for the long haul.

Brogan stretched one arm across his body like he was warming up to get in the water. He waited until Pri delivered his drink to launch into his story. "You may have heard this already, but Kelly was crushing it. She was doing stuff that no one could compete with—revolutionizing the sport. The poster child for conservation. She was using her power and fame as a force of good. I was grateful to be in her wake. Every coach and agent on the planet wanted to sign her."

"Which were you?" I interrupted. It could be an important distinction in terms of Brogan profiting off Kelly's success. "Coach or agent?"

"Both. It's not uncommon. Brands reach out to me first. The surfing world is fairly small—we're one big family."

"So you made a percentage of her brand deals."

"Yeah, but you make it sound bad. It wasn't like that. It was a win-win for both of us. I was invested in her and her success. I only wanted the best for her." He ran his fingers through his immaculate, untamed hair. "Most surfers don't know or care about the management aspects of the sport. Surfing is a religious experience for most of us. When you're out there riding, you're in the flow. It's a moving meditation, our form of church. There's money to be made, but that's the almost dirty, little secret side of the sport. Surf culture is completely different than the big sports. We surf because we *have to* surf. That was Kelly's philosophy. Brand deals and sponsorships are a means to an end—a way to fund her passion projects. They give you the freedom to surf, but I wouldn't say most surfers I know are actively trying to land sponsors; they need dudes like me for that."

"Dudes like you, huh?" I chuckled, taking down notes. "Still, brand deals must be lucrative."

"Not always. Depends on the brand and the surfer." He flicked his bracelet like a rubber band, snapping it against his wrist again and again like he was trying to inflict pain.

"It sounds like Kelly was special." I took a drink of my coffee, gauging his reaction and body language. Nothing about his posture suggested he was uncomfortable or closed off, but that still didn't mean he wasn't lying. Reading body language was a key part of the job, and everything about him was shouting that something wasn't right.

"Kelly was incredible. You should have seen her ride the waves. She had such a tender touch, an ease. She was a natural." His voice became dewy, like he was swept up in the memory and sucked back into the past. "Everyone could see it. You didn't need to know anything about surfing to appreciate her talent. It was effortless. She was one with the water."

He spoke with such reverence that it made me sit up and pay attention. "She would have done all the things—won regional, national, and international competitions without even trying. She was already starting to break through, not just in surfing circles but with the general public, especially because of how vocal she was about saving the beaches for future generations. She would have been a household name. You know, surfing is an Olympic sport now. She was going to be captain of the US national team."

"Wow, that is big." I made a note, wondering about Allison's comment that Kelly was signing with a new coach.

His eyes welled. He twisted his onyx wedding ring and brushed away a tear with the back of his hand. "Sorry. It's just tough to think about it again. Her life was cut way too short. Young kids would have wanted to be her. She would have been on cereal boxes and had her own brand of surf gear."

I reached for a napkin and offered it to him. "Do you think the pressure got to her?"

"Kelly? Nah. She was chill. That's what made her so good—so different. She was always loose when she was in the water."

That didn't exactly match what we had learned. I wanted to keep him on track, but I also needed to know if his story had holes. "I heard she was quitting."

He balled up the napkin in his fist, wadding it tightly. "That's a lie. No chance. She had her sights set on the Olympics. We had just signed a major deal. She wasn't quitting." His ultramarine eyes were the color of the sea. They were equally mesmerizing and unsettling as they fixed on me. "There was some stuff going on with Kelly, but she wasn't quitting."

"Okay. Can you expand on what kind of stuff?" Was he hinting about Kelly wanting a change? If she intended to sign with a new coach, that could give him a motive for killing her. Maybe she confronted him, and he snapped.

He stuffed the napkin in his shorts pocket. "That's why I thought it would be better to talk here. Things were rough with her and Jake. You know they dated, right?"

"Yes. I'm aware of their history." I flipped through my notebook. "They broke up shortly before she died."

"That's right. He was messed up about it. It shook him. He thought she was the one. He was planning to propose after the team got back from Hawaii."

"Really?" That was a new piece of information.

"I warned him not to. She was done. She was singularly focused on her career, and Jake was a distraction. He's a decent dude, but he has some anger issues. If he has a bad day out in the water, he can't shake it. He brings it home with him. Kelly tried to model how to let it ride—be in the flow. He can get there sometimes. When he does, he's great, but when he doesn't—" He didn't finish the thought.

I didn't want to make any assumptions or fill in the words left lingering, so I pushed him for more. "When you say anger issues, do you think he took out those issues on Kelly?"

"No, no, I mean, yeah, kind of, sure, when he was pissed, but he wouldn't hurt her, not physically, anyway." He ran his finger along the inside of his bracelet, circling it around his wrist absently.

"But mentally?"

"Yeah, sure. He isn't chill to be around if he has a bad day, and watching her catapult to the top was hard. Her career was skyrocketing, and he was stuck."

I paused to take another drink of my coffee before it went cold. "Is that why she broke it off?"

"Partially, but more than anything, she was ready for the next level. We had a long talk a couple of weeks before she died, and she told me she needed a reset. She was determined to prioritize surfing. It's funny because she was so calm and fluid in the water, but she was a fighter. She wanted to compete, and she wanted to win. That's one of the things that made her so unique and made sponsors and other surfers pay attention."

"So she broke up with Jake to focus on surfing and her Olympic goals," I clarified. But internally, I was hyper-focused on his word choice. *Reset.* Did Kelly have plans to make a major change in her career trajectory? And what if those plans *didn't* include Brogan?

He ripped off a hunk of his chocolate hazelnut croissant. "That's right. She would have taken home the gold. I guarantee it. I already had dozens of sponsors lining up to sign her. She might have broken records for ad deals—become the first woman to amass over ten million in sponsorship money."

"Was she on track to make that kind of money?"

"Oh yeah. For sure." He tugged at his ring. I recognized the telltale sign of guilt. "My wife used to say that Kelly was our retirement plan."

I winced and quickly recovered, making my face passive. It was impossible not to wonder about Brogan's motives. Was he altruistic about her career, or could he have been putting an inordinate amount of pressure on her to succeed? Maybe we had it wrong. Maybe it wasn't Jake placing pressure on her, but her coach.

"How does Jake play into this?" I asked, hoping to shift the conversation back to why we were meeting at Cryptic.

"He was messed up with the breakup, and then since she died, he's been a total wreck. He can't get it together. My world kind of fell apart, too. My wife and I separated. Kelly's death sent shockwaves through the entire surfing community. We're all trying to make sense of it and get a grip, but it's tough. It's still such a shock, you know?"

"I understand. I've lost someone I loved and have a sense of how life-altering that experience can be." I wanted to lean harder into the cause of his breakup. How was that connected? He was setting me up perfectly.

He blinked hard and tore off another piece of the flaky croissant, sending crumbs flying everywhere. He brushed them away. "It was so unexpected. We surfed that morning, and then a few hours later, she was dead. Part of me still doesn't believe it."

I nodded, staying quiet.

"God, that day was awful. I hate even having to think about it, but Jake went to see her that afternoon. They fought. She told him to leave her alone for good. She wanted to end things peacefully. They were going to see a lot of each other. It was impossible to avoid having contact with him, but he couldn't let it go. He was desperate to try and change her mind and get back together."

"Could that be what they fought about?" I furrowed my brow.

"Uh, yeah, uh, I guess." He shrugged and rolled his neck from one side to the other. "He accused her of having an affair. He was sure there was someone else."

"And was there?" I reached for my phone and pulled up the photos of him and Kelly looking anything but professional at a competition shortly before her death. "I know you denied it, but be honest with me—were you and Kelly an item? Is that why you didn't want to talk in front of Jake? Is that why you and your wife are separated?"

"Damn." He swallowed hard, slowly raising his head, transfixing his eyes on me as he nodded. "Yeah. Yeah, Kelly and I hooked up."

CHAPTER 17

"So you and Kelly were having an affair?" I asked. *I knew it!*

But I wanted to hear every detail from him. I had suspected as much since our very first conversation, and Brogan's tell was his wedding ring. He'd been fiddling with it through our entire conversation as if it were a physical reminder of his guilt. But I'd caught him in a lie. He'd started our chat by insisting there wasn't anything going on between him and Kelly. Now he'd done a complete one-eighty. What else was he lying about?

"We hooked up a few times," he admitted, staring at the artwork on the far wall. "It wasn't anything serious, at least not at first, but things got complicated."

"Because you're married?"

"Technically, we're separated. It's actually been a few months." He tugged the ring off and held it between his finger and thumb. "My wife found out about Kelly a few months before Kelly's accident. I explained that it was a mistake, but she kicked me out immediately. I don't blame her. It was a bad move on my part. I should never have crossed that line. I got caught up in the moment, the excitement of what Kelly was doing, but I love my wife. I still do."

"What about Jake? Does he know?" I kept my feet planted on the floor. My mind was already three steps ahead, trying to make new connections and form fresh theories, knowing that Brogan had confirmed he and Kelly were romantically involved. This added another layer to her mental health and stress.

The more I learned, the less confidence I had in June's theory that Kelly had been murdered. Kelly was dealing with a breakup, having an affair with her coach (who happened to be ten years her senior and married), training for a spot on the Olympic team, and who knows what else—maybe quitting entirely or about to sign with a new coach? There was a strong possibility she had succumbed to the mounting pressures and stresses. But on the flip side, her romantic entanglements could have put her in serious danger. If Jake learned Kelly and Brogan were having an affair, he might have killed her in revenge, or could Brogan have silenced her to protect his marriage?

"Jake doesn't know." He paused as if searching for the right words. "Not about me. He knows Kelly was seeing someone else. That's why they were fighting that day. That's why this is so hard." He hung his head, flipping the ring through his fingers like it was a toy. "It would break him if he knew it was me."

"But you live with him?" Brogan appeared remorseful or at least conflicted, but I had many more questions for him and didn't trust that I was still getting the complete picture of his relationship with his client and student.

He nodded his head, not looking up. "Yeah. We've been roommates. When my wife kicked me out, I needed a place to crash and Jake had space. I get how this sounds. It's bad, but like I said, surfer culture is family."

I wasn't sure our definitions of family were aligned, but I let him continue.

"Jake is a good guy. His temper has gotten better. He's done the work. Put in the hours. His surfing has improved." His tone shifted into coaching mode.

"You're coaching him, too, now? And he signed with Kelly's sponsor. Is that correct?" I hoped I didn't sound judgy. That wasn't my intent, but it was hard to extrapolate the tangled layers with this group of surfers.

"I get it. I get it. It's a bad look for me, but there's no reason for Jake to know. It would kill him. He thought he had a shot at getting back together with Kelly. He didn't, but it's better to let him believe that."

"What about your wife? Aren't you concerned she'll tell him?"

"No. She knew it meant nothing. See, I've had a few flings in the past. Kelly wasn't the first. It happens." He shrugged and pushed his ring back onto his finger. "We spend long hours together. People crash together. Sometimes, there's drugs and drinking involved. My wife knows I love her, but she'd finally had enough. Kelly was the last straw. She kicked me out, and Jake took me in."

"And you're not worried she'll say something to Jake?" I was having trouble believing this part of his story. It made me doubt his sincerity.

Was there another reason he was telling me this?

"She's not like that." He forced his lips together, shaking his head like he was trying to convince himself. "She looked the other way. We kind of had an open relationship. Nothing was ever going to happen long-term with Kelly. We hooked up a few times. We both realized it was a mistake. That was the end of it."

He made it sound so simple, but I knew situations like this—or *situationships*, as Pri liked to say—were never as easy or uncomplicated as he was trying to make it sound.

"Who ended it?" I asked.

"It was mutual. Kelly wanted to keep things professional, and I was just having a little fun, so that was fine by me. She told me I was the catalyst for finally ending things with Jake, and she was appreciative."

"Were you worried she would tell your wife?" I made a couple notes to follow up on—like having a conversation with his wife.

He scowled, his cheeks growing redder. "No, I told you. It's not like that. It wasn't a big deal."

And yet his marriage had ended because of the affair. Something wasn't adding up.

"Did you tell the police any of this when they were investigating Kelly's death?" There had been no mention of the affair in the case files.

"They never asked."

That wasn't exactly an answer. I tried another angle. "Why are you telling me now?"

A group of high school students bustled into the coffee shop, bringing the sound of laughter and heavy backpacks with them. They crowded toward the espresso counter, boxing each other out to get in line to order hot chocolate and after-school vanilla bean cupcakes and sausage pastries. I glanced at the clock. I couldn't believe Brogan and I had been chatting this long.

He thought about it for a minute. "I don't know. A few reasons. Guilt, maybe. I guess it feels good to get some of this off my chest. You figured it out. You seem smart and determined. You kind of remind me of Kelly, actually; not in appearance, but in the way your jaw is set and how your eyes are constantly darting around the room, taking everything in and observing me like I'm a specimen. She was like that." He gave me a nod of what I could only interpret as approval. "I overheard you talking to Jake. I could tell you were serious about getting to the bottom of her death, and I guess I figured you were going to ask a lot of questions. I was worried that if I didn't tell you about this first, it would get back to Jake."

For someone so protective of his friend and roommate, I wondered why he had slept with Kelly in the first place and if there was another reason he was concerned about the truth getting out. He still hadn't answered my questions about his professional relationship with Jake. Could that be because he needed Jake as a client? If Jake learned about his affair with Kelly, that would likely put an immediate end to their partnership. Not to mention, Jake would probably kick Brogan to the curb just like his wife had. Suddenly, Brogan would be down a client and homeless. That was a fairly strong reason to want to protect his secret.

The coffee shop buzzed as more teens spilled inside. The smell of espresso grew stronger, and Pri cranked the music higher to be heard over the chatter. I needed to get back to the Secret Bookcase soon.

"I heard Kelly was potentially signing with a new coach, and what can you tell me about Jake landing her branding deal? It seems fairly convenient for him to swoop in and take the deal meant for her."

"A new coach? What? Nah, that's a rumor." He scraped his hands through his hair as he shook his head. "And Jake was just in the right place at the right time. The deal was already a go. They needed a surfer, so he jumped in."

Before I could ask him a few more final questions, he stuffed his half-eaten croissant into a paper bag and chugged his coffee, which had to be lukewarm at best by now. "But I'm worried about Jake."

"You mentioned that already." I closed my notebook, sensing our chat was coming to an end.

"No, this is different." He leaned his elbows on his knees and stole a quick glance at the doors. "There's something I haven't told the police. I should have, but I was wrapped up in my own problems, and I guess keeping this secret was sort of my penance for sleeping with Kelly."

Secret? My body went still in anticipation of what he was about to say. The noise in the coffee shop faded away as I waited for him to continue.

"Jake had a key to Kelly's place. She made him give her his key back when they broke up, but he made a copy."

I reached for my notebook. This was too important not to jot down. "You're sure?"

"Positive. He still has it. It's like a talisman. He's been surfing with it—on a chain around his neck. No one else knows it's the key to Kelly's place except me."

"How do you know?"

"He showed me the key the day she died." Brogan's voice was so low I could barely hear him. "He went over there, and they fought."

"You already said that." I'd read as much in the police report and heard it repeated by pretty much everyone I'd spoken with.

"No, I wasn't done." He held up a hand to stop me. "He went back that night. The night she died. He let himself into the house."

I gasped audibly.

Brogan nodded. "Yeah, it's bad. He told me he snuck back in with flowers and a box of chocolates. He was going to propose. Don't ask me why. He thought maybe if she knew how serious he was about her and their relationship, she would say yes. She wouldn't have said yes, but he wouldn't listen to reason. He was obsessed with winning her over, so he used the copy of the key he had made and snuck inside with the flowers and candy, intending to take a knee and ask her to marry him, but instead, he found her dead in the bathtub."

"Wait, what? Jake found her in the tub?" That definitely was not in the police report.

"He freaked out and told me the next morning. He was worried the police would arrest him and think he did it, so we agreed never to speak about it." Brogan blew air from his lips like a motorboat, mimicking the sound. "It's bothering me. I don't think he killed her. I don't want to believe he killed her, but there's a chance, especially if the police really aren't sure what happened. I'm not throwing him under the bus, but since you're smart and looking into this, I figured you should probably know." He picked up his coffee cup. "I need to go. Thanks for the talk."

I watched him leave, my mind reeling and my body humming. Maybe June was right. If Jake had snuck into Kelly's house, he could have killed her, mopped up the evidence, and taken off long before Allison returned home from the night shift. This changed everything.

CHAPTER 18

My mind buzzed with a combination of caffeine and new possibilities. I needed to parse through what Brogan had revealed and figure out how much of it was true. One of them was lying about Kelly quitting. Jake insisted Brogan sent him to Kelly's place to talk her out of leaving the sport, but Brogan had glossed over the question. Had he lied to Jake to cover up their affair or was there truth to the rumors that Kelly was giving it all up or signing with a new coach?

Currently, there were two incongruent pictures of the young surfer being painted in my head. Fletcher and I needed to sort through stories to find a clear path to the truth.

I gathered my empty cup and dishes and took them to the bar.

"How did it go with your *bro*?" Pri asked in her best surfer accent.

"I don't know yet. Everyone I've spoken with thus far seems to have a different impression of Kelly, with one exception—they all think her drowning was an accident. Every single person has repeated the same sentiment about her accident, almost to the letter. Well, except for her landlord, but he's another story." I tapped the long counter in rhythm with my words.

"And it sounds like you think that's odd, right?" Pri repositioned glossy pastries in the glass case next to the espresso machine. I was seriously tempted by the chocolate eclairs and cardamom orange tarts. Pri sported a new sleeve of temporary tattoos. Her intricate designs always told a story. The imagery of a black-and-white line drawing of Cryptic with people cozied up cradling warm drinks made me want to step right into her art.

Pri preferred the temporary nature of her tattoos. She enjoyed the process of drawing more than displaying her final creations, so she would print them on temporary tattoo material, wear them for a few weeks, and then design something entirely new.

I sighed. "Yeah, maybe. I'm not sure yet." I dragged my teeth over my bottom lip, wishing I could put my finger on exactly why the similarities were bothering me. Talking to Pri always helped. "It's almost like they're actors in a play, and everyone is reading the same line. Almost everyone is repeating the same thing verbatim—she ate her usual nighttime gummy, poured a hot bath, and slipped. It feels rehearsed, but collectively. As if each of them is reading off a script."

"Watch out, you're slipping into conspiracy territory here, Annie." Pri winked as she wiped down the counter with a mixture of lemon and rosemary soap. "What's the Agatha Christie book where they all did it? Is that what you're hinting at?"

"*Murder on the Orient Express*," I replied, thinking of Hal reading his well-loved copy at the store. "It's a classic, but, no, I don't think it's that. It's more that everyone, except for June, can't even entertain the possibility Kelly was murdered. The unanimous sentiment is that her death was a tragic accident, likely brought on by stress. Minus her seedy landlord, who told me in no uncertain terms she killed herself. I can't rule out that the most obvious answer could be the answer, but June is so insistent. She stopped by the bookshop with a press release this morning. She wants as much attention on Kelly's case as possible to keep it top of mind, and she seems to think that approach will somehow force the killer out of the shadows. I've been trying to convince her otherwise."

"What do you think that means?" Pri spritzed the pastry case with the natural cleanser.

"That's what I'm stuck on. The consensus seems to be that June is a busybody and nosy neighbor. Part of me wonders if she's engineering more to the story, trying to make it seem like Kelly's death was murder, when in reality, she knows it was just an accident. It is a way to get attention. She's bored and lonely and needs a reason to be actively engaged in the community again."

"Maybe she should take up knitting." Pri twisted her face as she gave the top of the counter one last spritz.

"Right? But on the other hand, I can't dismiss her claims. The more I speak with people, the more that surfaces about Kelly's personal life and career—things that could have put her in harm's way and made someone stage her murder to look like an accident."

Pri washed her hands and opened the pastry case, packing an assortment of house-made cookies—giant, chewy snickerdoodles, almond sugar cookies with cherry compote, and triple chocolate chip cookies still warm and oozing with melted dark chocolate. "Here, take these to the store to share. Maybe they'll help inspire you." She thrust a white pastry box with the tangerine Cryptic logo at me.

"Thanks." I took the box and blew her a kiss. "Keep me posted if any of the surfer bros swing by anytime soon."

"By the way, are we still on for soup and grown-up grilled cheese this weekend?"

"Uh, yeah. Count on it." I shot her a thumbs-up and took off. Pri, Penny, Liam, and I had been having grown-up grilled cheese, soup, and movie nights a couple of times a month. This weekend was my turn to host, and I was leaning toward going with a classic—a creamy tomato and basil soup.

The air was brisk outside, but not a single cloud showed its face as the late afternoon winter sun splashed onto the sidewalk. Every storefront in the village square was lit with gauzy, warm interior lights, beckoning anyone passing by to stop and stay for a while. Huge terra-cotta pots filled to the brim with colorful succulents lined the sidewalk. Garlands of clementines and

Meyer lemons twisted together with eucalyptus were strung in a sweeping pattern along the eaves of Spanish-style haciendas and mid-century modern buildings. The eclectic nature of the square made it infinitely more interesting than any big-box shopping complex. Every shop was unique in its architecture and offerings.

I considered my next move as I meandered slowly, taking my time to admire a bouquet of blushing pink roses mixed with dainty stalks of salvia and English lavender in the flower shop window. Seeing the crime scene was at the top of my list. As Allison had mentioned, there wouldn't be any evidence left at this point, and too much time had passed. But just being in the space Kelly had inhabited might spark something new.

I turned off Cedar Avenue onto the stately drive leading to the Secret Bookcase. There was never a time when seeing the sprawling estate draped in ivy and glistening under the butterscotch sun that my breath didn't catch for a moment. I paused and took a second to drink in the beauty. Birdsong filled the air like a sweet serenade. Deep green topiaries and manicured hedges in the garden sat in stark contrast to the soft creamy shades of the estate with its arched windows and pitched roofline.

At the bookshop, I shared the cookies with Fletcher and Hal and snuck upstairs to compile my notes from my conversation with Brogan. I also emailed Allison to see if there was a convenient time to drop by. To my surprise, she responded almost instantly, saying that she was fine and she had another hour before her shift at the hospital if I wanted to stop in now.

Do I? Uh, yes!

I replied to let her know I was on my way and hurried back downstairs to find Fletcher enjoying a quarter of the snickerdoodle. He had cut each of the cookies precisely into four perfect sharing slices. "That was fast." He brushed cinnamon and sugar crumbs from his chin.

"Allison responded right away to my request. She's available now." I pointed to the vintage typewriter clock behind the cash register. "Do you want to come with me? It shouldn't take long. Mary Jane can handle the store, and Ash should be here any minute." Since Ash was a junior in high school, he worked three days a week after school and on weekends.

He shook his head, pointing to the phone. "I'm waiting for a call. I've been reconfirming everyone's alibi, and her boss is supposed to be calling any minute. You go. I'll hold down the fort."

"Anything else we need while I'm out?"

"Nope." He twirled his hand with a flourish. "Work your magic. Channel your inner Sherlock. Maybe you'll notice something with fresh eyes."

"Don't get your hopes up on that. This crime scene is pretty cold, but I'll do my best. You never know, just being there might spark something. I want to see the bathroom and the cottage layout. I've been considering the possibility that perhaps the killer scaled the wall outside and got in that way?" Even as I said it, it sounded outlandish, but at this stage of an investigation, we needed to keep every possibility open. "It's a long shot, but I'll take whatever shot I can get right now."

"My faith is in you, Annie." He snatched a slice of the chocolate cookie. "Let's compare notes when you're done."

I didn't waste any time getting to Allison's house. Since the rain had cleared, I opted to cut through Oceanside Park and take advantage of the fading light.

I observed the exterior. Allison's cottage was painted in a light apricot with a cream trim and a stone pathway that led to a covered porch with a swing and two large potted palms flanking the front door. Allison greeted me at the door and ushered me inside, checking over my shoulder before motioning for me to hurry. "Get in here, quick. June's probably watching us," she said, shutting the door behind me the minute my feet had crossed the threshold. She wore a pair of mint green scrubs and tennis shoes. Her hair was tied up in another ponytail and I noticed a gym bag resting in the entryway. She was clearly ready for work, so I needed to make the most of what little time I might have.

"Now that you're investigating, June has been over here twice." She locked the door, bolting it shut.

"Why?" I glanced out the long, rectangular windows, gazing toward the end of the street. It was too far to see if June was stationed at her telescope, but I suspected she probably was. Once I was done at Allison's, I should probably drop by and give her another update. Hopefully, that would bring her some reassurance.

"I have to say, it's like she's excited about the case being open again." Allison leaned against the door like she was trying to reinforce it. "I'm the opposite. I'm trying to put Kelly's death behind me and find a way to move on."

"I understand," I said softly. "I know how hard it is to lose a friend, and I greatly appreciate you letting me take a look. I'll try to be as quick as I can."

"No, it's fine." She sounded resigned as she pulled away from the door. "I'm just not sure there's anything here for you. Her parents took most of her things. I don't know what I'm going to do with her room. Maybe turn it into an office or workout space. I'm not sure I can face getting another roommate. Not yet. It's too soon…" She trailed off, glancing upstairs.

"That's okay. You don't need to make any major decisions. In fact, I know from previous experience that it's better not to make any massive life changes right after a death." I surveyed the entryway. The cottage was a mirror of June's space, with a curved archway leading to a living room on one side and a kitchen on the other. A staircase with a banister lay in front of me. The extent of the similarities ended with the layout. Allison's aesthetic was minimalistic. Modern artwork hung on the walls featuring geometric patterns, bold colors, and sharp angles.

"Would you mind showing me the bathroom?" I didn't want to elaborate on the many reasons I wanted to see the spot where Kelly had died. First and foremost, I was curious to see if there was a chance the killer could have climbed up the side of the house, opened the window, and climbed back down again. It was a long shot, but every possibility was worth exploring. Secondly, I wanted to feel the space. It was a technique I'd learned in my criminology studies. Some of my classmates found the practice too woo-woo, but I appreciated the concept of sharing a space with the victim and imagining every possibility, literally putting myself in their perspective. Dr. Caldwell encouraged us to tap into our feelings and senses versus trying to shut them off and approach a crime scene from a completely clinical standpoint.

"It's this way." Allison gestured to the stairs. I followed her to the second-floor bathroom. It wasn't particularly large. There was a clawfoot tub and freestanding shower, a small sitting area with extra lighting, a medicine cabinet, and a large window looking out onto the street below.

"Do you want me to stay?" Allison asked, already backing out of the room.

"No, no. Go ahead." I didn't want to make her relive the ugly memories of that night. "This shouldn't take me long. I just need a few minutes to study the space. I'll come downstairs when I'm done if that's okay?"

"Sure." She left without another word, hurrying away like she wanted to be anywhere but here.

I felt bad bringing the unpleasant memories to the surface. She had found her friend and roommate in this very tub. I could only imagine that having me revisit the scene was making it all come back. Even living in the cottage where her best friend had died must be challenging. I wasn't sure I could have done that after Scarlet died. It would have been too painful.

I would do my best to gather what I needed as quickly as possible.

I closed my eyes and took a long breath. I'd studied the crime scene photos and knew exactly how Kelly was lying in the tub. I paced from one side of the bathroom to the other, considering whether there was a way the killer could have drowned her without leaving any evidence behind. As per the police report, there were no water marks or footprints and no fingerprints on the door or windows other than Kelly and Allison's, which was to be expected. But there was a long chunk of time between the time Kelly died and when Allison discovered her. The killer could have brought supplies with them—a towel to mop the floor and gloves.

If someone like Jake were the killer, I knew he had a key. He could have entered the house through the front door, killed her, mopped up the bathroom, and left the way he came. What about Brogan? Did he have a key as well? Could he have gotten in another way? An open window on the main floor?

I pulled back the curtains and peered out the bathroom window. Unless the murderer had extra limbs or magical powers, there was no chance they could have scaled the exterior wall. But what if Allison or Kelly hadn't locked the front or back doors?

Or could Kelly have let the killer in?

I scanned the ceiling, spotting a smoke alarm near the recessed light fixture.

That was odd. Smoke alarms weren't usually installed in bathrooms. Fires rarely started in a bathroom, and there were ample water sources to put one out. I wondered why the extra precaution was necessary.

I moved to the medicine cabinet and inspected its contents. There were a few prescription pill bottles remaining, a tube of lip gloss, and a jar of expensive sunscreen. Otherwise, as Allison had mentioned, none of Kelly's personal items remained. I picked up the prescriptions—each bottle was labeled with Allison's name, not Kelly's. I snapped a few pictures of the medications to check them against what had been found in Kelly's system. Was there a chance she could have taken her roommate's medication and unknowingly overdosed? Or perhaps the medication caused an adverse reaction with her sleep gummy?

I mentally reviewed my suspect list. Harvey likely had a master key to the property, which meant potentially everyone had access to the house.

The police hadn't found any evidence—wet towels, used gloves, etc. But the killer could have been clever and disposed of them immediately after committing the crime.

From what I'd gleaned reading the case notes, it didn't sound as if the police had done a huge sweep. There were no subpoenas for any of the suspects. Since they were treating Kelly's death as accidental or suicide there wouldn't have been a need to search further.

I took one last look before heading for the stairs. I'd promised Allison I wouldn't linger longer than necessary, and there was nothing more for me to see here.

A text message dinged from Fletcher as I shut the bathroom door behind me.

> Breaking news! There's a hole in Allison's alibi.

> What kind of hole?

> Too much to share in text. I'll fill you in when you get back. Ask her where she was and if she left the hospital.

Will do. Good work. Also, can you research these medications? See if any of them match what was in Kelly's system. Found them in the bathroom.

You got it, Watson.

He signed off with a sleuth emoji.

I took a second to compose my thoughts and calm my surging heartbeat. If Allison lied about her whereabouts the night of Kelly's death, was I on the verge of coming face-to-face with the killer?

CHAPTER 19

I found Allison in the living room. The décor and furnishings were distinctly minimalistic, like the rest of the house. There were two gray loveseats arranged in front of the huge bay windows, a sleek coffee table, and a gold bar cart with pretty bottles of expensive liquors, a cocktail shaker, and fancy glasses. A canvas with rushed brush strokes in black and red took up the wall behind the couch. Just looking at the piece evoked a sense of anger, like the artist had taken out their rage on the painting. It was an interesting statement, but not my style.

Allison scrolled through her phone, only looking up and noticing me after I cleared my throat to announce my presence. "Did you divine a new revelation about Kelly's death up there?" She clicked off her phone and turned it upside down on the coffee table.

"Unfortunately, no." I gestured to the empty loveseat. "Do you mind if I sit for a minute?"

"Go ahead." She sounded less than thrilled, but I tried to keep in mind how I would have felt if someone had re-opened old wounds about Scarlet. She pulled her head to one side, stretching her neck. "I have to leave soon, though."

"I understand, I'll make this quick." I took out my notebook and flipped to a fresh page. "I've been considering who had access to your place. You have a key, of course. What about Brogan and Jake? And I'm assuming Harvey must have a key as well?"

"Harvey has a key, for sure. That's part of our lease agreement. He must be able to access the property. But neither Jake nor Brogan had keys." She reached for her copy of *Blood on the Page*, which rested on the coffee table. "Tell your colleague thanks for the rec. I stayed up way too late reading it the other night." She flipped to a page she'd dog-eared. I bit my tongue. Dog-earing books was a criminal offense in the indie bookselling world, but it was her copy. She was free to inflict as much harm as she wanted on the poor, unwilling pages. "It's a bloody gem."

"I'll be sure to tell Mary Jane you're enjoying it." I tapped my notebook. "Okay if I take a few notes?"

"Yeah. Fine." Her tone was crisp and curt, but I couldn't jump right to her alibi. That was a sure way to get her to stop talking or find myself uninvited.

"When you came home after your shift, the front and back doors were locked, right?"

She put the book down and grabbed a charcoal gray throw pillow with black-and-red embroidery. Then she clutched it to her lap like she was giving herself a much-needed hug. "Yes. Kelly always locked up at night after I left because she was asleep."

"The back door, too?"

"The back door, windows, the garage. She was kind of paranoid. I used to tease her—this is Redwood Grove, after all, one of the safest places in California, if not anywhere—but she didn't like being alone. That's why she wanted a roommate in the first place. She was such a force out in the water. No wave fazed her, but she was a scaredy cat at home. It used to irritate me because there would be at least half a dozen lights on when I got home. She'd leave the entry, hallway, kitchen, and bathroom lights on. I never understood how she slept with that much light. I need a black room to sleep in—not an inch of light can get in. I guess that's probably because my days and nights are flipped, but still, Kelly could sleep through anything once she was knocked out with her supplements."

That was interesting. Kelly was a hard, sound sleeper, and she'd consumed a gummy. Yet another check in the "accident" box.

"Let's say Kelly knew her killer." I intentionally used the word "killer" and watched her carefully to gauge her response.

"Killer?" Allison interrupted me with a severe scowl, clutching the pillow tighter to her chest in a show of protection.

"I'll rephrase that: Assuming Kelly was murdered, if she knew her killer, do you think it's possible she could have let them in, and they locked the door on their way out?"

Allison's gaze ping-ponged from the hallway to the front door. "I don't know. I never considered it, but, yeah, sure, I guess it's possible."

"You don't happen to have any security cameras installed that might have recorded someone at the front door?" I shot a glance to the front of the house.

She shook her head. "No, but Kelly wanted to get some. Maybe if we had—" She paused and fought back tears, blinking rapidly like she was trying to force them away. "I guess we'd know for sure whether it was an accident or murder. I hate the idea that someone could have done that to her and been in our house." She shuddered, squeezing the pillow so tight I was worried it might rip open.

"What about Harvey? Is there a chance he used his key?" I doodled in the notebook, pretending to make a note while really trying to assess her reaction to each of my questions.

"What about him? He's the worst, vile, gross. He doesn't mess with me, though. I know how to deal with a bully—you attack back. Kelly hadn't figured that out. He walked all over her. She reported him to the housing authority and had written a scathing review to post online. She was also looking for new places for us to rent. She wanted to get away from him." Allison's eyes grew wider as she considered this, her grip on the pillow loosening a touch.

"Do you think he singled her out?" This time, I actually made a note about Kelly looking for new places to rent. That could be an important thread to follow, especially with Harvey.

"I think he had a thing for her. She was gorgeous and young and semi-famous. He harassed her—crossed a line for sure. I was in full support of a move and anything we could do to get eyes on his shady business practices. We made a pact that only I would deal with him. I didn't want her anywhere near the guy. Don't get me wrong, she was a strong woman and could take him if necessary, but he was super creepy with her and he did come around more than necessary. About a week before she died, she caught him in the house without either of our knowledge or permission. He claimed to be fixing a broken water pipe in the bathroom—there was no broken pipe. She called and read him the riot act for coming into the house without telling us."

"What bathroom?" A lump swelled in my throat, constricting my breathing.

"Kelly's. Upstairs." Allison pointed to the ceiling.

I swallowed hard, forcing the knot in my chest down. No broken pipe. What was Harvey doing in the bathroom? The bathroom Kelly died in? Could Harvey have been scoping out a way to spy on her? Installed a hidden camera? Surely, the police would have found something like that. But then again, if they weren't looking…

My mind went on a wild ride, mapping the room I'd just observed. There were plenty of places he could have installed something to spy on Kelly, from the showerhead to the lights to the mirror on the medicine cabinet, or the smoke alarm, which had immediately flagged my attention. I hated the thought, but I couldn't ignore it either.

"What's wrong? You went white." Allison sat up, tossing the pillow to the side and studying me like I was one of her patients in danger of passing out.

"We need to go back upstairs right now." I was already on my feet. My heart thudded in my head as I took the stairs as fast as I could.

"What? What is it?" Allison sounded confused as I whipped open cabinet doors and scanned the ceiling.

"I have a bad feeling about this," I told her, truthfully. "Can you shut off the light and close the door?" I tugged the curtains shut, trying to make the room as dark as possible.

"Okay, what are we doing, though?" She followed my directions as I pulled out my phone and turned on the flashlight app.

I carefully ran the flashlight around the room, keeping it at eye level. "This is a trick we learned in my criminology classes to scan for any hidden cameras."

"Hidden cameras?" Her words came out in a squeak.

I nodded, continuing to survey the dark room as I moved the light toward the ceiling. "We're looking for any little blue or purple reflections—anything that shines when my light hits it."

"Oh, God, like that?" She threw one hand over her mouth like she was about to be sick, and she pointed to a tiny ribbon of purple light streaming from the smoke alarm.

My heart dropped from my chest like it was in a free fall. This was worse than I imagined. "I'm afraid so—that's a camera. Someone was spying on Kelly."

CHAPTER 20

"I think I might puke." Allison dropped to her knees. "A camera? In our bathroom? That can't be legal, right?"

I flipped on the lights and knelt next to her, rubbing her back. "It's going to be okay. We need to call the authorities immediately. This is a massive violation of your privacy, and yes, it's also highly illegal."

"How long has it been there? This whole time?" She sat up, rocking on her knees, wiping sweat from her brow, and clasping her hand over her mouth as she shook her head. "Thank goodness I never use this bathroom, but Kelly did. It has to be Harvey. He was spying on her? Here? What a creep. What a monster."

"We don't know anything definitive yet, but it appears that way." I helped her to her feet. "I'm calling my friend Dr. Caldwell. We're going to want the authorities to document this so that you have a solid case against Harvey."

"Is June right?" Allison rubbed her temples and squinted up at me. "Did he kill her?"

"I don't know. Depending on the footage, there could be evidence here. Or he may have come back and destroyed it. Has he been in the house recently? Like since she died?" The fact that Harvey, unlike the rest of the suspects, immediately insisted Kelly killed herself suddenly seemed like a very important point of differentiation.

"Not that I know of." She sounded dazed as she shook her head again. "But who knows now. Maybe he's been coming and going without either of us knowing." She shuddered at the thought, wrapping her arms around herself tighter.

"Let's go downstairs and wait for the police." I placed a call to Dr. Caldwell, who agreed to come right away. "Can I get you a drink of water or something?"

Allison rubbed her thighs, continuing to shake her head in disbelief. "I can't believe this. I can't believe it. Will he go to jail?"

"I don't know. It depends on the charges and what the police are able to gather. That's why it's important we let them take over from here." In my training to obtain my private investigator's license, I studied when it was necessary to involve the police. This was one of those times. Finding the hidden camera gave me much more reason to suspect Harvey, but I still needed to follow up on Fletcher's text, and this was my best chance. I knew once Dr. Caldwell and her team arrived, it would be a whirlwind. "You were at the hospital the entire night when Kelly died, right?"

A shiver rippled through her body like a miniature earthquake erupting inside her. "What? Yeah, why?"

"I'm piecing a new timeline together now that we know Harvey installed a camera," I said, hoping she bought my lie. "You never left? You didn't happen to swing home to grab a snack or check in with Kelly?"

"No. I didn't come home." She gnawed on her pinkie. "It was my usual routine all night. Like every night."

"And you didn't leave?" I tried again. Her body language told me she was on the brink of cracking.

She sucked in a breath and started to respond, but the doorbell rang. Dr. Caldwell was true to her word. She must have dropped everything to get here that fast.

I let the team in. Dr. Caldwell was short and petite, like me, with oversized, black-framed glasses and cunning eyes that didn't miss a single detail. Her silver-white hair was cut in a neat, clean bob with sharp angles that accented her apple-like cheeks. She greeted me with a warm yet curt smile, glossing over any niceties to get straight to work. "Annie, you found a hidden camera? Can you fill me in on the basics?"

I gave her a brief overview of what Fletcher and I had uncovered in Kelly Taylor's case since we last spoke and shared my theory that Harvey Wade may have installed the camera under the guise of fixing a leaky bathroom pipe.

She took a few notes on a small, black leather notebook and then directed the police officer who had accompanied her to stay with Allison while I showed her where I'd found the camera.

"Do you have gloves?" she asked on our way upstairs, already reaching into her bag to offer me a pair.

"Thanks." I pulled the blue latex gloves over my hands. "I didn't bring any because I wasn't anticipating this. I dropped by to take a look at the bathroom, hoping maybe seeing the space might paint a clearer picture, just like you taught us, but when Allison mentioned Harvey had entered the house without their permission, claiming to do repair work on a pipe that wasn't leaking, I had a sudden realization that something more could have been at play, especially because I've never seen a smoke alarm in a bathroom before."

"Well done." She nodded with approval. "I ran his name through the system after you called, and he has a long list of tenant complaints. The housing authority has been investigating him, but if this turns out to be his camera gear, we'll have a much different case on our hands."

"I've been torn about Kelly's death, wondering if maybe it was an accident, but now I'm wondering if Harvey was stalking her. He could have come by that night. If she refused his advances or realized he was watching her, he could have killed her, cleaned up any evidence, and left without being seen. He obviously had access to the property and likely knew Allison wouldn't be home for hours. His story is the only one that varies from the rest of the suspects—he told me she killed herself, whereas everyone else thinks it was an accident."

"All solid points of consideration." Dr. Caldwell snapped a glove over her hand. "Let's remove the camera first. Then I'll have my team dust for fingerprints."

I repeated my magic trick for her—shining my flashlight toward the ceiling where a beam of purple split through a tiny hole in the smoke alarm.

She took a few photos and videos. "Go ahead and turn on the lights," she said when she finished documenting the crime scene. Now it was officially a crime scene. A strange mix of horror and relief flooded through my system. It seemed more and more like that June's theory could be correct. A new theory formed in my mind—Kelly realized that Harvey had hidden the camera in her bathroom, confronted him, and he'd had to silence her.

I blew out a breath and took a minute to compose my thoughts.

I was familiar with the California Penal Code. Harvey would face "invasion of privacy" charges for installing a camera without consent. Typically, that would result in fines and jail time, but given the placement of the camera, he'd captured sensitive material, which would allow Dr. Caldwell to charge him with a felony. Allison could also pursue a civil suit against him.

Dr. Caldwell moved the cushioned stool from the makeup seating area and positioned it under the device. I gave her a hand to steady her as she climbed up and unscrewed the alarm. Sure enough, fit into the base of the plastic was a tiny camera. The lens itself was the size of a pinhole. Unless you were looking for it, you'd never know it was there. "Looks like we have a new crime here," she said with a frown.

"It's Wi-Fi enabled, right?" I asked, examining the device more closely. Fletcher had an entire catalog of spyware flagged for future potential stakeouts, and I'd seen many models like this. Anyone could purchase a camera like this from an online retailer these days, so now the task would be linking this particular device to Harvey.

"Yep." She rested it on the stool and snapped more photos. "I'll send my team to do a sweep of the entire house—check the other smoke detectors and any likely places other cameras could have been hidden. Then I'll take this to our tech department and bring Harvey Wade in for questioning."

"Do you think you'll be able to trace the footage back to the night Kelly died? If the camera was installed then and recording, we might be able to close the case quickly."

"It's possible. It will depend on a variety of factors. I will keep you abreast of everything we learn. Good work, Annie. This is a major breakthrough, and if Harvey installed this camera, I will also be sending a team to every other property he owns to check for similar devices, immediately."

That thought brought me some relief. If Harvey was spying on any of his other tenants, then this case would be worth it even if we couldn't definitively determine the cause of Kelly's death. Although finding the hidden camera gave me even more resolve and a fresh jolt of energy to piece together the puzzle and provide June with answers.

CHAPTER 21

I didn't stay much longer. There was a frenzy of police activity, and Allison, understandably, wanted to accompany Dr. Caldwell's highly skilled team room by room. I promised her I would check in later. I considered dropping by June's house but decided to return to the bookstore instead. I wanted confirmation from Dr. Caldwell that Harvey was in custody before I gave June false hope or potentially put her in harm's way.

The sun was already making its evening descent, covering the village square in a veil of dusky eggplant. Shops and restaurants hummed with life. The intoxicating aromas of smoke puffing from chimneys and savory sauces bubbling at the pizzeria made me suddenly hungry. Artifacts, Caroline's boutique, was already closed, but her window display caught my eye. I stopped to admire it.

She'd created a whimsical winter garden scene with plush felted snowcap mushrooms and woodland creatures—spotted deer, chipmunks, and skunks. Moss and bundles of white birch logs finished off her temporary forest floor. Strings of golden twinkle lights draped around the window frame gave it an ethereal glow. Caroline used more birch logs to showcase her current wares—cashmere scarves, woolen mittens, jewelry, candles, and boxes of chocolates in painted tins. Her eye was exquisite. I hoped Fletcher and I would have news for her about Hal's mysterious brooch soon.

I continued past the Stag Head and down the long gravel drive where the Secret Bookcase sat, bathed in the warm glow of fading periwinkle light. My feet crunched along the pressed pebble path as a cool breeze kicked up, stinging my cheeks and bending the tree branches in a slow, solemn wave.

Fletcher was bringing in the chalkboard sign. "It's about time. I've been eagerly waiting your arrival." He folded the sign flat and waited for me. "Spy cameras! This is straight out of a novel or movie, Annie. Why didn't I accompany you?"

"I invited you, remember? You said you were checking alibis, and it sounds like that paid off, yeah?"

He tucked the sign under his arm and propped the door open. "Let's chat inside. It's freezing out here."

Freezing in California meant something different than it might in the Midwest or Northeast, but he wasn't wrong. January storms blew in from the Pacific Ocean, one after the other, battering the beaches and leaving palm branches and pinecones in their wake. But snow was never in the forecast, and many days, like today, broke with clear skies and cheery sunshine.

"Hal's upstairs and Ash is doing a quick walk-through before he takes off," Fletcher said, turning the sign on the door from OPEN to CLOSED. "I'm nearly done with closing procedures, but tell me everything. You really found a hidden spy camera in the bathroom? Very good, although I expected no less from our fearless detective."

"I'm still in shock. It's so disturbing to think that Harvey—I mean, assuming it was him—was spying on Kelly in the bathroom."

"Terrible. Absolutely appalling." Fletcher shook his head in disgust. "I hope Dr. Caldwell uses the full extent of the law on him."

"Me too." I nodded, rubbing my hands together for warmth. They'd gone white on my short walk, a side effect from Raynaud's, a condition I'd dealt with since my teen years, which left my extremities numb and tingling if exposed to the cold for too long. I filled him in on my initial conversation with Allison and how I'd come to realize Harvey might have been spying on his female tenants. "Tell me about this alibi situation," I said when I finished. "Allison made a point to say she was at work and did her usual routine that night, but I felt like she was leaving something out. It was crummy timing because right as she started to crack, Dr. Caldwell arrived. I think she's lying."

"Oh, she is," Fletcher said with a sly smile. "I spoke with her manager, who backed up her claim that Allison was indeed on shift for the duration of the night, but I used my stellar deduction techniques to press her further, and I, too, had an epiphany, you might say."

I could tell he was enjoying this. Fletcher was in his element and stretching the moment for as long as possible.

"And?" I pressed my lips together, jutting my chin out. "Are you going to say more or keep me in suspense?"

"I rarely get these opportunities. Allow me the luxury of savoring them, won't you?" He flashed me a sneaky wink and then turned serious. "I checked the prescriptions you found at Allison's, and two of them are sedatives, so we could be on the right track there. I also confirmed with the hospital that Allison never left the building. I suppose you could say it was simple semantics, and when I asked that question, I jogged something in her memory. Apparently, Allison goes on midnight snack runs. The all-night convenience store around the corner from the hospital has far superior snacks than the cafeteria, and Allison has a habit of running over to pick up snacks for the team on her break."

"So she left the building that night?" I couldn't believe he'd learned such a critical piece of information. Not that I ever doubted him. Fletcher was relentless when it came to following every lead and chasing every angle.

"She did. No one mentioned it initially for a few reasons—the police were trying to establish Kelly's state of mind versus looking for a killer, and Allison's snack runs were quick. I guess nobody thought it was a big deal, except for me." Fletcher couldn't contain his Cheshire grin. "What are the odds that anyone clocks how long her snack runs take? She could have slipped home, killed Kelly, and returned with an armful of chocolate chip cookies and spicy potato chips."

"Right." I bobbed my head in agreement as the tiny hairs on my arm stood at attention like soldiers falling into formation. "That could explain was she was evasive when I asked about her shift that night."

"Exactly." He motioned outside where the purple had muted into darkness. The twinkling lights of the village square dotted the horizon like little stars. "You know what this means?"

I shook my head.

"Stakeout! Tonight. You and me—we meet up at the hospital shortly before midnight. I wonder if there's more to Allison's late-night snack runs. I also think we should time exactly how long it takes to get from the hospital to her house and back again."

"That's a great idea." I wasn't about to put up a fight. We were so close to finding the answers we needed to close this case. "By the way, Allison loved Mary Jane's rec. You definitely should order more copies."

"You say that as if you're surprised. I'm not the least bit shocked. Mary Jane wasn't exaggerating. She's been hand-selling copies of *Blood on the Page* like wildfire. I've been considering reading it again. Although I hesitate because I might not sleep again. That book is dark, really dark."

"Surprisingly, so is Allison's vibe." I told him about her artwork.

"All the more reason we follow my method and watch her every move tonight. The game is afoot."

"Oh, no, you're not planning to wear a deerstalker and a houndstooth cape, are you?"

"I wish, but sadly, tonight calls for us to blend in with the background. I say we both don black from head to toe."

"Okay, where exactly do you want to meet?" I was going to need a cat nap with Professor Plum and some serious coffee for a midnight stakeout, but Fletcher's plan was solid. I was in complete agreement that we needed to figure out if there was another reason for Allison sneaking out of the hospital and if there was enough time for her to have killed Kelly before any of her colleagues noticed she was missing.

Why had she left this critical detail out when the police originally questioned her and now again with me? She was hiding something, that was for sure.

"Let's meet on the corner across the street in Oceanside Park. You know that bench right by the entrance? I'll be there with our own reinforcements."

"Reinforcements?" Was he inviting someone else to join us on night watch?

"Snacks, Annie. Snacks." He licked his lips eagerly. "I've waited my entire adult life for a proper stakeout. I'll come prepared to last the duration."

I chuckled. "Great. You bring the snacks. I'll bring hand warmers."

We parted ways. I finished closing up the bookstore, texted Liam to let him know about our plans, and grabbed my car, which was still parked out back. I'd never done a legitimate stakeout either. We'd had some practice runs in college, just for fun, but tonight could give us new insight into Allison and her potential involvement in Kelly's death. I had to admit I was as excited as Fletcher.

CHAPTER 22

I texted Liam to update him on my plans with Fletcher.

> Heading out on night watch.

I added two googly-eye emojis and gave him a brief overview of the agenda for our evening adventures.

> Do you need a bodyguard? Extra backup?

> I have my own personal Sherlock.

I shot him a picture of Fletcher dressed up as Mr. Holmes for Halloween, complete with the deerstalker cap, cape, and fake plastic pipe.

> Okay. But be careful.

> Will do.

I ended our exchange with thumbs-up and kissing emojis.

I felt better knowing that Liam was aware of our outing. I was confident in our ability to remain out of sight. We'd invested in the necessary gear for occasions like this— cameras with telescopic lenses and night vision goggles. Fletcher and I had even taken a weekend seminar offered by the local police on the art of surveillance. I knew we were prepared, but it was always good to take extra precautions, and Liam's offer to be my bodyguard or extra backup made me feel all fluttery again. I knew I could count on him for anything, which was the ultimate romantic gesture in my book.

A few hours later, bundled head to toe as if we were about to take a trek through the Arctic, I met up with Fletcher in the park. The park was eerily quiet. The silence seemed to stretch out as far as the redwoods. A deep cold loomed overhead, along with a scattering of stars and thin clouds that shrouded the moon like a veil. I hated feeling so on edge.

Was it my imagination, or did the trees seem almost sinister tonight? Like someone was tucked behind them, waiting to jump out and strike?

I shivered and pushed my anxiety away.

I had managed a short twenty-minute nap, although much to Professor Plum's disappointment, my alarm forced me awake again before I had a chance to slip into a deep sleep. I brewed a pot of coffee and layered with leggings, winter boots, a turtleneck, and my puffy jacket—it wasn't black, but it was navy, and that should suffice. I was confident Fletcher and I could hang in the shadow of the park and avoid being seen by Allison or anyone else who happened to be out and about in the village late at night.

Oceanside Park was like our version of Central Park—taking up acres and acres of protected land in the heart of the village square. The hospital was on the opposite end of the park from the Secret Bookcase.

I grabbed a stocking hat, gloves, two sets of hand warmers, and a carafe of coffee.

"There you are!" Fletcher jumped to his feet, looking like he was ready to camp out for the night. He had already staked out his claim on the park bench. An unzipped sleeping bag served as a cushion and a barrier from the cold. He'd brought an extra blanket and two grocery sacks of snacks.

"How long are you planning to be here?" I asked as I joined him. I checked my watch. It was eleven thirty. We only had a half hour before Allison was due to make her supposed snack run.

"You never know." He shrugged and began unpacking containers. "You've met me, right? I always over-prepare. Here, have a slice of zucchini bread while it's still warm." He thrust a container at me. "I baked batches of it last summer when zucchini was in abundance at the farmer's market and froze them for occasions like this."

"Like a midnight park stakeout?" I teased.

"Yes, absolutely." He pretended to be put out as he practically forced the container into my hands.

"Well played, and I don't mind if I do." I sat on the sleeping bag, glad for his tendency to overdo it as I helped myself to a slice of the bread. "I brought an extra set of hand warmers for you."

"No need." He reached into the bag, which was suddenly starting to feel like something from *Mary Poppins*, and retrieved a portable heater. "I know you get cold. This should help." He cranked on the fan and an instant wave of heat washed over me like a hot summer breeze.

"Ah, Fletcher, what would I do without you?" I patted his arm with my glove.

"Freeze." He passed me a napkin and a slice of the bread. Then he made himself cozy on the other side of the bench and we settled into our stakeout. "This is the boring part. The waiting and watching."

I checked the time again. "We still have a while, but I'm so curious about her snack runs. It seems suspicious, but this could all be for nothing. Doctors, nurses, hospital support staff work tirelessly, and the night shift has to be the worst—your circadian rhythms are all thrown off. She might just be a generous co-worker who likes an excuse to take a quick break and return with junk food."

"Maybe. We'll see." Fletcher chomped on a dried mango, offering me the bag. "Want one?"

"No, I'm good, and this bread is delicious by the way." I took another bite of the tender, moist slice. It was balanced beautifully with notes of warming spices—nutmeg, cinnamon, and cloves. Everyone in my friend group knew their way around a kitchen. Fletcher had surprised me during the holidays with his incredible royal icing talent. He had constructed a gingerbread showpiece that could have graced a museum. He'd complained endlessly about the painstaking task of gluing spiced cookies together with buttercream and vowed never to bake another gingerbread house again. I didn't blame him. That particular bookstore event had left a bad taste in my mouth after a participant in our first-ever gingerbread competition had dropped dead. I shuddered at the memory and took another bite of the zucchini bread. "So, what are you thinking about the summer program?"

He sighed audibly. "Will you get off my back if I tell you I sent in my application last night?"

"Did you?" I asked too brightly, feeling a newfound burst of excitement.

"I did." He bowed his head and placed his finger to his lips. "However, I won't hear whether I've been accepted for a while, so can we agree to table it for now?"

"Yes, but you're getting in. I have zero doubts, Fletcher. That's so exciting." My knee bounced with eager anticipation.

"We'll see. I hear it's highly competitive."

"You're a shoo-in." I gave him a squeeze.

"We can't let Allison clue into what we're doing," Fletcher said, stating the obvious and changing the subject. As if he realized that, he gave his head a little shake and continued. "I'm not saying anything you don't know, but I was surveying the route from the hospital to her house. I timed myself on the way here, and it took me exactly eleven minutes and twenty-seven seconds. I think we should see what she does first, and then maybe tomorrow, we can time it again to make sure. I'm slightly amped up about our stakeout, and my legs are a lot longer than yours, so it might be worth double-checking the time."

"Sounds like a plan."

While we waited for any sign of Allison, we reviewed our case notes and munched on Fletcher's snacks. If nothing else, we wouldn't go hungry.

My breath puffed out in bursts of little clouds. Stars scattered across the inky sky, and the earlier breeze turned into a full-force wind. I was glad for the blanket and hand warmers.

Finally, shortly after midnight, Allison emerged from the sliding glass doors. She wore a puffy coat that hit her at the knees over her scrubs. She looked like a woman on a mission. She didn't hesitate; she made a sharp left turn and headed straight for the convenience store.

"There's our mark." Fletcher jumped to his feet. "Leave all this. No one is out this late, and if I have to sacrifice the rest of the zucchini bread for the deer, so be it."

I stuffed my hand warmers in my pocket and followed him. We skirted along the edge of the park, careful to avoid the glow of the antique streetlamps and remain out of sight. The night air was heavy with the scent of pine. We kept our footsteps light, barely making contact with the ground as we tiptoed slowly, keeping an eye on Allison. Fortunately, the park extended the length of the village square, allowing us to stay safely in the shadows beneath the sheltering canopy of the redwood trees. There was no need to venture out in the open to watch Allison's movements. Our vantage point was perfect -concealed, safe, and secure.

Sure enough, she stopped at the connivence store, but she didn't go inside. Instead, she waited off to the side of the building in the parking lot. Fletcher grabbed his binoculars and zoomed in on Allison. "What's she doing?"

"It looks like she's waiting for someone." I pulled out the tiny pair of binoculars Fletcher had ordered for me as a gift. At the time I'd teased him about whether it was more likely we'd be using them for stakeouts or birdwatching, but it turned out he was smart in securing sets for a situation like this. "She's holding something in her hand. A bag. Can you see it?"

"Yep." I zoomed in. "I saw the same bag at her house earlier. By the door. I assumed it was her gym bag, but it's unlikely she's getting a parking lot workout in, is it?"

"Maybe it's a new trend," Fletcher said, keeping his voice low.

Allison rocked from one foot to the other. I couldn't tell if she was cold and trying to keep blood flowing by doing a little dance or if she was nervous. She checked her watch twice.

"Whoever she's meeting must be late," Fletcher said, his eyes still glued to the binoculars.

"Does she seem nervous to you?"

"Without a doubt." He started to say more but a car pulled into the parking lot. "Is this her meetup?"

"She's moving toward the car." My teeth chattered slightly as I spoke. I wasn't sure if it was from the cold or from the excitement. Our stakeout looked like it was actually yielding results.

Fletcher tossed the binoculars at me. "Here, hold these. I want to take photos with a high-range lens. Maybe we'll be able to see what's in the bag or if any money changes hands." He positioned the camera, aiming it at them, and snapped photo after photo as if he were a paparazzi member on assignment. "Can you make out the guy's face? I think it's a guy?"

I shook my head. "No, but he handed her something—money? Does that look like money to you?" I squinted through the binoculars, which were starting to fog up from the heat of my breath.

"A stack of cash." Fletcher twisted the camera lens to zoom in closer. "What is our emergency room nurse up to?"

We watched in utter silence as Allison unzipped the guy's bag and handed him a white paper bag that looked suspiciously like the kind prescriptions came in.

The exchange was brief. As quickly as the car appeared, it sped off again. Allison went into the store and returned a few minutes later with a bag of snacks. She walked back to the hospital as if she hadn't a care in the world.

We waited long enough to watch her vanish back into the sterile hallway.

"What was that all about?" Fletcher asked.

"My most educated guess—or maybe the better phrase is 'working theory'—is that she's selling prescription drugs. It makes sense, don't you think? That white paper bag looks exactly like the kind they give you at the pharmacy." Voicing aloud what I'd been wondering internally made me more convinced that the theory had legs. "As a nurse, she has access to prescription medication. What if she's been stealing from the hospital and selling the drugs on the black market? The medication I found at her house had her name on it. Maybe she has an arrangement with a doctor on staff who writes her prescriptions that she fills and then sells illegally?"

"Who would have thought that Redwood Grove had a black market." Fletcher carefully secured a lens cover on the camera and packed it away.

"You know what I mean—selling to a supplier, someone who distributes the drugs illegally."

"I think you're right, Annie." Fletcher slung the camera pack over his shoulder and gathered up our snacks. "Now, we need to take a closer look at the photos and see if we can make out a face."

"We can do that first thing tomorrow." It was already late, and I didn't want to be wrecked for the workday. Allison was up to something shady, for sure. Her cover was going on the late-night munchie run, but could she be covering up for something bigger? Something like killing her roommate?

CHAPTER 23

"Okay, well, that was certainly eventful. Tomorrow, we'll clock how long it takes to get from here to Allison's house, right?" Fletcher asked. His arms were loaded down with the bags and gear.

"Yeah, that sounds like a plan. Do you need help with any of that?" I danced from one side to the other because my toes were frozen and my nose had started to drip. Time to head home and warm up under a layer of blankets with Professor Plum.

"Nope. I'm good. And for the record, I doubt I'll sleep a wink tonight. I'm buzzing with this new intel. I might take a look at the photos and see if I can come up with any leads. Meet you at the Secret Bookcase at oh-dark-thirty?"

"I don't like the sound of oh-dark-thirty, but yes, I'll see you in the morning. Hopefully, by then, Dr. Caldwell will have a report on Harvey for us, too."

"Okay, sleep tight, Annie. Don't let the bed bugs—or should I say dead bugs—bite." He let out an evil cackle as he walked away, waving one arm in the air.

I headed for home and curled up with Professor Plum, who had kept my spot warm for me. I had no problem falling asleep, but my dreams were filled with images of prescription pill bottles washing up on the surf and cameras watching me in every room at the Secret Bookcase. When I woke the next morning, I had to remind myself they were just dreams, and there weren't hidden cameras tucked in the bookstore's many nooks and crannies.

I took my time getting ready, enjoying a leisurely hot shower and two cups of coffee. I opted for a pair of black leggings, knee-high boots, and a flannel sweater dress. I paired it with black glasses and tied my hair in two braids.

"Don't nap all day," I said to Professor Plum, giving him a kiss on the head as I grabbed my coat.

A frost settled over Redwood Grove, dusting the grass and leaving car windshields shrouded in white. I was eager to hear if our stakeout had garnered any results, but Fletcher wasn't at the store when I arrived.

Not a surprise.

He probably stayed up late reviewing the photos and ended up falling asleep with his laptop on his face.

I used the quiet of the early morning to tiptoe through the store, turning on lights, cranking up the heat in the gas fireplace, and making sure everything was ready for customers. Soft sunlight poured into the windows as I tied back the curtains in the Sitting Room. I fluffed pillows and rearranged books we wanted to feature with the covers facing out. There was something wonderfully special about having the entire bookstore to myself. I loved being alone with thousands of gilded spines and faded covers. It was as if the world belonged just to me and the endless possibilities waiting inside the pages.

When I returned to the Foyer to heat water in the tea kettle, brew a pot of coffee, and arrange a plate of almond sugar cookies, Fletcher still hadn't arrived. When he didn't show by opening with Hardy and Mary Jane, a tiny worry spread through my chest, but I didn't give it much thought. I set the chalkboard sign outside and flipped the sign to OPEN. Hal padded downstairs shortly after the first eager customers made their way to the Parlor and Mary Westmacott Nook.

"Morning, Annie, I followed my nose to the scent of coffee." He poured himself a cup in in his favorite ceramic mug with a skull and crossbones. "My little gray cells could use a boost."

"Your nose *knows* the way," I joked.

"Clever, clever." He stirred cream and a packet of sugar into his coffee. He wore a patchy cardigan and corduroy slacks. Hal would have made a perfect detective in one of Agatha Christie's books, like Miss Marple's male counterpart—a sweet grandfather with a cunning ability to cut through to the truth. "Where's Fletcher?"

"I think he's sleeping in. I hope he's sleeping in." I told him about our late-night antics and our progress on the case.

"A stakeout. You kids have all the fun. Of course, these old bones don't like to remain up much past ten p.m., so I'd be worthless." Hal helped himself to a cookie, dunking it in his coffee.

"Hal, you're never worthless. Don't say that. And, also, should I be worried about Fletcher? He's never late. I guess I'm a little paranoid about our current case." I gave him a hug. My mind drifted to our other investigation. We should have news from the other appraisers and the auction house soon. I didn't like keeping secrets from him, but I agreed with Caroline's decision. It would be nothing short of cruel to get his hopes up, just to dash them.

"This case makes me think about Agatha," Hal said, using a napkin to dab his chin as he took a bite of the coffee-soaked cookie. "As I'm sure you well know from my endless stories, she loved the sea and swimming. Her time in Torquay informed and inspired so many of her novels. Did you know she was also quite the surfer?"

"Surfer? Agatha Christie?" I shook my head. That was news to me.

"Oh yes." He dipped the remaining half of the cookie into his drink. "She was one of the first women to surf. She started with belly boarding in South Africa and then progressed to riding surfboards in Waikiki. The matronly images of her in her golden years are such a part of the zeitgeist, but as a young woman she was very athletic, and the sea had her heart until her very last days."

That explained the old surfing photos in his private quarters of him posing on the beach next to a vintage orange VW van. In those days, he had long hair and a permanent tan. I wondered if he'd picked up the sport because it had been a favorite of Agatha's. His Christie knowledge knew no bounds, and the slight touch of longing in his tone when he spoke about the queen of crime made me even more resolved to find answers for him.

"You could check on Fletcher," Hal said, shifting the conversation back to the present. "I can cover the register. I saw Mary Jane unpacking a new shipment, and Hardy's getting some great pictures of the new display in the Library." Hal plunged another cookie into his coffee.

I considered it, but I didn't want to wake Fletcher if he was simply getting some much-needed rest after our marathon night. "I'll give it an hour or so."

My phone rang, pulling my thoughts away from Fletcher. It was Dr. Caldwell. "Annie, I don't have much to report yet, but Allison's house came back clean. There were no other hidden cameras. My team has reached out to Harvey's other tenants, and we'll be doing sweeps today. He has not confessed, but we have him in custody."

"Thanks for letting me know. What about the footage from the camera? Anything yet?" I knew it was likely too soon, but it never hurt to ask.

"Nope. I sent it to our tech department, and I'm waiting for the judge to approve a warrant to search Harvey's property. I'll keep you posted. Anything else on your end?"

"Maybe. I'm waiting for Fletcher to review some footage we shot last night." I gave her a brief recap of our stakeout. "It may or may not be related to the case, but I'll let you know either way once I see what we captured last night."

"Annie, at this rate, I might need to deputize you and Fletcher. You're uncovering criminal activity everywhere you go."

"Which is why I can't help but wonder if there could be a connection to Kelly's death." I felt pleased by her praise, but there were still too many questions lingering.

"My best advice is to remain open to every possibility." She repeated a sentiment I'd heard her share many times during our coursework together. She was right. I couldn't jump to conclusions yet or try to see patterns that may or may not be there. It was better to let the case come to me rather than force it. "More from me soon."

After we hung up, I helped a few customers with book recs and wrapped packages in our signature craft paper wrap with our Secret Bookcase stamp and a plaid ribbon. Mary Jane restocked the thriller section, and Hardy scrambled between rooms, helping customers find new reads and taking pictures for social media.

Fletcher still hadn't shown up.

I was almost ready to go to his apartment to check on him when the door burst open, and he rushed in. "Annie, hey, sorry I'm late. It's been quite a morning." His angular cheeks were flushed with heat, and his tone was rushed and flustered.

"Did you sleep in?"

He shook off his coat and hung it on the antique rack by the front door. "Sleep in? No, why?"

"I figured you must have stayed up later last night after we left, since you weren't here when I arrived."

"Wait? What? You didn't get my texts?" He pulled out his phone and stared at it. "Oh, wait, no, sorry." He shook his head.

"No, what texts?"

"These." He approached the checkout station and thrust his phone in my face. "I went to the beach before dawn. I haven't slept at all. Once I got home and saw who Allison was meeting with, I knew sleep was out of the question."

"Slow down. Start from the beginning." I pointed to the screen where three text messages had a red exclamation mark, pointing out that his texts had failed to send.

Fletcher looked at his phone, frowning. "Sorry, yes. I guess they didn't go through because service is so spotty on the coast." He glanced toward the Conservatory, making sure no customers were within earshot and then scrolled through his photos until he found the one he was looking for. "Check this out. Recognize who Allison met last night?"

My jaw practically dropped to the floor. The picture was grainy, but the driver's face was unmistakable—it was Jake Harken. Allison had met with Jake Harken.

CHAPTER 24

"Allison and Jake met last night?" I nearly dropped Fletcher's phone. "Oh, my God. This means it must be connected to Kelly's death."

Fletcher nodded rapidly like he was glad I was catching up. "That's why I went to the beach early this morning, which technically still felt like the middle of the night. I have to give credit to the surfers' determination. They are out in the cold, cold water before the sun."

"Did you confront Jake about the exchange?" Fletcher had taken on a large investigative role lately, but I couldn't picture him trying to shake down a suspect on his own.

"No. I followed up on your theory." He flipped through a few more zoomed-in photos of Allison and Jake, moving to the counter for me to see. "We never see what's in the bag, but that's definitely a stack of cash crossing hands." He pointed to the picture. "Once I realized it was Jake, I deduced your idea about Allison stealing prescription medication must be the solution. If she was selling to Jake, he must be selling to someone else, so I decided to tail him."

I scrolled through dozens of photos of Jake and other surfers warming up on the beach in their wet suits and waxing their surfboards.

"Here's what I think has been happening—likely for years: Allison steals the medication, Jake pays her for it and then distributes it to his surfing buddies. You can see right here." He tapped his phone with a bony finger. "He's making exchanges.

More cash, little ziplock bags of white pills. Do you think this is enough for Dr. Caldwell to make an arrest?"

My mind spun like I was twirling around in a circle too fast. Jake and Allison were working together? Had they met through Kelly? What medication was she stealing? And could Kelly have put it all together, too?

This certainly gave Jake and Allison cause to kill her. What if she hadn't taken a sleep gummy? What if Allison had drugged her and Jake finished her off?

A cold, tingly feeling spread to the tips of my fingers. I let my gaze drift around the Foyer for a moment, landing on the display of bookish stickers that needed rearranging, as I tried to make sense of it all.

"I can see you're trying to connect the dots. Sorry. I've had a few more hours with this." Fletcher turned off his phone and strummed his fingers on the counter. "This is proof, isn't it?"

"Yeah, I think there's a lot Dr. Caldwell can do with this, but I'm stuck on the relationship between Allison and Jake. They seemed like archenemies, although this would explain his frantic phone call. He must have realized that our digging into the case would expose him and their arrangement. I wonder if Kelly realized what her roommate and boyfriend were doing. Could that be the reason she broke it off with him? Is that why they fought the day she died? And how does Allison play into it all?"

It made sense why everyone had been sticking to the same story about Kelly's death—they wanted the police to think it was an accident. They *needed* the police to believe it was an accident. No one, aside from June, wanted the police to continue the investigation.

"Excellent questions." Fletcher snapped his fingers together like he had put it all together and stuffed his phone back in his pocket. "Here's my theory: Jake knew Allison had an easy in at the hospital, or maybe she approached him?" He paused and pondered it for a moment. "Anyway, we'll figure that out when we come to it; but for the time being, we're operating under the assumption that the two of them arranged some kind of a deal—Allison swipes the drugs, they meet at the convenience store for the drop, Jake pays her, distributes said drugs amongst his surfing friends, and the cycle repeats."

"Yep, I'm with you." I nodded, encouraging him to continue.

"Let's say Kelly found out. It wouldn't have been a stretch. She and Jake hung out with the same people. Maybe someone let it slip that Jake was their dealer. She confronted him, and he confessed that Allison was the mastermind behind their 'business' endeavor?" He used air quotes to emphasize the word *business*. "Kelly flips out. Tells them she's going to the police. Allison would lose her job and probably serve some jail time. Jake would lose any potential sponsorship deals, and I need to check the regulations for the competitions, but certainly, illegal drug use would ban him from competing in, say, the Olympics."

"Right, so they conspired to kill Kelly together? Allison gave her something to knock her out before she left for work, and then Jake snuck in and drowned her while Allison was at the hospital since we know he had a key and she covered for him." Everything was falling into place.

Had we done it? Had we solved her murder? I was tempted to think so, but there were still too many pieces of the puzzle that didn't fit, like Harvey's hidden cameras and Kelly's affair with Brogan. Plus, there was the lingering question of Kelly's future with the sport.

"Or, Allison used her meetup with Jake, snuck home, and killed Kelly. There's also the possibility that only one of them killed her and the other has been blackmailing—using their history with drug dealing—to buy their silence."

"This is huge, Fletcher." I took a minute to consider everything. "I'm ready to officially say Kelly's death was a murder, whether it was one of these two or Harvey. Well done." I reached out to give him a fist bump.

"We're not done yet." He bumped his fist against mine. "We still need to time the walk from the hospital, but I feel like we should loop Dr. Caldwell in now. What about you?"

"Absolutely. I spoke with her not that long ago, and she mentioned that she has Harvey in custody." I was glad that we were going to have plenty to report to June. Her continuing to care about Kelly's story and seeking justice for her death had led us here.

"I'll call her now and text her the photos." Fletcher reached into his pocket for his phone.

"What happened with Jake?" I asked. "Did you speak to him at the beach?"

"No. I was a silent observer. He had no idea I was there. I blended in with the sand and kept my distance."

"Good." We needed to regroup and decide on our next move. It would be better if Allison and Jake were in the dark. If they figured out we were watching them, we might spook them, or worse—have one of them take off to avoid speaking with Dr. Caldwell. I had no doubt she would act swiftly and bring them both in for further questioning immediately.

While Fletcher stepped outside to call Dr. Caldwell, I reviewed my conversations over the past few days, walking around to the front of the checkout counter to fix the sticker display. Someone had accidentally placed a PLOT TWIST AHEAD sticker in the wrong compartment. Was Brogan aware of Allison and Jake's arrangement? I couldn't imagine he would be pleased that one of his star surfers was dealing. His career and reputation would also be at risk. But there was also a chance he was in the loop in terms of what was happening and had opted to turn the other cheek and ignore it. Or, he could be part of it, too.

"What now?" Fletcher asked, returning to the Foyer after he'd spoken to Dr. Caldwell. "She's on her way to interrogate both of them. Should we time the walk from the hospital to Allison's house, or do you think it even matters in light of this new development?"

"I think we should. It could help us eliminate her as the killer. Maybe not as an accomplice, but if it takes more than twenty minutes round trip, I would think that might interfere with her break time, especially because she still had to stop and purchase snacks to maintain her cover." I made sure each of the stickers were facing upright and then ducked behind the counter to check the staff schedule to make sure we had coverage. Hardy was scheduled for the morning, Mary Jane was here all day, and Ash had an afternoon shift. There wasn't much on the event schedule at the bookstore. We tended to keep things light during the day and host our bigger events and author talks in the evenings and weekends.

Today, we had a crafternoon on the calendar for our younger readers that Mary Jane would oversee. We arranged fun crafts and a selection of our crafting books and let the future generation of artists create their hearts out. "We can drop by June's after and give her a full report."

"Hopefully, that will help her chill out about the press release and trying to get Kelly's name in the headlines again." Fletcher scowled as he swiped a spiced cookie like he was a kid about to be reprimanded for eating a sweet treat before lunch. "That still strikes me as odd. Does it seem odd to you, too?"

"Without a doubt." I scrunched my face. I wasn't sure what was bugging me, but something about June wanting to go to the press didn't sit right. "I don't know. It's weird, and I'm going to keep thinking about it, but the only thing I can come up with is that she's old-school. The newspaper was the key way her generation learned what was happening in the world and the community around them. Maybe she's clinging to that? Assuming it will bring much-needed attention to the case?"

"Mm-hmm, probably, or she liked the attention herself?" Fletcher countered.

"Oh, most definitely," I agreed. The door jingled as a group of women who frequented the store after their morning yoga class came inside with a gust of wind and a flurry of laughter. The women stopped at the tea station to pour steaming mugs of Earl Grey and chai, which they took with them as they shopped. I said hello and told them about some new titles on display in the Parlor. "I'll make sure Mary Jane is ready for crafternoon. Should we plan to leave in an hour or so?"

Fletcher nodded. "That gives me time to touch base with Dr. Caldwell again. And I got a text alert that the back order of book candles came in. I want to unpack those because we can't seem to keep them in stock."

The book candles were always a hit. We shelved several brands, but by far the most popular were a collection of fictional mystery settings like the "abandoned mansion" and the "remote island." The frosted glass candles were wrapped with comic-strip-style images depicting aging, haunted mansions and creepy islands. They came with a synopsis explaining the story behind the candle and scent profiles with aromas like cedar wood, quince, and dusty paperbacks.

I left Fletcher to the candle unpacking and headed to the Dig Room to set out the supplies for crafternoon. The kids' book room was quiet as the morning toddler and preschool crowd had left for lunch and naps, and the after-school crowd wouldn't arrive for another few hours. I tidied up the whimsical space, returning plastic dinosaurs and treasure chests to the sandbox and pushing long tables together. I covered the tables in craft butcher paper so that participants could doodle on the table while working on their crafts. Then I retrieved a large tub of yarn, felt, glitter, beads, glue sticks, pens, colored pencils, and markers from the supply cabinet.

Next, I arranged platters of cookies and bowls of crackers, along with a selection of juice boxes. At the Secret Bookcase, we liked to go beyond the basics and make sure every event, whether for our most mature readers or burgeoning picture book lovers, was special. That's what set us apart—we were more than a bookstore; we were a community hub and a third space for so many of our loyal customers and friends.

Once the crafts and snacks were ready, I organized a stack of craft reference books, including everything from nature and paper art to stitching and finger knitting. There was nothing better than knowing we were creating a space for young readers that hopefully would spark a lifetime love of books and reading.

I cherished the thought, letting it warm my chest, spreading across my body like butter melting on toast. I really did have the best of both worlds—a thriving bookshop and an emerging private detective practice. If we could close Kelly's case soon and determine the origin of Hal's brooch, we would have a bona fide agency on our hands.

CHAPTER 25

Fletcher and I reconvened in the Foyer a while later. We met with the team to do a rundown of what to expect with crafternoon and made sure they were up to speed on everything before we took off.

"Should we start at the hospital and walk from there?" Fletcher asked, pausing at the front stoop and glancing toward the village square and the gardens.

"Yeah, great idea. That way we can give June a report, too. Hopefully, an update will help appease her." I grabbed my parka from the coat rack near the seasonal display.

Our walk took us through the English garden and across to Oceanside Park. Arriving at the hospital felt like déjà vu, yet everything looked different in the afternoon light than it had under the veil of midnight. Jekyll and Hyde swooped down to greet us, grazing my shoulder as they swept over the grounds in a figure-eight.

Fletcher tossed them peanuts, which they snapped up in one fluid motion.

"No late-night window sessions, you two," I warned with a quick shake of my finger.

"Just wait until they start following us home," Fletcher said. "They're probably telling their friends we're the go-to source in town."

"Great. Just great. That's what I need, a murder of crows waiting for me on my front porch."

He laughed deviously. "It's an honor. You know, studies have shown crows recognize human faces. If you've been kind and helpful, they'll share that with other crows. But you don't want to get on their bad sides. They hold serious grudges to people who have mistreated them, for years."

"I would never be mean to you," I said, blowing a kiss to the sky. "But I could do without the surprise visits."

Fletcher prepped his timer on his phone and his watch. "You ready?"

"Is this a race? Should I have stretched?" I teased, pulling one hand behind my back. "I should have prepared better."

He huffed in mock annoyance. "No, there's no need to sprint, but I do believe we should maintain a brisk pace. If Allison is the killer, she would have needed to hurry before any of her colleagues realized she'd been missing for more than her usual snack run."

"Agreed," I replied with the utmost seriousness, making my face stern. "I'm ready. Let's do this."

"Okay, on my count. Three... two... one... go!" Fletcher hit start on both his timers and took off in the direction of Allison's house.

I had to practically run to keep up with him. One of the curses of having short legs. It didn't help that Fletcher was naturally tall and lanky. We power-walked to the opposite side of the park, cutting past the kids' splash pad and the amphitheater in the center. The ground was soft from the rain. Bark chips squished under my feet. Everything smelled slightly damp and earthy yet equally refreshing. My glasses fogged as I kept pace with Fletcher, my heart rate rising and warmth spreading through my body.

I was glad for our speed because, if nothing else, it was keeping my heart rate up and my blood pumping. When we made it to the far side of the park and spilled out onto the street leading to Allison's, Fletcher checked the time. "Not bad. We're looking good, and we're just a few blocks away now."

"And there wouldn't have been anyone out and about at that late hour or traffic. Not that there's ever much traffic on the village square, but she likely wouldn't have had to wait to cross the street," I added, pointing to the car slowing to wait for us. I gave the driver a wave of thanks as we hurried across the street.

"And no prying eyes unless June was spying on the neighborhood."

"True, although I'm going to guess that might be late for her."

We continued on the sidewalk until we reached Allison's front yard. "Thirteen minutes and thirty-five seconds," he announced proudly, as if we had actually won a race or hit a personal best.

"Doable," I said with a nod. "Although she'd still need time to kill Kelly, cut back through the park, and stop for snacks. Realistically, it seems like that would have taken at least a half hour altogether. Do you think she had that kind of time? Would one of her fellow doctors or nurses have noticed if she was missing for that long?"

"Good question." Fletcher typed something with his thumbs on his phone. "I'm making a note to reach out to the hospital staff again and see what Allison's colleagues have to say about her snack runs. Are they usually ten minutes, like last night? If so, I'm guessing being absent for thirty minutes might have raised a few red flags."

"Agreed. I'm leaning toward the possibility that Jake did it and Allison is an accomplice. The only thing I can't decide is whether she was a willing partner in the crime or if Jake blackmailed her about their illicit drug deals to keep her from talking." The neighborhood looked bucolic, with pastel houses and vibrant yards. My mind drifted to Harvey. I still couldn't believe he had so grossly violated Kelly and Allison's privacy. Had he done the same to other tenants?

"It seems like the latter, doesn't it?" Fletcher made another note.

"Maybe, but the mere fact that Allison is involved in stealing prescription drugs from the hospital to sell illegally calls into question her entire character. I'm not ready to rule her out yet."

"Fair enough." He stuffed his phone into his satchel and pointed to the end of the street. "Should we pay June a visit?"

"What are the odds she's watching us as we speak?" I stole a subtle glance in that direction and would have sworn there was a flash of movement in the front window.

"Ten out of ten," Fletcher retorted without hesitation. "But she is a paying client, so she should be happy to see us in the neighborhood."

As expected, June's front door swung open before my knuckles had a chance to make contact with the wood. "Come in, come in. I saw you at Allison's and was putting on my coat to come meet you, but you two are much quicker than these aging bones." She made a show of returning her knee-length wool coat to its hook.

Her house smelled of lemon tea and something almost fruity that I couldn't quite place. "I made a batch of my peach-cobbler muffins. Would you like one?" She shuffled toward the living room, where the gas fireplace was blazing. It had to be pushing eighty degrees in the room. I could feel my cheeks warm instantly.

"I hope it's not too cold for you," June said. "I cranked up the fireplace earlier. This wind has been the death of me."

I tried to keep my face passive, not wanting to offend her, but the small living room felt like a sauna. The last thing I wanted her to do was turn up the heat. The room was already hotter than the beach in the middle of a July heatwave.

"This is excellent," Fletcher replied for me, taking off his coat and pointing to the chair farthest away from the fireplace. "Should we take a seat?"

"Please. I'm interested in hearing what you've learned about my dear Kelly, but first would either of you like a muffin, tea, a glass of water?" There was a touch of hopefulness in her tone like she'd been expecting us and eager for guests.

Truth be told, I didn't want to linger, there was so much more to do, but I could tell June was desperate for company, so

I caught Fletcher's eye and nodded. "Tea and a muffin sound lovely, thanks."

"Yes, thank you." Fletcher bowed his head in agreement. Once June was out of earshot, he whispered, "We're going to be here for hours now, Annie."

"I know. Sorry. She seems so eager to have us." My initial take on June hadn't altered drastically. She was obviously desperate for company or attention, but given everything we'd learned about Kelly, she had wisely sounded the alarm and hired us.

June returned, carting a wobbly tray with teacups and muffins. I jumped up to help her. "Thanks, dear. Put it there on the coffee table, would you?"

She eased into her rocking chair next to the fireplace. I had no idea how she could tolerate the heat. "Shall I pass these around?" I asked, not wanting to make it seem like I was taking over.

"Yes. I didn't bring any cream or sugar, but it's in the kitchen if you want any." She draped a throw blanket over her knees and tucked her hands under it.

"I'm fine. Fletcher?"

"I wouldn't mind a splash of cream, but I'll help myself." He stood, picking up one of the dainty mugs. "Be back in a flash."

Fletcher never took cream in his tea. Was he taking a momentary reprieve from the oppressive heat and humidity, or up to his usual tricks?

"Help yourself, dear, don't just stand there. The muffins are hot from the oven," June said.

I took a muffin and a teacup and returned to my seat, hoping she wouldn't notice that I scooted my chair back against the wall as far as it would go.

"What were you doing at Allison's yesterday? I saw the police arrive shortly after you, but they wouldn't tell me anything, and Allison went to work, so we haven't had a chance to speak yet."

"That's one of the reasons Fletcher and I wanted to drop by. There have been several developments with the investigation, and we want to make sure you're in the loop."

"In the loop? That sounds like my knitting is all in a bunch." Her eyes drifted to a basket with yarn and pointy knitting needles at her feet.

"Are you a knitter? We're hosting a crafternoon at the bookstore today. It's a monthly event. Maybe you'd want to drop by and teach the kids some basics?" If I could expand June's connection in the community, it might take some of the pressure off her neighbors.

"No. Oh, no, thank you. I despise children." June's face soured like she'd tasted something tart. "Their sticky fingers. Drippy noses. It's not for me." She tossed the blanket off her legs and reached for one of the pill bottles resting on the TV tray next to her rocking chair.

I was taken aback by her response. "No worries. I just thought you might enjoy an excuse to get out of the house. We have plenty of other activities for adults—book clubs, teas, author signings."

"I'm fine. I prefer to stay right here in the comfort of my own home." She unscrewed the bottle, popped a pill, and then tightened the blanket around her knees. "Where did he disappear to?" Then she raised her voice higher, hollering toward the kitchen. "Cream is in the refrigerator. Second shelf. You can't miss it."

"Found it, thanks!" Fletcher replied, returning with his teacup carefully balanced in his hands. "Some detective I am. I should have tried the fridge first."

June frowned and studied him with new interest like she didn't believe him.

I tried to catch his eye, but he didn't look my way as he sat down. What had he been doing?

I took over, clearing my throat and setting my cup on a hand-crocheted coaster on the coffee table. The intricate lace pattern must be June's handiwork. "Yesterday turned out to be a bit of a breakthrough in the investigation. I visited Allison to take a look at the property, check to see if there was another way in that the killer might have used, but the police overlooked."

"There isn't," she snapped. "The layout is the same as my house."

I nodded. "Yes, I realized that fairly quickly, but while I was in the bathroom where Kelly drowned, I noticed a hidden camera. It was disguised in the smoke alarm. That's why I called the authorities. We believe that Harvey Wade, Kelly's landlord, installed the camera and was spying on her."

"In the bathroom? I'd say that he was doing more than spying." June hmphed under her breath as she shook her head.

"Agreed. It's a major violation of privacy. The police are looking at all his other rental properties to determine whether this is a pattern for him."

"I never trusted the man." June's voice turned icy. "I saw him lurking, sneaking around the yard, checking to make sure no one was watching when the girls weren't home, and then going inside. See, this is why the police are completely incompetent. They should have listened to me. I warned Kelly about him."

"Right, it sounds like she was ready to make a formal complaint against him," Fletcher chimed in. "One of our working theories is that he learned of her plans to report him to the housing authority, and he took matters into his own hands before she could do that."

"Wouldn't surprise me," June said with a shake of her head. "He's sleazy. I don't like him, and I wouldn't be sad at all to see him behind bars. It sounds like you've done it. I admit, I'm impressed. I had my doubts about you two—you're both so young, but well done. I'm proud of you."

I tried to keep my expression neutral in response to this, though Fletcher and I exchanged a quick look and I pressed my thumbs and forefingers together to help from cringing outright. It wasn't as if we were in our early twenties. I supposed we were young in comparison with June, but we both had over a decade of experience. I also didn't want to lead her astray in terms of the case. "Well, we don't know that he's the killer yet. The police need a search warrant to enter his property to see if there's any hard evidence of his illegal camera placement."

"Their digital team is tracing online breadcrumbs," Fletcher added. "If we're lucky, they may be able to trace the footage back to the night Kelly died."

June's hands trembled as she lifted her tea to her lips, spilling a little down the front of her sweater. She patted it with her napkin, appearing pensive. "That can't be possible, can it?"

"Almost everything is possible when it comes to technology these days. Unless you're living off the grid, they can find almost anything," Fletcher answered with a wry smile. "Everything is in the cloud. It's nearly impossible not to leave a digital trail, and we don't think Harvey is any kind of a mastermind, so that should work in our favor."

I hesitated to go into too much detail about Allison and her activities. I didn't know whether Dr. Caldwell had had a chance to bring her in for questioning yet, and I had zero doubts that June would march down the street the minute she spotted her neighbor and confront her.

"Fletcher's right," I said to June. "We have some solid leads on a few of our other suspects that we're also pursuing. But we're feeling very confident with the investigation and hoping that we might have enough evidence to share with the authorities soon."

"We're confident an arrest will be pending," Fletcher said, backing up my claim.

I hoped it was true for June's sake and for Kelly.

CHAPTER 26

June lifted her tea to her lips with a shaky hand while her attention was focused out the window. "An impending arrest certainly seems reason enough for you to alert the press."

"I don't think that's a good idea," I replied, ripping off a small piece of the crumbly peach muffin. "We don't want to interfere with Dr. Caldwell at this stage of the investigation. She and her team are gathering evidence, and we don't want to tip the killer off. It's better to play our cards close to our chest for the moment."

Why was she so stuck on media coverage?

"Nonsense." June sloshed more tea as she set the cup on the side table and tossed the blanket away. "If the police had done their job properly when Kelly was murdered, I wouldn't have needed to hire you. Alerting the press puts more pressure on them."

There were so many flaws in her logic that I didn't know where to start. I could tell she believed the only way to close the case was to keep Kelly's story in the spotlight, and I understood her frustration, but we needed to convince her to be patient a bit longer.

"I felt the same way after my friend Scarlet was killed," I said, leaning forward and meeting her eyes, which were glassy and narrow. I couldn't tell if she was on the verge of tears or about to explode with anger. "I realize how hard it is to wait, but I promise that Fletcher and I are doing everything in our power to bring Kelly's killer to justice and that Dr. Caldwell, who is head of the police now, is extremely competent."

June cleared her throat and pressed her hand to the side of her face. "I disagree. If you don't share this news with the local press, I will." She pushed to her feet, using the armrest to steady herself. "I won't allow another young woman to come to harm under my watch. It's obvious they need to arrest Harvey before he kills again."

Fletcher caught my eye and shrugged like he didn't know what else to say to persuade her.

"They have Harvey in custody," I said, gathering my cup and uneaten muffin. "Like we discussed earlier, please give us a few more days—until the end of the week, okay? Let's schedule another meeting for Friday, and if we're still in limbo by then, we can revisit going to the press with the story."

June shuffled to the window. "It doesn't sound like I have another choice, but I don't like this. I'm extremely concerned that someone else will meet the same fate as Kelly. I know you think I'm a senile old lady, but I've been right about everything so far, haven't I?" She swiveled slowly, turning to face us.

"We don't think you're senile," Fletcher said, sounding serious. "Anything but senile. If it weren't for you, we never would have uncovered Harvey's hidden cameras. Think of how many current and future tenants you've saved from his spying. This story will make the news, but as Annie mentioned, we just need to make sure the timing is right. You'll receive the credit. I'm already writing the story in my head."

June perked up, rolling her shoulders back as her eyebrows pulled toward her forehead. "Fine. Friday. Meet here at the end of the day—sharp. Do not be late."

"Great." I picked up my dishes and put them on the tray. "It's a date," I said brightly, hoping we had appeased her enough in the short term.

"Leave it," June commanded. "I'll let you see yourselves out while I clean up, but I do want to warn you that I have a terrible feeling about this. I don't trust that man, and I will remain here, vigilant at my post until he's behind bars."

I didn't have a great response for that other than a platitude, which I knew would only make her more upset, so we said our goodbyes and promised to update her immediately if there were any new developments between now and the end of the week.

We walked down the block in silence, waiting until we got to the park before rehashing our client visit.

"Well, that didn't go super great, did it? I didn't picture having our clients irritated with us, did you?" I asked Fletcher. "And what were you doing in the kitchen? You don't even like cream in your tea."

"I barely like tea." He stuck out his tongue and made a face. "I used the opportunity to sleuth. We're private detectives, aren't we? It seems a shame to waste our sleuthing skills, and I'm very curious about June's obsession with the news. Check this out." He stopped and grabbed his phone. "I took a bunch of photos of her fridge. There must be at least forty articles about Kelly's death pinned to it, and several about other cold cases all involving bathtub drownings."

I scrolled through the photos, a prickly sensation spreading up my arms.

"Is she some kind of a voyeur? Obsessed with drownings?" Fletcher asked when I handed him the phone.

"Do you think she could be involved?" Whatever had been bugging me about June wouldn't loosen its grasp, and her refrigerator homage to drownings made it feel like a vise, tightening around my chest.

Something was off. I just couldn't figure out what.

"Yes, but how? Look at her. She's frail. She never leaves her house. It sounds like she's basically a recluse. I don't think she has the physical strength, and then there's the key issue—why come to us? Why the insistence on getting the story back out into the zeitgeist? If she killed Kelly, wouldn't she be content to let her death remain a mystery?" Fletcher stabbed his fingers together, raising his eyebrow pointedly.

I sighed. Fletcher put into words exactly what I'd been struggling with since our first meeting with June. But like him, I couldn't piece together how June could have pulled off killing her neighbor or what would have made her want to hire us. "Let's talk it through," I said, turning onto the pressed-bark pathway that wound through the park and out onto trails leading deeper into the surrounding forest. "What if June did somehow manage to kill Kelly? Although I'm drastically lost on a motive, we can loop back to that. Could something have happened recently that made her realize she was in danger of being revealed? One of our other suspects discovered evidence linking her to the crime, or maybe she accidentally let something slip. That could have forced her hand and made her come to us—to put suspicion on someone else." Even as I worked through the possibility, it sounded weak.

"Maybe." Fletcher nodded, sounding more open to the idea than me. "Or, she's the ultimate narcissist and can't handle not having Kelly's name in the paper and on news sites any longer, so she brought it to our attention."

"Yes!" I didn't mean to shout. I lowered my voice. "Sorry, but yes, I'm with you on that. It's been bugging me. She's so determined to get us to reach out to the press. She *needs* the story to be headline news again. The only issue with that is it comes with a huge risk. Our looking into the case brings it attention, but it also puts a huge spotlight on her. If she is the killer, I can't imagine taking that kind of a risk." But images of the prescription medication on June's TV tray invaded my mind. I had no idea what medication she was taking, but there was still the nagging question of what had been in Kelly's system.

"Exactly. It's a conundrum worthy of Sherlock." Fletcher twisted his scarf around his neck, sounding as perplexed as I felt.

We strolled through the park, where winter birdsong greeted us like an outdoor symphony. An elderly couple sat huddled together on one of the benches with a bag of peanuts, tossing the unshelled nuts to the birds. The children's play area was filled with happy kids chasing each other up slides and scampering up the rock climbing wall. Parents gathered nearby with cups of coffee, watching from a safe distance as their little ones burned off steam.

Fletcher stopped suddenly and tossed his index finger toward the sky. "Sherlock, that's it, Annie. That's what's been bugging me."

"What?"

He clasped his cheek with his hand. "Remember our first meeting with June?"

"Yeah." I had no idea where he was going with this.

"She paraphrased Sherlock, remember?" He circled his wrists like he couldn't contain the energy in his spindly body. "The quote—that's it. I can't believe it's taken me this long to figure it out. Mr. Holmes would be quite dissatisfied with my deduction skills."

"Uh, I vaguely remember her quoting Sherlock." I tried to recall the quote. "But I'm not as well-versed as you. What am I missing?"

"She didn't quote *Sherlock*, Annie. It took me a while to remember where I'd heard the reference, and then it hit me. That sentiment is from a novel by Kim Newman, who wrote a pastiche in the style of Sherlock, but the quote, which she paraphrased, isn't from Sherlock." He sucked in a breath and held it for a minute before releasing it slowly. "Not Sherlock."

"Huh?" He was losing me.

"The quote she was referencing is said by none other than Moriarty."

I drank in the cool air, letting the implication sink in.

"Moriarty, Annie. Sherlock's most vile and cunning nemesis."

CHAPTER 27

My pulse quickened. I could feel the blood rushing in my ears as I considered the possibility that our sweet, elderly client could be the killer. But was it actually possible June had orchestrated Kelly's death, and why?

"She quoted *Moriarty*," Fletcher repeated like he was worried I hadn't heard him the first two times. "Moriarty, Annie. That has to mean something."

"I get it. It's kind of weird she would quote a villain, but it's not enough to go on. We don't even have a motive. Plus, we know Harvey installed hidden cameras, Allison and Jake are dealing drugs on the side, and Kelly was having an affair with Brogan and potentially about to fire him as her coach—all of those are potential motives for murder, but where does June come in?"

Fletcher pressed his lips together and shook his head as we proceeded along the path. "No clue, but it's worth putting our energy into, isn't it?"

"Yes, for sure. Everyone I interviewed mentioned June being a creepy and meddling neighbor—Jake, Brogan, and Allison all reported her watching them around the clock. Could her story be a lie? What if Kelly wasn't a dear friend? What if she didn't drop by for tea and muffins but instead complained about June's spying?" A new theory started to take shape. What if Kelly had been fed up with June's meddling? Could that have sent June over the edge? If Kelly were truly her only friend, maybe she'd snapped. It wasn't a strong motive, but it was a start.

"I'll do a deep dive into her past," Fletcher said, stepping over a downed tree limb from the earlier storm. "If our elderly client has any skeletons in her closet, you can count on me to find them."

"I don't doubt that. Let's take a closer look at the other cold cases she had pinned to her fridge," I suggested. "We should be able to zoom in on the photos you took and look them up. Maybe there's a connection."

"Good. Yes. I'll get right on that." He bobbed his head seriously.

We made it back to the bookstore in record time, probably because we were both buoyed by this new turn of events. I wasn't ready to declare June a killer, but I was ready to get a better understanding of our client and ask some new questions about her relationship and connection to our victim.

If Kelly confronted June about poking into her personal life, could that give June a motive to kill her? We'd already established June was lonely and reclusive. One possibility was that Kelly had initially befriended her neighbor, but maybe she'd quickly realized June was unstable. Their relationship could have been more volatile than June had initially let on.

But how?

Was it physically possible for a near-eighty-year-old woman with self-proclaimed aging bones to have drowned an Olympic surfer in her bathtub? Doubtful. But could she have slipped Kelly something? Possibly.

"What now?" Fletcher asked, holding the door open for me.

"Why don't you start researching June's background and follow up on the cold cases?" I suggested. "I'll check in with Dr. Caldwell and see if she's made any progress with Harvey and had a chance to interrogate Jake and Allison. After that, I'd like to swing by and have another chat with Brogan. I'm curious about his involvement with both of them. Did he know about the drugs? Could he be part of their circle or are the two of them acting independently?"

"It's a plan, Watson." Fletcher held up a finger. "Be careful, though. We've clearly uncovered ample information, and someone has killed once, I wouldn't put it past them to kill again."

"Agreed." That was the one point I had also agreed with June about. "I'll head that way as soon as I speak with Dr. Caldwell, before it gets dark." Since I'd been unable to fully shake my nerves, the last thing I wanted was to be traipsing through the village alone at night.

I wandered down the hallowed hallways of the Secret Bookcase, following the sound of happy laughter and children's voices. Crafternoon was in full swing. The Dig Room looked like a glittery tornado had swept through. Kids were covered in glue up to their elbows and deep at work, creating colorful collages and watercolor masterpieces.

"It looks like the crafters are crafting," I said to Mary Jane. "We should do a gallery display in the Conservatory."

She was seated at one of the craft tables in a kid-sized chair up to her elbows in glue and glitter, too, right along with the gaggle of young readers. "Yes, let's do it. When my kids were young, they would puff up like little proud peacocks whenever their artwork was hung on the walls at school."

"Great idea," a mom hovering nearby with a packet of baby wipes chimed in. "I know we'd love to see the kids' art featured here at the store."

"Consider it done." I chatted with the other parents. Mary Jane took on the task of getting the names of any of the young artists interested in letting us showcase their talents. I loved that I could make a decision like this on the fly, and I knew Fletcher and Hal would be all in for a gallery showing. It would be a great way to bring families back into the store, and if it was a hit, which I had a feeling it would be, we could make it a monthly event.

Crafternoon, followed by a gallery display in the Conservatory for a week or two.

I returned to the Foyer with an extra spring in my step. Creating spaces for our community to connect was by far the best part of owning a bookstore. I was about to shift gears and head up to my office to call Dr. Caldwell, but I didn't need to go far because she was waiting for me in the Foyer.

"Annie, hello. I thought I would drop by and give you an update." She extended a hand with a touch of formality. She'd been my mentor since college, and while she wasn't particularly effusive, she was astute, kind, fair, and extremely intelligent. Her sharp eyes missed nothing as she scanned the entryway, looking for a private corner or nook to chat. She wore a charcoal gray suit and oversized black glasses, which contrasted starkly with her cropped white hair.

"We can go upstairs." I pointed above us. "I can show you our official headquarters if you have time."

"Perfect." She nodded crisply and waited for me to lead the way. "I've been eager to see what you've done with the place. I bumped into Hal at a library fundraiser a while ago, and he said you've completely transformed it."

Upstairs, I showed her to our client meeting room. She surveyed the space with the same keen eye for detail. "This is very well arranged. Comfortable yet professional. I'm impressed, as always. It's lovely, Annie." She gestured to the couch. "Shall I take a seat?"

"Please. Can I get you anything?"

"No, thank you." She waved me off and sat, pushing her oversized black frames up to the bridge of her nose. "I was in the village square, so I decided it might be nicer if we went over everything in person. My team finished scanning Harvey's other properties and found similar cameras in four of them."

"Ugh." I shuddered. "I mean, I sort of anticipated you would find more, but it's terrible for his tenants."

Her frown tugged her entire face down, making the fine lines on her forehead more pronounced. "It's thanks to you and Fletcher. I agree that Harvey's behavior is unconscionable as well as illegal, but without your diligence, he may have gotten away with it."

"Did he confess?"

She tilted her head from side to side as if hemming and hawing about her answer. "Yes, he finally admitted to installing the cameras after we'd amassed too much evidence for him to continue to insist he had no idea how they'd gotten into Allison's bathroom, but he claims that he never hooked the cameras up."

"Meaning what? They weren't operable?"

"Exactly." She adjusted her glasses to read her notes. "Harvey confessed he purchased the cameras online with the intent to spy, but he couldn't figure out how to connect them. I'm waiting for the report from the tech department, but as I'm sure you've already deduced, the man is hardly a tech wizard or a criminal genius. I tend to believe him, although that in no way negates the severity of the charges against him."

I exhaled deeply. "No, but if that's true, it does bring me a small glimmer of relief to know that he wasn't successful in his quest to spy on his unsuspecting tenants. It's not much, but I'll take it. I still can't believe he violated his tenants like that. It creeps me out."

She ran a hand through her hair, pressing a strand of silvery white back into place. "I intend to pursue the strongest charges against him."

"Good." I shook my head, unable to believe Harvey had spied on the roommates in such a horrific fashion. "What about Kelly's murder? Do you think he had anything to do with it?"

She pondered the question, pausing intentionally before answering. "I'm not ready to say yes, and I'm also not ready to release him. First and foremost, I want confirmation as to whether video footage of any of his tenants exists. I went back through the case notes, and he doesn't have an alibi for that night, so we can't rule him out."

"What about Allison and Jake?" I was curious how their behavior may have played into Kelly's death. "Allison had pre-scription medication in the bathroom. I wondered if Kelly could have accidentally taken it, but now I'm wondering if Allison just had a stockpile of drugs."

"She certainly does." Dr. Caldwell nodded. "They've both been questioned independently, and their stories match."

That was typically a sign that a suspect was telling the truth, although they'd also had ample time to get their stories straight. They could have rehearsed what they would say should they ever get caught.

"Allison has admitted to stealing prescription medication from the hospital," Dr. Caldwell continued. "Jake first broached the subject when they met through Kelly. Allison needed cash to pay off her nursing school debt and apparently got sucked into Jake's scheme. He approached her, knowing that he had built-in buyers among his surfing friends. Although he continues to claim he's clean. He admitted to distribution, but not to using himself as that would immediately disqualify him from competition. They've been running the same exchange once every few months for years now. I'm quite shocked that the hospital hasn't tracked the missing medication. I have an appointment with the administrator shortly."

"What was she stealing?"

"She had quite the list—opioid painkillers like oxycodone, hydrocodone, and codeine, as well as testosterone and other steroids, and fentanyl patches, which are highly valuable on the black market. I think that's one of the reasons she wasn't caught soon. She rotated through different drugs in order not to call too much attention or drastically reduce the hospital's supply at one time."

"And Jake sold them to surfers?" I asked.

"Among others, yes." She nodded. "We are pursuing charges against each of them, and I'm confident the hospital will terminate Allison. She'll likely lose her nursing license. Jake's brand deal is sure to be short-lived, too. It's a shame they both got caught up in something like this, but I'm appreciative you and Fletcher have brought the issue to light."

"I can't believe how much has come out in our investigation." I let out a small sigh, feeling pleased with our accomplishments but also not wanting to lose sight of the real reason June had hired us—to solve Kelly's murder.

"Well done, Annie. Not that I expected less from you, but well done." A smile replaced her earlier frown, softening her face and spreading to her eyes.

I wasn't fishing for compliments. I appreciated Dr. Caldwell's faith in me, but I never would have anticipated that taking Kelly Taylor's case would have led to all this. Now it was time to finish it. If we could just figure out who had killed her, we could successfully close our first case and bring her justice.

CHAPTER 28

"I was planning to speak with Brogan shortly," I said to Dr. Caldwell. "Will that interfere with what you're doing? I don't want to overstep my bounds, but I have some additional questions for him, and I'm curious whether he had any awareness or involvement in the drug dealing that's been going down."

"Feel free to proceed," Dr. Caldwell said with a bob of her head. "I'll be interested to hear what you learn. We did ask Jake and Allison, and both insisted no one else was involved or aware of what they were doing, including Kelly. I think a chat with Brogan is an excellent idea."

"Fletcher's also looking into June's background." I went on to explain our conversation with June and some of the red flags it raised.

"Keep me posted on all accounts, and I'll do the same." She stood, bringing an end to our conversation. But she didn't leave right away. Instead, she picked up one of our Novel Detectives business cards and studied it, like she was considering what she wanted to say next.

I felt a touch of worry creeping up my spine. Was she upset about something? Had we accidentally done something outside the boundary of my private investigator's license? But no, I'd been meticulous about following the proper procedures. It couldn't be that.

Fortunately, she put me out of my misery by picking up another few cards. "Do you mind if I take these?"

"No, of course not, but why?"

"I'd like to propose a joint workshop with my team. I think it would be highly beneficial for some of our younger staff to meet with you and Fletcher. Would you be up for a special collaboration?"

"Yes, absolutely." I felt a flush of warmth come over me. Dr. Caldwell wouldn't suggest a collaboration if she wasn't happy with our work. I was equally happy for Fletcher. He'd put in as much effort as me to make Novel Detectives a success. I knew it would be a boost to his ego, especially in light of his recent revelation that he felt the need to prove himself. He had—in spades.

"Excellent. I'll reach out soon to discuss the details, but I must say, Annie, I hope you're proud of the work you've done. I'd like to use this as a case study and potentially discuss you and Fletcher having a look at some of the other unsolved cases that we have yet to close."

Her praise made me puff out a bit and sent a swelling sensation through my chest. I was happy that she was pleased with our results. "I'm a yes for all of it," I said, showing her out. "And I know Fletcher will be, too."

We parted ways in the Foyer. I checked in with the staff to make sure everyone was in good shape before I took off to see if I could catch Brogan at home. Since both Jake and Allison were currently in police custody, this might be a chance to speak with Brogan alone again.

I used the short walk to ruminate on each of the suspects—Harvey had been caught spying on Kelly and had installed similar cameras in his other tenants' properties. Whether or not he had actually been able to set up the cameras to film was almost secondary. Clearly, he had major issues. And no alibi on the night of her death. What if Kelly had realized what he was up to and confronted him? Or caught him in the process of installing the camera? That would give him a strong motive to kill her. Silence Kelly and silence any accusations about spying and violating tenants' privacy.

Then there was the dynamic drug-dealing duo of Jake and Allison—an unlikely pair, to say the least. I was curious if their claims were true. Were they working alone? Or had Kelly discovered their secret partnership? If she threatened to tell the police, the hospital, Brogan, or the World Surf League, both of their careers were in jeopardy. Could that have led the two people seemingly the closest to her to kill her?

My thoughts turned to June as I turned onto Brogan's street. Were we missing a critical detail about her interest—or obsession—with Kelly? Hopefully, Fletcher's search into her background would shed some much-needed light on our client. She didn't have an alibi for the night of the murder either.

And then there was Brogan. What else did he know? It was time for me to find out.

I pondered the question as I knocked on the front door. He answered right away, wearing a rash guard and board shorts, and with a towel tossed over his shoulder like he was on his way out.

"Hey, I was just leaving. What do you need?" he asked abruptly, like he wasn't particularly pleased to find me at his doorstep.

"I was hoping I could ask you a few more questions about Kelly's neighbor. June Munrow. Did you know her?" I launched right in, not wanting to give him any leeway to take off.

"June, yeah, the nosy one. Why?" He tugged at the towel, running it back and forth behind his neck.

"There have been a few developments in the case, and since June is the person who hired us, it's important we paint a complete picture of her as well as the other suspects in Kelly's death."

"Suspects, you say?" He took a small step backward. "So you're sticking with the murder angle for sure?"

I nodded. "We are. The police have several people in custody at the moment."

He squinted like he was trying to make sense of what I was saying. "Wait, Jake? He told me they called him. My God, you don't think…" He dropped to his knees, unable to finish the thought. "I mean, when he said he went back to apologize and try to win her back, I believed him."

"What do you know about Jake and drugs?" I asked, holding my ground. Instinctually, I was drawn to want to console him, but he could be playing me, and I wasn't about to take any chances.

"Drugs? What are you talking about?" He rocked back on his knees like he was practicing a deep yoga stretch.

"Jake has been arrested for selling prescription medication, serious stuff like opioids and steroids, to many of your fellow surfers."

"Hold up. What?" He tossed his towel on the floor and stood up again, pacing from the surfboard propped against the wall to the door and back again. "No, not Jake. Not anything hard. Some pot but that's legal. He knew he had to be to compete in the Olympics."

"He may be clean, but that doesn't mean he wasn't dealing. He and Allison Irons have had a secret partnership for a few years. She steals the medication from the hospital. He distributes it." I was glad I'd had a chance to speak with Dr. Caldwell and get the green light to share information with Brogan. It gave me more bargaining power.

"Damn. No." He shook his head like he refused to believe me. "I can't believe it. I thought Jake was a good guy. How did I not see it? I live with him. This is going to blow up our deal with TideBreak Apparel, too." He thrust his thumb toward the staircase, which had been transformed into a drying rack for brightly colored board shorts and beach towels.

"He was probably very subtle about it." I watched Brogan's body language. Everything about his jerky movements and the way he kept shaking his head like he'd been left in the dark made me believe he was telling the truth. His reaction seemed genuine.

"And God, with Allison. Her roommate? I can't believe they were doing this behind Kelly's back." He ran his hands through his hair. "I don't think Kelly knew. I bet she had no clue."

"That's one of the many things we're trying to determine," I replied truthfully. "Do you think Kelly could have been involved? Maybe it was initially the three of them, and something went south? She wanted out, and they couldn't let her?"

"No chance. No way. She was focused and determined. She was super uptight about what she put in her body. She was surrounded by nurses and only took medical advice from Allison and June. She struggled with her sleep, and they both gave her plenty of tips and tricks to try."

She sought medical advice from her roommate and neighbor? A tingling sensation spread across the base of my neck. I wondered if one of them could have given her bad or misinformed advice, especially given what I now knew about Allison. Could she have encouraged Kelly to take a higher dose of her gummies or mix medications?

"Plus, what would be her motivation?" he continued with a shrug before I had more time to ponder it. "She was loaded. She didn't need the money."

"She was loaded?" I repeated. This was new information. I'd seen her bank records in her case file, and she had a decent sum in her savings account, which I assumed was from the sponsorship money. I made a note to discuss it further with Fletcher. He'd reviewed her financial records more closely.

"She'd been making good cash by winning so many titles, and then, with the sponsorship money, she was set. I get Jake needing cash, but not Kelly. The only reason she was doing sponsorships was to donate whatever she brought in to her conservation projects. That's where her heart was—that and surfing. Plus, like I said, there's no way she would have risked her career and future for something like that. No way." His tone was adamant and unyielding.

"Could they have roped her in somehow?"

"Like what?" He balled his hand into a fist and punched the wall. "God, I can't believe I missed that. Jake, what the hell are you thinking, my man?"

"Yeah, he's facing serious charges—we're talking a felony for trafficking and possession with intent to distribute. If he's convicted, he'll have a significant prison sentence, fines, and a long-term criminal record. The same is true for Allison, only she'll also lose her license and be barred from working in the medical field."

"They killed her. They freaking killed her, I know it." He could barely get the words out. His voice was breathless, like he was struggling for air. He yanked his ring off and tapped it to his forehead.

"We don't know, but that's why I'm here. Anything else you can share is critical right now."

He rolled his shoulders like reality was sinking in. "Okay, yeah. I'm all yours. Ask me anything. What else do you want to know?"

"Is there a chance Allison and Jake found out about you and Kelly?" I had a feeling he was going to immediately dismiss the thought, but instead, he mulled it over, staring at the ceiling and running his hands together.

"Ah, yeah, okay I see where you're going with this—they killed her in retaliation." He curled his lip into a snarl. "A few minutes ago, I would have said no way, but I also never would have believed that Jake would be dealing drugs, so I guess my answer has to be maybe, but why Allison?"

"One possibility is that Kelly discovered what they were doing and threatened to go to the authorities."

"You know, she did say something briefly—just in passing—about going to the police, but I assumed she meant because of Harvey, her landlord. You know he was awful to her. A super creep. Stalker. Bad vibes all around."

He sounded way too casual about this piece of news. Why hadn't it come up before? "You didn't follow up?" I knitted my brows together, wondering how he was so relaxed about Kelly being harassed by her landlord and why he hadn't intervened.

"I should have paid more attention, I guess," he said, voicing out loud what I was thinking. "We were in the middle of a training session, waiting for the waves. When they hit, you have to go. They hit, and we never had a chance to get back to the conversation."

Interesting. And maybe a bit too convenient.

"You asked about June?" Brogan said, sliding his ring up and down his finger. "I can't see her being involved in drug running."

"No, not in the drug dealing, at least not as far as we know at this point, but there have been several additional things that have come to light, including that Harvey installed a camera in Kelly's bathroom with the intent to spy on her."

"What is going on right now?" He leaned toward me, glancing in both directions. "Am I being pranked? You've got to be kidding me. Isn't this sleepy Redwood Grove? Stuff like this doesn't happen here."

"I wish I were kidding." I shook my head softly and explained the situation.

"Well, then he did it." Brogan threw his hands up. "The police should arrest him now."

"They have. He's in custody, too."

"This is nuts. No wonder Kelly was stressed. How much do you think she knew?"

I shrugged. "That's what I'm trying to determine now. Since you and Kelly were, uh, well." I paused, trying to find the right word to describe their affair. "Uh, close, I was hoping you might be able to give me a better understanding of her friendship with June. You must have spent time at Kelly's place. Did you meet June? Did Kelly mention June watching her?"

"Dude, they weren't friends. Kelly was terrified of June. She thought the old lady was batty, and she went out of her way to avoid seeing her at all costs."

CHAPTER 29

"You're sure Kelly hated June?" I asked Brogan. My heart ticked up like things were starting to finally click into place.

"Positive. She hated her. She was talking about trying to get a restraining order. Even moving. At first, I teased her about it. You know, it was kind of a joke. Strong, world-class surfer, terrified by an eighty-year-old lady, but she was serious. June was always pushing special teas and sleep remedies on her—claiming she used them when she was a nurse. Kelly mentioned something about June's past. A story she'd read. No, it's not that, but something like it." He sighed and massaged his temples like he was trying to force the memory. "Oh, wait, I know. Yeah, that's right. Kelly told me she saw a newspaper article at June's house. I totally forgot about it until this minute, but I remember it creeped her out."

The ticking in my heart turned into a full-fledged pounding. Special remedies and teas? A newspaper article like the ones Fletcher had photographed in June's kitchen? Kelly had taken medical advice from June? Suddenly, a new theory was taking hold. "Did you ever mention it to the police when they questioned you after Kelly's death?"

"No, why would I? They thought it was an accident or suicide, and what would the old lady do anyway? It's not like she could have killed her."

"Right." My heart was beating so fast, like I had downed one too many of Pri's strong espressos. I knew exactly what I needed to do next. "Thanks for the info. It's been very helpful," I said to Brogan.

"You'll get whoever did this, won't you?" A tear fell from his eye, streaming down his cheek like a trickling waterfall. "Seriously, she was one of a kind. She would have gone far. She could have been one of the first surf Olympians and if anyone could have saved the beaches from over-development it would have been her."

"We're doing everything we can," I told him truthfully. "Hey, about her Olympic hopes, are you positive she wasn't quitting the sport or looking for a new coach?"

"One hundred percent. She was determined to make the Olympic team, and she knew I was the person who could get her there." He paused and hesitated, stealing a look behind him. "I have some notes and cards she wrote me. They're kind of personal. I hid them in my closet upstairs because I didn't want Jake to accidentally find them. I can show you, if you want to see them. Kelly talks about our partnership and how excited she was to work with me on realizing a dream. It was awkward because I was still trying to get back together with my wife, so I never wrote her back." He choked up again, holding back tears. "Sorry. I just wish I would have."

"That's okay. I think we're good for now, but if Dr. Caldwell feels differently, I'll let you know." I believed him. I didn't need to pry deeper into Kelly's love notes. "Thanks again for your time."

I left him and stopped at the end of the sidewalk to text Fletcher.

> I just had a breakthrough.

I told him about my conversation with Brogan.

> Now we have to prove it and I think I have a way.

> You're not going to believe this. Two of June's prior acquaintances also drowned. She's quoted in the other articles on her fridge. Three bathtub drownings. She is our Moriarty!!!

I filled him in on my plan. I needed to confront her alone, but I needed him as backup.

We worked out the details in text.

I couldn't believe our client was the killer, but suddenly, everything made sense. Her insistence that we go to the press. She wanted the fame of having her name and her villainous act in the news. She thrived off the notoriety. Her odd behavior, quoting Sherlock's archnemesis, spying on the neighbors—all fit together like a perfect puzzle. Those pill bottles on her TV stand. Cozy cups of tea. The only piece I was missing was exactly how she'd done it. I had an idea, but I needed to hear it from her.

I needed to make tiny moves. It felt like I was about to enter a chess match. I thought about Hal and his weekly chess games. No sudden shifts. I had one huge advantage at this stage of the game I'd inadvertently fallen into with June—I was already many steps ahead. She had no idea we were onto her, and I needed to keep it that way as long as possible.

I made a beeline for June's house—cutting straight through the park. The sky turned gauzy and overcast. A fine mist spritzed my face as I raced past the play structure and toward the opposite end of the park. I wondered how many miles I'd amassed in the past few days of trekking from one side to the other. I never imagined my private detective work would skyrocket my step count, but I was definitely surprising my daily totals with this case.

A rush of excitement and trepidation surged through me as June's house came into view.

You can do this, Annie.

I texted Fletcher again to let him know I arrived and that it was time to prep for the next phase of our plan.

I took in a deep breath for courage and knocked on the door.

June wasn't at her usual post at the front window, nor did she answer on my first knock. Could she sense we were onto her? But how?

I tried again. This time a bit louder.

Still nothing.

I checked my watch—it was just barely after five. She couldn't be asleep already. Or had she gone out? But she never left the safety of her personal fortress.

I knocked for a third time.

If June wasn't home or wouldn't answer the door my plan was about to be very short-lived.

"One minute, I'm coming," she hollered from inside.

Thank goodness.

I let out a sigh of relief and planted my feet firmly.

Showtime, Annie.

CHAPTER 30

The door creaked open after another minute. June peered at me with beady eyes, squinting to get a better look. I had clearly surprised her with my unexpected arrival. That was good.

"What are you doing back already?" She kept the door open just a crack.

"I have some news I think you'll want to hear. Can I come in?"

She hesitated for the slightest second but then nodded, swinging the door open wide and stepping to the side to make way for me. "You already have an update?"

Given our earlier conversation, I would have expected her to be much happier to hear we had news on the case, but then again, I knew the truth—she didn't want closure. She merely wanted Kelly's tragic death to be on top of everyone's mind again. She wanted to revel in the glory of getting away with it.

But there was just one problem. She hadn't met Fletcher or me.

I followed her into the living room. Any remnants of our earlier visit had been cleaned and put away.

"Would you like another cup of tea? Something a bit stronger? A shot of whiskey?"

"No, thank you. I won't take up too much of your evening, but I know how important getting closure on Kelly's death is to you, so I didn't want to wait until morning." I glanced around the living room, trying to think about how I was going to pull this off. First, I needed to get her out of the space. The room was incredibly hot. Even hotter than earlier in the day. Or maybe it was a combination of the blazing fireplace and my nerves, but either way, tiny beads of sweat pooled on my forehead.

"Hey, I meant to ask you about where you were the night Kelly died." I tried to keep my voice light and breezy. I didn't want to set off any alarm bells.

"What do you mean?" June leaned against the doorframe, watching me carefully.

"Well, I read in the case files that Kelly dropped by that evening, right?"

"Have a seat," June commanded, staring at me with distrust and gesturing to the couch.

Was it my imagination, or did she seem different? More irritated. More closed off?

"Did she stay long?" I asked. "What exactly did you discuss?"

"No. We chatted. She left, and then she was dead." June's beady eyes narrowed into slivers. "What does this have to do with the investigation?"

I cleared my throat and clutched my neck, pretending to have swallowed wrong. Then I launched into a coughing fit.

Time to bring the drama, Annie.

I was worried she might not buy it, but I was pleased with how well I must have sold it because June craned her neck like a turtle emerging from its shell and held up a hand.

"I'll get you some water." She shuffled to the kitchen while I continued to cough.

"Sorry—uh—um." I coughed again. "I must have swallowed wrong." I kept up the gig as I slid over to the side table and picked up the first bottle of medication. "Thanks," I called, allowing my voice to go gruff like I was still struggling to breathe.

It wasn't the right one. I checked the next bottle and the next. None of them matched the medication found in Kelly's system.

Was I wrong?

Had I made a mistake?

I picked up the last pill bottle, holding it to the light and straining to read the fine print.

Nope. There it was—a sedative! The exact sedative found in Kelly Taylor's system.

My heartbeat whooshed through my head.

I could barely steady my fingers as I snapped a picture and returned the bottle to the TV tray.

I texted the picture to Fletcher.

Got it!

Then I stuffed my phone behind my back.

I heard June returning and swept back over to the couch, clutching my stomach as I sputtered for air. She offered me the water glass with a disapproving frown.

No, I wasn't mistaken. Something had changed. But how could she possibly know that we were onto her?

You're being paranoid.

Stay the course.

I took a sip of the water, tapping my chest and then rubbing it softly as I allowed my breathing to return to normal.

"Drink more of that," June said, settling into her rocker next to the fireplace. My heart skipped a beat. Suddenly, everything about the claustrophobic space—the telescope pointed out the window, the newspapers, pictures, and notes—took on a new and much more sinister meaning.

I pretended to drink more. I wasn't an idiot. There was no chance I was trusting her. I could picture that this was exactly how she had managed to kill Kelly. Slip the sedative into her drink, encourage her to go home and pour a long, hot bath, and sit back and let nature take care of the rest. That had to be how she'd done it. It was the only explanation that made sense.

How could I get her to admit it?

I considered my options as she lasered her gaze at me.

"What did you want to tell me?" She peered around me toward the window, using her elbows to push herself up halfway.

Was she expecting someone?

An accomplice?

"The police have made an arrest," I half lied. It was partly true. Dr. Caldwell had technically made three arrests—Harvey, Allison, and Jake, but none of them were being held on murder charges.

"Who?" June sounded skeptical. She threw the blanket on the back of the rocker, stood, and adjusted the gas fireplace, cranking the heat to the highest setting. "There, that's better. I can't get it warm enough in here." Then she moved over toward the window and opened it a crack, poking her head outside.

What was she doing? Did she know that we knew?

If she was cold, why was she next to an open window?

I felt like I was trapped in this chess game, and maybe I had underestimated my opponent. I had to keep playing my part.

Don't let her crack you, Annie.

I swallowed hard, feeling the slightest touch of dizziness. Was it the room? The fire? It couldn't be the water. I'd barely taken one sip.

I tried to ignore the woozy feeling and the wavy lines crossing my vision. I blinked hard, steadying my gaze on her. "It's Allison." The lie escaped my lips effortlessly.

June smiled almost triumphantly, but there was no joy or humor in her face. It lacked any ounce of empathy or warmth. It was in that instant I knew I was dealing with a psychopath. "Is it, dear? Is it?"

"Yes. Dr. Caldwell arrested her earlier today. She was stealing medication from the hospital and selling it illegally. We've theorized that Kelly must have realized what Allison was doing and threatened to go to the police. She decided she had to kill her to keep her quiet, so she slipped her the medication—she obviously had access to a litany of sedatives and opioids. Once Kelly was groggy, she probably helped her into the tub and left her to die. Fletcher and I timed the walk from the hospital to her house and the timing works. She would have had to make it quick, but she could have pulled it off on her break without any of her colleagues realizing she was even gone. She does a nightly snack run, which is her perfect cover." My head felt heavy. It bobbed forward and to the side. "She must have slipped Kelly something and waited for the effects to kick in."

"You mean when she began acting like you?" June sneered.

"What?"

"Dear, you're about to pass out. You can hardly keep your eyes open." Her tone was cloying and sweet but laced with darkness.

What had she done?

I gasped for air, blinking as hard as I could to fight the effects of whatever she'd given me. But it didn't make sense. One sip of water wasn't enough. It wasn't enough.

"Oh, I can see you trying to work it out, but I'm afraid you're not going to get there." June clicked her lips together like she had already won. "You remind me of her, you know. So attached to your principles. So determined. That's why I chose you."

"Chose me?" Were my words coming out in slow motion? Everything felt surreal like I was inside a silent, old black-and-white film.

"Yes, dear. You've been my target all along. Although I will say I did think it might take you longer to put it together. You're the fastest of them. I'll give you that." She smiled broadly, her shoulders arching back in triumph. Suddenly, nothing about her movements looked frail or timid.

What had I missed?

How was I going to get out of this?

"You won't. You can't. Fletcher. Dr. Caldwell…" I struggled
to string a complete sentence together as the room began to close
in. My vision tunneled into one long black, never-ending line.

This is bad.

Focus, Annie.

Do not pass out.

I fumbled for my phone.

I had to get in touch with Fletcher—stat.

I was losing this battle and fast.

CHAPTER 31

June remained at the window, watching for any sign of the authorities. "It won't be long now, dear. Sadly, you were so disorientated from that nasty fall. I didn't realize you had a concussion until it was too late."

Darkness enveloped me. It had to be the fireplace. That's why she was at the window, drinking in gulps of fresh air while carbon monoxide filled the living room. I had to get out of here.

I tried to stand, but my limbs felt like Jell-O.

"They always underestimate us, don't they?" June's voice was shrill and tinged with a bizarre delight. "You pretty young things. You can't imagine what it's like to be old and decrepit like me. You want to talk down to me. You condescending little imps—you get what you deserve, just like Kelly. She acted like I was a child needing to be pacified. I didn't need her pity, and I certainly didn't need her snooping. She could have left it alone and been fine, but then she started digging and digging."

"You killed her—like this?" My mouth felt dry and gummy at the same time. I kept one hand in my pocket, trying to find the emergency call button on my phone.

"Not exactly like this. I have many methods. For Kelly, it was a nice cuppa and a little chat about how stressed she was. She seemed almost tipsy when we finished our lovely get-together, so like any good neighbor, I walked her home and helped her into a hot tub to soothe her nerves."

"And the others?" I asked, pressing wildly all over my phone screen.

"What others, dear?" June cocked her head to one side and glared at me. "I have no idea what you mean."

"The fridge. The articles. All drownings."

Please, Fletcher.

Please come.

"Oh, those poor, unfortunate young women. We often worry about the elderly slipping and falling but seldom consider the dangers to those in your age group, do we?" She leaned out the window further, drinking in the fresh air.

I willed my body to move.

I was running out of time.

After I passed out, she must be planning to stage a fall. What would she do? Hit me over the head and position my body in front of the fire? Or drag me outside and make it look like I'd taken a deadly tumble down her front stairs?

She was diabolical.

This was an entirely different level of delusion. I'd read about serial killers like her, but never imagined I'd come face-to-face with one.

I tried to stand again. My knees buckled, and my arms flailed like they were puppet strings.

Annie, move.

Move.

I grabbed the back of the couch for support and dragged one leg forward. It felt like I was trudging through clumps of wet, heavy sand.

"Dear, go ahead. Feel free to try, but you're not going to make it. You've consumed way too much carbon monoxide. It's such a shame that the gas fireplace was faulty. I will have a lawsuit on my hands. Rest assured, the builder will pay for your most unfortunate death. What a stroke of luck I had just happened to be fortunate enough to be near this window." She tapped the frame with pleasure. "Proceed. You won't feel a thing. I predict in less than two or three seconds, you'll be out for a nice, long, eternal nap."

No.

This can't be happening.

Not now.

Not after every good thing I had started in Redwood Grove. My thoughts went to Liam and Pri, Penny, Fletcher, and Hal. I couldn't leave them. Not yet. I had so much to live for—wonderful friends who cared deeply about me, the bookstore, the detective agency, and Liam Donovan. Oh, Liam. His face flashed in my head. I could see his impish grin and practically taste his lips brushing against mine.

I took another step forward and then fell flat on my face as everything went black.

CHAPTER 32

The next thing I knew, someone was standing over me, shaking my shoulder and calling my name. "Annie, Annie, are you okay?"

I opened my eyes slowly, trying to get my bearings.

Where was I?

The ceiling didn't look familiar.

The house smelled like tea and old lady perfume.

Oh, God, June.

That's right.

I must have passed out.

I tried to sit, but lights flashed across my vision like hundreds of fireworks putting on their own personal show for me.

"Easy. Take it easy," the voice said.

I strained to see, feeling a strong hand supporting my back. Fletcher hovered over me, along with two paramedics. *Thank God.*

"She's awake." Fletcher threw his hands over his cheeks. "Dr. Caldwell, she's up. She's okay!" he called, turning toward the kitchen.

"Take it easy," the paramedic repeated. "Nice and slow breaths. Let's oxygenate your lungs." He held out an oxygen mask, encouraging me to breathe through it.

I sucked in the air, feeling my lungs burn with relief.

The fireplace was off, and every window was wide open. A breeze blew inside, bringing with it the sweet, sweet smell of clean air.

"June?" I asked, removing the mask.

"Dr. Caldwell has her," Fletcher assured me, nodding in the direction of the kitchen. "We were so worried about you. When we got here, you were on the floor. Passed out. I was worried we were too late."

"No." I shook my head. "It was a rookie move on my part. I should have realized it when she cracked the window open, but I was fixated on her drugging Kelly, so I figured she must have done the same to me. Like we discussed, I knew not to drink or eat anything she offered me. I took one tiny sip of water, but I knew that wasn't it. Once I realized what she had done, it was too late. I can't believe you came. I hadn't even texted you."

"You didn't think I wasn't going to back you up, did you?" Fletcher scowled. "We're partners, Annie. When you didn't check in, I called Dr. Caldwell, and then the emergency call came through."

"It worked?" I couldn't believe I'd managed to put through the call.

"Yep." Fletcher nodded.

The paramedics assessed me and gave me more oxygen. It was another thirty minutes before they were willing to release me. Dr. Caldwell checked in. "I'm on my way to the station with June, but we have ample material to arrest her for all three murders plus an attempted murder."

"Our first client is a serial killer," Fletcher said, tapping his finger to his chin. "Now that Annie's okay and we've closed the case, that sounds like a title we'd shelve at the Secret Bookcase, doesn't it? Maybe we need to pitch the idea to one of our favorite mystery writers."

"You were clued into her from the start," I said, stretching. It was a relief that my extremities had finally stopped tingling and the spots in my vision had disappeared completely. "That Moriarty quote was her downfall."

"I should have figured it out sooner," Fletcher scoffed. "If I had, you never would have ended up like this."

"I'm fine, all things considered." I blinked, trying to center myself back into the room.

"Get some rest," Dr. Caldwell said, walking us to the door. "I'll need official statements from each of you, but those can wait until tomorrow."

Fletcher helped me down the stairs and wrapped a protective arm around my shoulder. "I'm under strict orders to deliver you to the Stag Head. Liam is concerned, obviously, and doesn't want you to be alone tonight."

I wasn't about to argue with that.

I didn't want to be alone either, and I was eager to see Liam. When I thought I was about to die, he was the first person who came to mind. I couldn't imagine my life without him.

We took it slow.

I was a bit shaken, but the paramedics had assured me there was no long-term damage or anything to worry about. I just might feel run-down for a while. Their orders were rest and relaxation, extra water, electrolytes, and some food.

Fletcher steadied me on the short walk to the village square. The stars appeared even more dazzling as I retraced my steps, watching my footing and gulping in the brisk air as if it were giving me new life, which it really was.

At the pub, Liam raced out to greet me with a hug that felt like it lasted for days. I collapsed in his arms, feeling the weight of the night, and the past few days started to slip away.

Fletcher stepped away to give us some privacy as Liam escorted me inside.

"Annie, how are you?" Liam finally pulled away, keeping his hands on my waist as he scanned my body from head to toe.

"I'm okay," I said with a faint smile. "I feel a little weak, but otherwise, I'm good."

"Let's sit down." He grasped me tighter and ushered me over to a booth. Fletcher joined us.

"Pri and Penny are on their way, too." He gave me a sheepish smile. "I hope you're not mad. It's just that everyone cares about you, and I thought they should know."

"That's great. I appreciate it, and I'm not mad." I nuzzled my head on his chest, inhaling the scent of garlic, onions, and his earthy aftershave. Thank goodness everything had worked out. Thank goodness for Fletcher.

Liam wrapped his arm tightly around my waist and pointed to the bench. "Take a seat. Rest your feet." He kissed the top of my head gently and tenderly ushered me into the booth like I was in danger of breaking.

Liam left momentarily and was back in a flash with burgers, tots, salads, fizzy water, and ginger ale. "Eat, drink, what else do you need?"

"Nothing. This is perfect." I helped myself to a tot, dipping it in Liam's signature fry sauce and sipping the ginger ale.

Pri and Penny arrived shortly after, squeezing into the booth with us and showering me with hugs and kisses. We spent the next hour rehashing the case and everything that happened while I inhaled tater tots and devoured a cheeseburger loaded with bacon, pepper jack cheese, tomatoes, pickles, and lettuce. Who would have guessed that carbon monoxide poisoning would leave me famished?

The food and conversation with friends energized me. I almost felt completely like myself by the time Liam passed around a new plate of gooey chocolate chip cookies and brought out a carafe of decaf coffee for us to share.

This wasn't how I'd expected to close our first official case as the Novel Detectives, but even if it hadn't gone exactly to plan, June was behind bars. Kelly and the two women who died at June's hand would get the justice they deserved. The same was true for Harvey's tenants and everyone who'd been impacted by Allison and Jake's drug dealing arrangement.

All in all, I would consider this a win. I'd learned some valuable lessons for next time, but tonight, I could sleep easy knowing that Fletcher and I had had a small part in making Redwood Grove that much safer for everyone I loved.

CHAPTER 33

I woke the next morning with a lingering headache, but I didn't care. We'd done it. We'd solved Kelly's murder, and June had been arrested.

I still couldn't believe it.

Our *client* had been the killer all along.

Who could have seen that coming?

I felt a deep sense of connection to Kelly. I wished I could have known her or watched her surf, but I took comfort in knowing that her family back in Michigan and those who loved her finally had answers.

On a whim, I shot a group text to Liam, Fletcher, Pri, and Penny.

> Anyone free tonight? Want to move our grilled cheese date? I could use some friend time.

Everyone was in.

Fletcher
> Yes, please for cheese.

Pri
> You had me at cheese!

Pri responded with three cheese emojis.

Penny
> I'll bring the wine

Liam

Count on it, Murray.

Liam signed off with a salute.

The day breezed by. I spent most of it writing up my final case notes to share with Dr. Caldwell and maxing out my step count, walking all around the store to help pair readers with their favorite next book and chat about the strange turn of events. News of June's arrest had already started to spread. Customers wanted to know if the rumors were true and how we had managed to solve the case. Talking about our progress and how June orchestrated such a devious and clever crime brought me even more relief and restored my sense of community.

On my way home, I stopped in for grilled cheese supplies, filling my cart with pesto, apple chutney, roasted red peppers, sundried tomatoes, pears, spinach, and three types of cheese.

At home, Professor Plum nudged at my ankles as I heated creamy tomato basil soup and sliced thick, crusty sourdough bread.

The doorbell chimed with a happy ding. Liam was the first to arrive.

He produced a bundle of flowers tied with a silky sage green ribbon from behind his back. "These are for you. I thought you might want something cheery after everything you've been through."

I stood on my tiptoes to kiss him. My body hummed with a contentedness I hadn't felt since taking Kelly's case. "Thank you, that's so thoughtful, and these are beautiful. Winter peonies are my favorite," I said when I finally pulled away and dragged him inside.

"How are you doing?" Liam followed me to the kitchen, scooping Professor Plum up and placing the tabby on his shoulder so the cat could see all the action as I filled a vase with water and placed the flowers on the dining table.

"Better." I nodded, returning to the sink to wash my hands. "I wish it could have ended differently for Kelly, but I'm glad we have answers. I hope that it's some relief to her family to know June orchestrated her death."

"I'm sure it is." Liam nuzzled Professor Plum's head. In return, the cat licked his chin. I couldn't believe what fast friends they'd become over the last year. Professor Plum had a discerning taste when it came to humans, and he clearly approved of my choice of boyfriend.

Penny and Pri showed up a few minutes later with wine and chocolate cupcakes. Followed shortly by Fletcher, who arrived with a gorgeous green salad and a bottle of sparkling water.

I buttered slices of sourdough and encouraged everyone to make their own grown-up grilled cheese creations with the spread of toppings. Soon, the kitchen smelled like toasted sourdough and fresh basil. We moved into the living room with our gooey sandwiches and bowls of creamy soup.

Penny passed around glasses of wine, and Liam lit a fire.

"Hey, guess who stopped into the coffee shop this afternoon?" Pri asked, dunking her sandwich into her soup. She didn't wait for an answer. "Brogan Blears!"

"What did Brogan have to say?" I bit into the crisp bread oozing with Muenster and Havarti cheese, thinly sliced pears, apple chutney, and spinach.

"He seemed pretty rattled about the news. He kept saying he couldn't believe it was June."

"You and me both," Liam replied, making room on his lap for Professor Plum.

"Tell me about it," I said through a mouthful of the sweet and savory sandwich. "My Spidey senses were up from the beginning with June. Same for you, Fletcher—that Moriarty quote had your head spinning, but it took us a while to peg her as the killer."

"Right? The little old lady—damn." Pri let her sandwich drip into her soup before taking a bite. "Brogan mentioned he got in touch with Kelly's family. It sounds like they're going to start a scholarship fund in her name for young surfers and are coordinating to donate a large portion of her trust to conservation efforts."

"That's so good to hear." I was glad something positive was coming from her tragedy.

"After June was arrested, the police found dozens more prescription pills stuffed all over the cottage," Fletcher said, stabbing his salad with his fork. "I've been tallying every bottle for our case files. It's essential to have an accurate record of what transpired, and it's been quite fascinating to research the various medications she kept on hand. Some of it seems to be benign, but some of it is quite potent—we're talking serious and deadly side effects. You should see my chart notes. I feel like I'm moonlighting as a physician. Dr. Watson would be so proud." He wiggled his eyebrows. "Is it overkill? Perhaps, but you never know when information like this might come in handy for a future case."

"But you're off duty tonight, yes?" Liam smiled, the edges of his eyes crinkling.

"True. True." Fletched looked at me. "I do have some more news on that *other* matter to share with you, Annie, but it can wait." He spoke in a code that I cracked instantly.

I knew exactly what he was hinting at—Caroline's case. And while I was eager to hear what he had learned, I agreed now wasn't the time. "We'll spare our friends the boring details of case notes for tonight, then."

Liam raised his glass, lifting it toward me and then Fletcher. "I think this calls for a toast to both of you for a job well done. Cheers to the Novel Detectives."

We all toasted.

Penny clinked her glass to mine, then looked at me pensively. "You know, on this topic of investigating, I might have a little case for you. Nothing as big as Kelly's murder, but I have a few candidates in mind for the vintner position, and I'm wondering if you and Fletcher might be willing to do some background checks. I don't know if that's too small for you. I figure if whoever I hire is going to be living on the property with us, it's probably best to be extra careful."

"Sure, yeah." I bobbed my head eagerly, glancing at Fletcher. "No case is too small for us."

The conversation shifted to plans for the weekend, winter hikes on the coast, and upcoming wine tasting at the farm. I drank it all in. I was so grateful that the peaceful feeling had returned to my body and that all was right in Redwood Grove again.

A week later, Fletcher and I were in the Novel Detectives office doing our final review of the Kelly Taylor case. Dr. Caldwell had managed to get a full confession out of June. She admitted to murdering three women—all by drugging them and then encouraging them to get in their respective bathtubs, whacking them on the head after they passed out, and leaving them to drown. It was still hard to wrap my head around June being the killer. It became clear that she thrived on the pattern of seeing her "successes" in the spotlight, and when she realized the police didn't intend to make Kelly's death a priority, she contacted us.

"Do you think she ever believed we would actually solve it?" Fletcher asked, stapling pages together for our case files. "It is fairly brazen to hire private detectives to solve a murder you committed."

"Yeah, but given the history, she had no reason to think we would suspect her. Everyone overlooked her. That was part of her issue." I typed a few final thoughts and closed my laptop. "Dr. Caldwell asked me to testify. She believes it's going to be an open-and-shut case with June's confession and the amount of evidence they gathered in her house. I still can't believe she had the medication she used to drug Kelly out in the open on her TV tray, but it just goes to show that she used her age to her advantage—she played up being the frail little old lady. You know, when we first visited her, I was struck by how much medication she had lying around, but I figured she was ailing, and the medication was for her. I can't believe I was worried about exacerbating a medical condition or causing her undue stress. I never considered that she was the killer until we were much further into the investigation."

"Right." Fletcher nodded in agreement. "She had her own pharmacy—an extensive pharmacy. I've already cataloged twenty-six different medications, and a bunch of dangerous prescriptions were simply sitting on the kitchen counter, and the TV tray and coffee table in the living room. She made no attempt to hide them. It was like she was taunting us. Daring us to find them."

"Yep, the evidence was literally right in front of our eyes. It wasn't until my conversation with Brogan that everything clicked and fell into place—he said that Kelly reached out to June for medical advice and June gave her special teas and things to help her sleep." I leaned back, swallowing hard. "She is diabolical to have left the evidence right there for us to find, but I'm confident that Dr. Caldwell should have plenty to pass on to the DA."

"That's right." Fletcher flipped through his notes. "Prescription drugs matching those in Kelly's system, photos and videos surveilling each of her targets, countless articles, and more. Yep, I wouldn't need much more to be convinced if I were on the jury."

We talked through Harvey, Allison, and Jake—all three were also scheduled for prison time.

"I'd say four arrests isn't bad for our first case." Fletcher pretended to fist bump me from afar. "Well done, Watson."

"You too, Watson," I shot back with a wink. Our ongoing debate as to who was the Watson and Sherlock on our team was cut short by a knock on the door.

"Come in," Fletcher called, getting up and moving to the seating area.

Caroline swept into the room with the grace of a ballerina, peering around the door and craning her long, elegant neck inside to make sure we were alone. "Am I early?"

"Not at all," I assured her, although I was kicking myself for not following up with Fletcher on his news regarding the brooch sooner. I guess I would be hearing whatever he had to share right along with Caroline. "We were just finishing up some case notes. Please have a seat." I joined them and gave Fletcher the nod to proceed. He'd done the bulk of the legwork for this case so far, so I was happy to have him share what he'd learned with Caroline.

He tidied a stack of papers and handed them to her. "We've done a thorough examination of the brooch and had it analyzed by three different appraisers to ensure that it wasn't an outlier. We've also enlisted an art investigator who has spent years tracking down stolen pieces and identifying forgeries. As you'll see in the documentation, each appraisal returned with the same assessment. The brooch is extremely valuable and aligns with the time that Agatha was spotted wearing it. What's more is that we were able to track down a receipt of purchase—the brooch was indeed bought by Agatha Christie as a celebratory gift for completing her fifth novel—*The Secret of Chimneys*." Fletcher couldn't hide the touch of pride in his voice, and I didn't blame him. It was great work.

"So the brooch did belong to Agatha?" Caroline sounded dumbfounded.

Fletcher nodded his head. "We're ninety-nine percent positive it did."

My heart sped up as I caught his eye and shot him a look of awe, mouthing, "Well done." This was huge news and could be the break we'd been waiting for.

Caroline looked anything but pleased, though. She frowned, glancing from the paperwork and over her shoulder and then back to us. "Oh no."

"I thought you'd be pleased," I said, catching Fletcher's eye again. The touch of pride had vanished, deflating his shoulders like a leaky balloon.

"I am. Yes, I'm sorry." She held out a hand to stop me from saying more. "It's just that this is revolutionary. It's the proof that Hal has been waiting for his entire life. I want to be sure. We have to be sure about this before we tell him. I refuse to give him false hope." She pressed her hand to her cheek. "I'd like you to keep going. To gather even more evidence. If we could find the birth certificate—something else tangible…" She trailed off like she was trying to decide what that might be.

"No problem," I said, feeling her concern radiate from her. I appreciated how much she cared about Hal, and I agreed. "I've put out records requests, but these tend to take a while," I said, trying to reassure her.

"That's fine. I'm not in a rush. I'd rather be confident than have any lingering questions."

"Understood," Fletcher said with a serious nod. "We'll continue the investigation. I have a few leads in the jewelry world I'd like to reach out to anyway."

"Excellent." Caroline handed him back the paperwork. "Keep these and the brooch. I don't want Hal to know about this." Then she reached into her purse and pulled out a small silver key. "I feel slightly bad, but when Hal suggested I get a key to his place, I made an extra copy for you." She passed it over to me.

"For us? Why?" I took the key, feeling an immediate sense of guilt. Was she suggesting we sneak into Hal's private quarters?

"There's another locked box in his closet. I think you two should take a look. We'll have to find the right time, but I can take him out for the evening."

That *was* what she was suggesting.

My stomach dropped. I wanted to find answers for Hal, but I wasn't sure I wanted to violate his privacy. That felt like overstepping our bounds.

"I know this might put you in an awkward position, and I know how much you both care about him like a grandfather. Trust me when I say you'll be doing him the biggest favor if we can prove his heritage. It will be the gift of a lifetime."

She had a point there.

"Go ahead and continue with your inquiries. Let's plan to connect soon and come up with a plan." She left without another word.

Fletcher let out a long sigh after she left. Then he rubbed his hands together and shot me a cheeky wink. "Well, what do you think?"

"I think it's stellar work. Bravo to you, my friend. This is a major win." I smiled brightly, impressed that he'd come through with a tangible link between the brooch and Agatha Christie. "I know I'm going to regret saying this and will probably never live it down, but I guess the game is really afoot now."

A LETTER FROM THE AUTHOR

I hope you enjoyed Annie and Fletcher's first case as the Novel Detectives. I have a long list of future cases that desperately need their attention and astute sleuthing skills, so there is more to come. If you want to hear all about my new releases and bonus content, you can sign up for my newsletter!

www.stormpublishing.co/ellie-alexander

If you enjoyed this story and could spare a moment to leave a review, it would mean so much to me. Even a short review can make all the difference in encouraging a reader to discover my books for the first time. Thank you so much for spreading the book love.

I'll be honest, I want the Secret Bookcase to be real, and to tell you the truth, it is inspired by a very real place, the gorgeous Filoli Gardens, which I have used as inspiration and made my own. I mean, who doesn't want to live in an Agatha Christie bookstore? Better yet, who doesn't want to run their own sleuthing agency out of a bookstore? Since I don't have a grand English estate with extensive gardens with sweeping views of the coastal Californian mountain ranges, the next best thing is to live *in the book*, fictionally. I spend hours and hours wandering the village square and hallways of the Secret Bookcase with Annie when I'm writing this series, and my hope is that you get to escape into the coziest bookstore and sweetest small town of Redwood Grove when you step into the story.

Thanks again for being part of this journey! Please stay in touch. I have many more stories and ideas that I'm eager to share with you!

Ellie Alexander

www.elliealexander.co

instagram.com/ellie_alexander

facebook.com/elliealexanderauthor

ACKNOWLEDGMENTS

I can't say enough good things about my brainstorming, cheer-leading, and all-around bookish team, which includes Tish Bouvier, Kat Webb, Flo Cho, Jennifer Lewis, Lily Gill, Courtny Bradley, Mary Ann McCoy, Ericka Turnbull, Spencer Calquhoun, and Kayla Baucom. Thank you, thank you!

To my writing group, who helped me think through how to spin off this series and are always game for plotting new cases that Annie and Fletcher can solve. Sharing space with other writers is a dream, and the snacks are next level too! Thanks to Melinda Hamilton, Tammy Qualls, Denise Lippmann, Jen Levine, Jessica Rosenberg, Lesley Taylor, and Leigh Odum.

In case you haven't heard, the publishing team at Storm is pretty freaking fantastic. Scratch that. They are outstanding and the best of the best in the industry. Vicky Blunden, Alex Begley, Elke Desanghere, Anna McKerrow, Becca Allen, Maheen Mehmood, Dawn Adams, and Oliver Rhodes—my deepest thanks for your editorial, design, and marketing expertise. My books are better because of you.

To Gordy, Luke, and Liv for the endless dinner plotting sessions, personalized tours of Filoli Gardens, and coming along on this wild ride that is the writing life, I couldn't love you more.